CHRISTMAS CRIMINAL

A WHIMSY CHRISTMAS ROM-COM

ALLY WILLIAMS

For my fellow Grinches.

CONTENT WARNING

Although this is a somewhat whimsy, fun Christmas novel, there are moments that may make some readers feel uncomfortable, including a mention of childhood cancer (as in, hoping to cure it), high school trauma, eczema, mentions of a dead parent, bullying, body image dysmorphia, potential alcoholism, parental neglect, and broken bones. And of course, plenty of explicit content and swearing. Please do not read if any of these things make you uncomfortable.

1

NOELLE

Friday, November 29th

"I'm here for community service."

I sound as crabby as I feel. There's nothing worse than having to walk into high school almost a decade after finally leaving and *thinking* you'll never have to go back.

Especially when you were the weird kid.

The guy sitting at the front desk peels his eyes away from the book he's reading to look at me, eyebrows high, and nods. "You must be Noelle."

I give him my best awkward smile and shrug.

I take it back: there is *one* thing worse.

Walking back into a high school almost a decade after you thought you'd never have to see it again, *with a reputation*.

His feet drop from the desk in front of him, and when he stands to his full height in front of me, I realize the man in front of me is built like a tank. All muscle underneath dark jeans and a Snow Falls High School T-shirt that makes my stomach churn. A light smattering of stubble lines his face. When he presses his glasses up onto his head, his chestnut hair flies out in every direction.

He holds his hand out to me to shake, smiling politely. "I'm Nick."

"Noelle," I say, doing my best to shake his hand harder than he shakes mine because *goddamnit, I refuse to let this community service arrangement take me down.*

He raises his eyebrows again, and for a second I think I impressed him with my strong handshake.

Then I realize it's because he already *knows* my name.

High school, one. Noelle, zero.

He gestures for me to follow him. "So today we're uncovering the Christmas float. See what we're dealing with and maybe clean it up a bit. We don't have a plan for the theme of this year's float yet, but we can get it all set up for when the kids want to work on it."

I nod, following him down a long corridor that leads to the garage. As we walk, I'm hit with a slew of memories from these halls. The door to the library, where I snuck in to eat my lunch every day because I never seemed to have the same lunch period as my few friends. The hallway where I used to wait for my high school boyfriend, who lasted all of two months, to make out for three minutes between classes. The quiet cove between banks of lockers where he broke up with me after implying to the whole school that I had an STD before promptly getting with Stacy Mann.

Stacy Mann–who didn't even know he existed before then–was more enticing than me, the girl who hung on his every word.

Because I was born with skin that reacts poorly to anything except air, apparently.

NOELLE

Friday, November 29th

"I'm here for community service."

I sound as crabby as I feel. There's nothing worse than having to walk into high school almost a decade after finally leaving and *thinking* you'll never have to go back.

Especially when you were the weird kid.

The guy sitting at the front desk peels his eyes away from the book he's reading to look at me, eyebrows high, and nods. "You must be Noelle."

I give him my best awkward smile and shrug.

I take it back: there is *one* thing worse.

Walking back into a high school almost a decade after you thought you'd never have to see it again, *with a reputation*.

His feet drop from the desk in front of him, and when he stands to his full height in front of me, I realize the man in front of me is built like a tank. All muscle underneath dark jeans and a Snow Falls High School T-shirt that makes my stomach churn. A light smattering of stubble lines his face. When he presses his glasses up onto his head, his chestnut hair flies out in every direction.

He holds his hand out to me to shake, smiling politely. "I'm Nick."

"Noelle," I say, doing my best to shake his hand harder than he shakes mine because *goddamnit, I refuse to let this community service arrangement take me down.*

He raises his eyebrows again, and for a second I think I impressed him with my strong handshake.

Then I realize it's because he already *knows* my name.

High school, one. Noelle, zero.

He gestures for me to follow him. "So today we're uncovering the Christmas float. See what we're dealing with and maybe clean it up a bit. We don't have a plan for the theme of this year's float yet, but we can get it all set up for when the kids want to work on it."

I nod, following him down a long corridor that leads to the garage. As we walk, I'm hit with a slew of memories from these halls. The door to the library, where I snuck in to eat my lunch every day because I never seemed to have the same lunch period as my few friends. The hallway where I used to wait for my high school boyfriend, who lasted all of two months, to make out for three minutes between classes. The quiet cove between banks of lockers where he broke up with me after implying to the whole school that I had an STD before promptly getting with Stacy Mann.

Stacy Mann–who didn't even know he existed before then–was more enticing than me, the girl who hung on his every word.

Because I was born with skin that reacts poorly to anything except air, apparently.

The hall is filled with that high school scent that's mostly stale with the hint of mildew.

And something... sweet. And a little smoky. Like a s'more fresh from the fire.

My mouth waters as I take another sniff, the realization dawning on me that it must be *him* that smells so delectable.

I inhale quickly again, like I might be able to put that scent in a little box in my brain and come back later for a midnight snack.

"Can't wait to get cleaning," I say, because I feel like I should say *something* before my inner obsession with the way he smells becomes outwardly obvious.

He looks at me from the corner of his eye. "Are you one of those people?"

"One of what people?"

"Who enjoy cleaning?"

I shrug. "I don't know. There was a lot of silence so I figured I should say words."

He nods. "Ah. You're one of *those* people."

I bite my lip, determined not to say anything else to prove him right. Or start sniffing for s'mores.

"So are you from around here?" he asks.

I pop my lips. "Yup. Went to this godforsaken school for four years."

He nods. "Ah."

And the fact that I'm back in this stupid high school reminds me of everything I'm sure people thought about me when I left.

When my older sister got her dream job in Philadelphia and moved to the city, I went with her and never looked back. While she became a corporate badass, my mom subsidized her apartment so I could live in her spare room while I got my GED and applied to college in the city.

Afterward, I started freelancing as a web designer, and one client turned into another, and that client turned into one more.

Before I knew it, I was running a whole damn business by myself.

I'm doing *so well* for myself, but coming back here puts me right back where I was all those years ago. Uncomfortable in my own skin. In a place where one picture of your thigh with an eczema outbreak suddenly becomes proof that you have an STD.

Never mind the fact that you're a virgin.

I don't speak to anyone from high school anymore. My college friends have stuck by me, and I love them for that. But as far as high school goes? I was over and done with it almost a decade ago when I left. I only ever come back here to visit my mom.

My dad lives here too, but I save those visits for when I have a carton of eggs with no better use.

Unfortunately *that* sort of decision-making is exactly what landed me back in this high school doing community service.

"I take it you're *not* from around here," I say, giving him a quick smile to cancel out the glare that settled on my face as we walked through my old torture chamber.

He shakes his head. "Moved here a few years ago. It's a nice town," he says, obviously not picking up on my hatred for it.

I opt to not burst his bubble. If he wants to believe this place is all sunshine and daisies, good for him.

He leans against the garage door, popping it with his hip and holding it open for me.

The door clangs shut behind us, and I pause in the dim light filtering in through the tops of the garage doors while he takes a few steps along the wall and flips on the overhead lights.

We're bathed in blinding fluorescents as we walk toward a large trailer covered in a multitude of white sheets.

He grabs a sheet and pulls it gently off, leaving it in a pile between us. When I don't immediately follow, he looks over his shoulder at me. "Are you going to help?"

I purse my lips as I grab one, tugging it off and dropping it into the pile with Nick's.

"Is it just us, for community service?" I ask.

"There aren't many criminals in these parts," he explains, shooting me a quick grin that sends a little zip of heat down my spine.

A surprised laugh jumps from my throat. "Ah. Should have known." I remove another white sheet, revealing a number of streamers and a thick ball of tinsel stuck along one side of the trailer. The only sounds around us are the humming of the lights above and the pillowy drop of sheets against the floor.

And the silence finally gets me. "Aren't you going to ask me what I did?"

He shakes his head. "No," he says, and pauses. "But you can tell me if you want to."

I glare at him. "What, are you trying to reverse psychology me?"

"No. I'm saying that if you don't want to tell me, you don't have to. But if you want to, that's fine, too."

I bite my lip as I watch him brush off one side of the trailer. He grimaces when a piece of a sticky streamer gets stuck on his hand and wipes it off on his jeans.

"Well, how did you get roped into doing community service?" I ask.

He raises his eyebrows. "I'm not *participating* in community service. I'm facilitating it."

"Right, but like, why? Are you actually a reformed criminal who went through community service yourself and realized his true calling was helping the degenerates of the world?"

He laughs, shaking his head. "That's an interesting story you've crafted."

I wait for him to continue. "I'll tell you why I'm here if you tell me why you are."

He pauses, crossing his arms and leaning against one side of the trailer. He fixes me with his gaze. "I work here."

I raise my eyebrows. "What are you, the grand marshal of the Christmas parade?"

He shakes his head. "No. I'm a teacher."

"Oh," I say, realizing that little bit of information should have been *obvious*. He's wearing a school T-shirt for Christ's sake. "What do you teach?"

"Math."

I raise my eyebrows. "*You're* a math teacher?"

"What's that face for?"

I fix my expression, struggling to hide my surprise. This man is entirely too attractive to be a math teacher. Gym teacher, maybe. But math teachers are supposed to have frizzy gray hair. Moles in strange places. Potbellies under blazers with ripped elbow patches.

"You don't look like a math teacher. And why are you here doing community service if you're a math teacher?"

"What, exactly, does a math teacher look like?"

He knows. Fuck, he knows I think he's unfairly attractive and I'm suddenly incredibly embarrassed about the poor decision-making that landed me here even though I don't regret a single moment of it.

"Not like you," I say, trying to keep things succinct as I turn to throw another sheet in the pile in an attempt to shield my reddening face.

He hums, and a moment later, he's right next to me, adding another.

"You didn't tell me why you're doing community service," I prompt, once I'm sure my face has returned to its normal color.

He turns to me, shrugging. "I like Christmas. I'd be doing this myself anyway, so when Hank asked if I had any ideas, it just seemed... serendipitous."

I laugh, the sound popping from my mouth in a definitely unattractive way. "Serendipitous?"

It's only when he raises his eyebrows with no hint of laughter that I realize he's serious.

I nod, swallowing down the laughter that so desperately wants to spill out.

"Serendipitous," I repeat.

He nods. "And apparently that's very funny." He cracks a small smile as I turn to detach a flattened streamer and a pile of silly string from one side of the float.

"That's more because you like Christmas but we're doing... *this*," I say. "Why would you ruin something you *like* by bringing degenerates into it?"

He shrugs. "I have never regretted inviting a person to help with the Christmas float before. Or the parade or the Christmas play or the Christmas concert. There have been a number of people who have come in to help who haven't wanted to, and every single time they've gotten something worthwhile out of it. And that's rewarding to me."

He walks around the float to grab an oversized broom that he uses to collect the bits of trash we're dropping to the floor.

"I thought you said you don't have many criminals around here."

He grins. "That's true. You're my first criminal," he says. My cheeks flush with his possessive wording. "But I have a lot of students who don't have the best home life, and giving them a bit of a reprieve from that during the holidays can sometimes work wonders. Or it can blow up in my face, but we don't focus on that possibility."

I nod. "That's... nice."

He shrugs. "I think it is."

"I feel like helping out kids and taking on degenerates are two different things, though."

He sighs, resting his hands on the top of the broom. "Why do I feel like you're going to be trouble, Noelle?"

I scrunch up my face. "I'm not trouble. I promise, I'm a good person. I'm just curious."

"Okay, Criminal." When my eyes narrow, his grin ticks wider. "I'm doing it as a favor to Hank."

I scoff. "Ugh, really?"

I turn back to the float, throwing another bunch of silly string to the ground.

Hank Grundy is the town sheriff.

The one who found me throwing eggs at my dad's window last week and called my mom to come get her unruly daughter from the police station. The one who told me very firmly that what I was doing could result in a misdemeanor if I didn't play my cards carefully. The one who told me he'd conveniently forget about this domestic dispute if I went ahead and stuck around for the Christmas season and took part in some good, old-fashioned community service.

I'm fairly certain he's in my mom's pocket and this

community service agreement is nothing more than an attempt to have me around more for the holidays.

I love my mom, but she's not subtle when it comes to Christmas.

"What do you have against Hank?" Nick asks.

"What do you *think* I have against Hank?"

He shrugs. "He was just doing his job."

I eye him. "You already know why I'm here," I accuse.

He turns with the broom to collect a small pile of trash at our feet. I cross my arms, waiting for him to explain. "I know that you were caught throwing eggs at the Hellermans' house," he admits, his eyes following the path of the broom before briefly flicking up to mine. "But I don't know why."

I purse my lips, debating whether I want to tell him. On the one hand, I've always found it easier to tell things to people I *don't* know. If they judge me, I don't care.

But on the other hand, I have to deal with math teacher Nick for another fifty hours of community service.

And I decide to take a chance and trust him. "He's my dad."

To Nick's credit, he doesn't seem surprised. "You have different last names."

"And isn't that the beginning of a fuzzy, feel-good family movie?"

"Ah. There's some friction there."

I snort. "Yeah, there's some friction there."

He nods. "Well, hopefully the egging was worth it."

I eye him. I can't tell whether he's trying to make light of the situation or reminding me that this is supposed to be punishment.

I press my lips together before responding. "I don't regret a moment of it."

He laughs, shaking his head as he walks off to one side of the garage and grabs a trash bin. He takes a pair of plastic gloves from the tool bench and begins scooping trash inside.

"So how many eggs did you get through before you got caught?" he asks, as he scoops and I waste time walking my bits of trash over to the bin so I don't have to pull on a pair of gloves and help him.

I give him my proudest smile as I turn back to the float. "All twelve."

WE CLEAR the trash from the float and take stock of what needs to be done before the kids can start decorating it. We throw last year's decorations in the trash and note that one of the steps is wobbly–and a little zip of heat runs down my spine when Nick waves that off as something he can fix when he brings his toolbox in–and that some of the paint on the floor has chipped off and could use a new coat.

We walk out together, the school eerily dark as he closes the door and locks up behind him. He scribbles quickly across my timecard and hands it back to me as we descend the concrete stairs to the parking lot.

"You know, I never really thought about schools having locks," I say, as we head toward the only two cars.

"Yeah, unfortunately there's always going to be some kid who has a bad idea."

I laugh. "Hence the community service."

He grins. "I think you're a little old to be considered a kid with a bad idea."

I glare at him. "Hasn't anyone told you never to comment on a woman's age?"

As we reach my car, he turns to me, ignoring my question. "So, what timing works for you? School nights or weekend hours?"

I shrug, leaning against my car. "Weekends, probably. Unless my sister has something come up," I say, before realizing how much of an excuse that sounds like. "She broke her leg," I explain. "So she's not totally mobile right now."

"Oh, I'm sorry to hear that," he says. "Well, I can give you my number and you can let me know what sort of schedule works for you?"

I swallow. "Yeah. I kind of thought the hours would be a little more rigid."

"Well, like I said, you're my only criminal." He pauses as if he's waiting for me to do something, and then clears his throat. "I, uh, don't have a card or anything, if you want me to put my number in your phone. For scheduling."

I nod, scrambling to pull my phone out of my purse. "Right. Sorry."

I pull up my contacts and hand it over.

A moment later, he hands it back, and I see on the screen he's saved his number under 'Saint Nick.'

"Seriously?" I ask. "Saint Nick?"

He shrugs, grinning. "So you won't forget me."

A smile spreads across my face despite my best efforts. I nod. "I *can't* forget you, or else Hank Grundy is going to show up at my door and drag me to jail."

Nick laughs. "Hey, whatever it takes to leave an impression." He pats the roof of my car before continuing on to his own. "Text me, Criminal," he calls over his shoulder.

I kind of want to flip him off.

Or throw an egg at that smug grin on his face.

And kind of maybe tackle him to the ground and kiss him.

2

NICK

Saturday, November 30th

Noelle shuffles through the doors of the high school at a quarter past eight, wearing leggings and an oversized sweatshirt. Big sunglasses cover her eyes, and she holds a coffee from The Lucky Mug, a little family-owned place that happens to be a two-minute drive from my house. She gives me a stiff wave as I stand from the desk.

"Good morning, sunshine," I say, and the way her jaw ticks at my words tells me she is *not* a morning person.

So, I guess she *was* annoyed that I suggested eight in the morning.

And I get that she's upset because of whatever contentious family situation she has going on, but she doesn't have to take it out on the town. No town is perfect, but when I was searching for a place to live a few years ago, Snow Falls checked off almost every single box.

Close-knit community with regular events, check.

A big high school where I'm not the *only* math teacher, check.

A local watering hole I can go to *without* getting in trouble with parents, check.

I've been alone for most of my adult life, but I didn't start feeling *lonely* until my friends from college started getting married and having kids and I realized that, as great as my friends were, I couldn't rely on them to consider me a part of their growing families.

I would have to go out and find my own, whether that's a person or a community. And I'm happy with where I ended up, even if I do get lonely every once in a while.

There was a time I thought I had found my person. Emily, who wanted a fancy life in the city I couldn't give her without sacrificing everything I've worked so hard for. Who picked fights like it was her job and then asked why I never raised my voice to her. Who used to poke and prod at me, "searching for an emotion" underneath my stoic exterior.

She left with a bluff, accusing me of being too scared to fight for her.

And I let her go.

So while I never found the right person, I did find the right community.

A place that feels like home. Especially this time of year.

When I was little, Christmas was my favorite. My mom would take me to all of the Christmas parades, and we would make paper snowflakes on Christmas Eve and bake cookies and put up the tree together. It truly was a magical time of year.

When she passed away during my senior year of high school, that was what I missed most. The smile on her face when the air turned crispy cold. The way her eyes would shut and her shoulders would hunch up by her ears. She'd pull me into her side and say, "You smell that, Nicky? Christmas is coming."

She raised me on her own, and despite struggling at times to make ends meet when I was young, she managed to leave me an inheritance that got me through college and gave me a reasonable down payment on a home just outside town.

In a way, it's like she left me with my favorite part of her–the part that loved this time of year.

Suffice it to say, I'm sure growing up and going to school here is a whole different experience than finding it as an adult. No one gets through high school unscathed, and although I'm sure Noelle doesn't want to bring up bad memories, sometimes it can be healing to go back and say, "Hey assholes, look who I am now."

She had a tough time here. Many students do. They're somewhere between a kid and an adult, hormones are raging, and not a single parent I've ever talked to has felt like they've figured out the teenage stage.

That's part of the reason I do what I do, especially around the holidays. I don't have a family to go home to and shower in love and support like I want, so I turn that onto my students. Onto the townspeople who seem to love Christmas almost as much as my mom did.

And for me, that's turned a time of year where I could sit and wallow in my grief into a time I look forward to.

I think my mom would be proud of me for that.

"Good morning," Noelle says stiffly, drawing me back to reality.

She starts down the hall toward the garage, and I'm left to follow in her footsteps and ignore the way her hips swing from side to side as she moves. The way her wavy brown hair cascades down her back.

When Hank asked if I was busy this weekend, he failed to mention the egg-thrower was pretty, a fact that threw me off for half a second when she showed up that first day. One second I was reading, and the next, a dainty brunette stood at the front desk, admitting to being the naughty egg-thrower Hank wanted me to take under my wing

Hank isn't the asshole that Noelle thinks he is. She happened to be throwing eggs in the wrong place, at the wrong time. And while she could have been dealing with a hefty fine or even jail time, she got a dose of small town community service work. The kind that skips a judge and gets brushed under the rug as long as you show up and do what you say you will.

There's a reason I like Hank as much as I do. I've seen a lot of good kids make one wrong step, and before they're able to correct course, they're tugged further in the wrong direction. Hank gives the benefit of the doubt when he can, and that's something I always appreciate.

Even if it means I get saddled with the pint-sized brunette with an attitude problem.

"How are you today?" I ask, taking a few quick steps to catch up with her.

She pushes her sunglasses up onto her head and narrows her eyes at me. "I'm doing great. I woke up at five in the morning to drive three hours to this stupid town to do community service for a *community* that can suck my ass, and instead of going home and relaxing with a glass of wine tonight, I have to go sleep in my childhood bedroom on a lumpy mattress while my mother rage-sings Christmas songs at me."

I snort. I can't say I was expecting the outburst.

"Oh, cool. So you think that's funny."

"Might I remind you that *you* picked weekend hours."

She comes to a stop and stomps. "I don't *live* here anymore!"

I hold up my hands, turning to face her. "Okay, I get it. What would have worked better? Start at noon?"

"Then I'm not done until eight!"

I shake my head, throwing my hands out in front of me. "I'm trying to work with you here, Noelle. You have hours to do. Tell me what times work."

She shakes her head, running her hand over her face. "I'm sorry. I think I'm tired. I don't usually get up this early and I had a long week at work and I just... ugh. I swear, I have a visceral reaction every time I walk into this building, like I'm shrinking back into high school. And I hate that I'm giving up my weekend to come back here." She lets out a long breath, resting her hands on her hips. "I don't like being here and I'm throwing a tantrum over it." She bites her lip, her face tipping up toward the ceiling. "I'm sorry. You don't deserve that."

I cross my arms over my chest as I look at her, raising an eyebrow.

"What's your worst memory of being here?"

She grimaces. "Oh god, no. We're not going there. It's bad enough that I can feel it. I don't want to talk about it and make it more real than it is."

"Humor me. Let's see if we can end the feeling by talking it out really quick."

She raises an eyebrow. "Isn't this supposed to be community service?"

"If we're helping someone, it's community service."

She narrows her eyes. "Why would you want to help me instead of using me for manual labor?"

I shrug. "We have all day for manual labor."

She eyes me and then throws her hands out in front of

her. "Okay, fine. When I was in high school, I used to have to sneak into the library over lunch to eat my food because I didn't have any friends so I had nowhere to sit in the lunchroom."

That hits me in the gut.

"You had to sneak in?"

She nods. "You weren't allowed to go to the library without a pass, and they wouldn't give you a pass over lunch because they were scared you wouldn't eat or something. So there was this kid who swiped one of the teacher's passwords, and when he got onto the shared file system, he found a printout of the pass sheets that he shared with the whole school. So as long as you could find the right color paper and make your signature terrible enough, you could write your own passes for anything."

I blink, vaguely wondering if we use the same passes as we did when she went to school here.

And if my students are passing out copies of them.

"You came up with quite the solution."

She shrugs. "It didn't always work." She's quiet for a moment. "I think the librarian knew."

I raise my eyebrows. "Yeah?"

She nods. "Mrs. Nguyen."

A grin spreads across my face. "Mrs. Nguyen is still here."

She swallows. "Is she?"

I nod. "And she does seem like the type of woman who would figure out what's going on. She's sharp. Kind of scares me a little, if I'm being totally honest. Did she send you away?"

Noelle shakes her head. "She never did. But every single day, she would look at my pass and mention that my teacher's handwriting looked a little off, compared to the one I handed her the day before." She bites her lip and lowers her voice. "I kind of think she was doing it to fuck with me because every single day I tried harder and harder to forge it better, and I think all it did was make it a little different every day, just like she told me it was."

I can't help my snicker, and a moment later, Noelle is laughing along with me.

"You know, I hated high school, but I *did* appreciate her. She used to let me check out more books than I was supposed to and every once in a while she would slip one into my pile that she thought I'd like."

"You should come back during the week. Say hello to her. I'm sure she'd like to see you again."

Noelle scoffs, turning and continuing toward the garage. "Please. I put her in a terrible position. She probably had to feign ignorance about why I was in the library for lunch every day."

I take a few quick steps to catch up and knock her elbow with mine, the touch sending a little jolt through my skin that I wasn't expecting. When she turns those piercing brown eyes on me, I clear my throat. "You know, just because she was an adult doesn't mean she knew *everything*. Speaking as one of the adults who has to take care of a bunch of teenagers all day, I feel clueless more often than not."

Her brow furrows. "Yeah?"

"She might have been doing you a kindness. Teachers will break the rules for kids who are technically stepping out of line but aren't a *problem*." And I can't resist making the joke once it occurs to me. "You know, like Hank, for you."

The glare takes over her face again. "You're lucky I have to be nice to you."

"This is being nice?"

She tries her hardest not to show her grin.

But when I break, so does she.

She shakes her head, laughing. "Stop making me laugh when I'm trying to channel my moody teenage self."

"Hey, if you really want to be miserable, go right ahead."

She shakes her head, letting out a long breath. "Okay, so I guess going to the library over lunch wasn't the *worst* thing in the world. And I do still love books. Now that I'm thinking about it, I'm actually kind of relieved I still love books after all of that."

We reach the door to the garage, and I open it for her to walk through. "What kind of books do you like?"

"Arguably porn," she says.

I blink, wondering if I heard her wrong. "What?"

"I mean, depending on the day, you know? Sometimes I like a nice clean romance, sometimes I like a nasty one."

The door clangs shut behind us as I struggle to catch up. "So a nice clean romance is... arguably porn?"

She rolls her eyes. "No. I'm just giving you the category you're going to put it in before you can judge me for it first."

I raise my eyebrows. "Who hurt you, Noelle? No one cares that you read *arguably porn*. Or anything adjacent to it."

She eyes me as she drops her bag on the ground next to the float. "Okay, that was a good answer."

"Was that a test?"

"I don't know, Teach. You tell me."

I point to my chest. "Math. No good at words."

"You sure do say a lot of them."

This girl is feisty. I take her coffee cup from her and take a sniff. "Huh. Surprising."

"What?" she asks, her face showing blatant confusion as she tugs it back from me.

"Thought for sure there'd be some alcohol in there."

Her jaw drops open. "I *drove* here!"

"You *are* a criminal."

"Nick!"

Her screech sends a little shiver down my spine. I grin.

"So, you want to do the painting or the drilling?" I ask, ignoring her ticking jaw. I grab my drill from where I left it on the step this morning and squeeze the button for a moment, listening as it whirs to life.

She shakes her head almost imperceptibly as she tugs her sweatshirt off.

"I dressed for painting," she says, gesturing to the minuscule tank top she had been hiding underneath. She drops the sweatshirt on the ground on top of her bag, and I have to force my eyes to anywhere but that thin line of cleavage that's now exposed.

Her shirt is covered in little specks of paint, and what looks like a hand print on one side.

A hand print that is far too large to be her own.

A spike of jealousy zips through me from my caveman brain.

I'm not thinking of her like that. I'm not attracted to her. I'm supposed to be helping her.

But god, the curve of her waist is absolutely riveting. The way her shirt bunches there. The tiny sliver of skin that shows between her shirt and her leggings.

And now she's tying her hair up, her arms above her head as she makes one of those messy buns that are always fifty percent adorable and fifty percent sensual.

Maybe she's trying to kill me. That must be it. Maybe she knows my weakness for small brunettes and someone has sent her here to take me out once and for all.

She raises her eyebrows. "That cool with you?"

"Hm?" I ask, accidentally starting my drill again and jumping at the noise.

"If I start with the paint?" She nods to it. "Unless you need help with your little drill?"

I shake my head. "Nope. I can drill just fine on my own."

NOELLE LOSES HERSELF IN PAINTING. She takes care of the worn areas quickly, but as we take a step back to look at the fresh coat, we realize that after years of use, the fresh paint of the same color doesn't match the worn areas.

So she kneels down again and drags the brush to the corners of the float in an attempt to hide the difference in color. I've finished my stair repair at this point, and there's only one brush, so I'm stuck waiting until she's done. And my eyes are drawn to her. The way her body stretches to paint the far corners. She's on her hands and knees, and my eyes are drawn to the way her body moves back and forth. How perfectly mine would frame hers.

When I snap back into my brain, I force myself to think about how else we can use our time today.

"I'm going to run out to pick up some lunch. What do you want?" I ask.

Her head snaps up, brush hovering over the float. "Um. Some sort of salad maybe? Where are you getting it from?"

I shrug. "I was going to run to a Wawa. Do they have a salad you like?"

She nods. "Chicken caesar?" She scrambles up from where she's kneeling to reach into her bag.

"Don't worry about it. You can get lunch next time."

"Oh," she says. "Well, thanks."

"You good to hold down the fort?"

She nods, returning to her painting. "I'll keep slaving away."

I take a good look at the floor before I leave, scrunching up my brow as I gaze at her work. She pauses when she sees me and sits back on her ankles. "What?"

I point vaguely in the direction of the far end, where she can't get to unless she wants to step in fresh paint or dangle over the side of the float and say, "You missed a spot over there," before zipping along the side of the float and out the door into the school.

Just as the door shuts behind me, I hear her shout, "Where?" A second later, as I'm speeding down the hallway, she shrieks. "Nick! What spot?"

NOTHING COULD PREPARE me for the sight I walk into when I return with my bag of food from Wawa.

She's hanging over one side of the float, angry-painting the spot I gestured to vaguely before I left. She found a step stool somewhere to hoist herself up over the edge, but now she dangles there, balancing by her hips with the paint can perched on the ledge of the float.

"Well fuck, it took you long enough!" she says, her foot moving in a small circle as she searches for the step stool. "I can't get this stupid spot. I don't know if the material is just, like, paint-safe or something but I've literally been painting this since you left and it won't freaking *stick*!"

Uh oh. Sounds like I've angered the pixie.

Her foot is still searching, and there's a part of me that wants to leave her there. At least while she's tipped over like that, she can't attack me, and something tells me once she finds out there never *was* a spot she missed, she's not going to be very happy.

I approach cautiously, nudging the step stool to where her foot can reach it, and peer over the edge of the float.

I look at the spot she's been working on and cock my head to the side when I see there *does* seem to be a darker line through the rest of the floor.

"I wouldn't worry about it," I tell her. "People are going to step on it anyway."

"But *why won't it be painted?*" she asks. "This is so frustrating. Like, I get that it doesn't matter. But it feels incomplete. If I'm going to spend this much time on a goddamn paint job, it better be freaking done!"

I glance down at it again as she looks behind her, one hand finding the edge of the float to push herself up.

And I realize the darker spot spreads with her movement.

I start snickering.

Her foot is still searching. "Jesus Christ, did you move my step stool? Are you playing a joke on me?"

I shake my head. "No, look," I say, pointing to where the gray spot continually moves. I wave my hand above my head, making our shadows dance. "It's a shadow."

She pauses, letting out a quick breath through her nose. "It's a fucking *shadow?*" She shakes her head, pushing herself up again. "Seriously, did you move my step stool? I can't get down."

I glance down and knock it another inch closer to her foot, but she seems to be doing everything in her power to avoid it.

I roll my eyes, dropping the bag of food to the ground and stepping behind her to grab her by the ankles and tug her feet down until they make contact with her stool.

And wow, even her ankles are attractive. A little bony, but her skin is soft and warm.

"Thank you," she says, clambering down to the floor and standing with her hands on her hips. "I can't believe a fucking shadow got us."

Got *us?* Yeah, it's probably in my best interest to let her believe that.

I lift the bag of food. "Hungry?"

"Yes!"

"Come on." I nod to the door and she throws her purse over her shoulder as she follows me out of the garage and through the empty high school halls to the cafeteria on the far side of the building.

"Ugh, this place," she says, wandering into the open space and spinning around slowly. Her shoes tap against the linoleum floor as she walks. "It always looks weird with all the kitchens boarded up and the tables up against the walls. Way better than when it's filled with a ton of kids, but still weird."

"Where do you want to sit?" I ask her.

She shrugs. "I don't care. It's a school cafeteria. No spot is a good spot."

"Well, you get to choose. Any spot."

Her eyes narrow. "Is this some sort of healing bullshit or something? Because if so, I don't need it. I'm an adult. I'm not still hung up on things that happened in high school."

Judging from the strange looks that overtake her face at random moments throughout the day, I'd have to disagree. Walking through the halls, she visibly flinches when we pass certain areas. And every once in a while when she doesn't think I'm paying attention, she cringes, her head shaking as if she's reliving some horrid experience.

I'm no stranger to what a bad high school experience

can do to someone. I was one of the lucky few who actually had an okay time in high school, but when you become a teacher and start looking at kids' behaviors as indications of what might be going on inside, you get a whole different picture.

And as much as we don't want to believe it, a lot of those reactions don't change as you get older.

You just get better at hiding them.

She lets out a long breath. "I want to sit by the cookie station."

I raise my eyebrows. "Yeah? Do you want a cookie? I made friends with Rita the lunch lady and she gave me a copy of the key to the kitchens."

Noelle scoffs. "No. And why do I get the impression that you're the sort of person who magically makes friends with everyone?"

"Because I'm a nice person?"

Her nose crinkles at this answer. "You can't say that about *yourself*."

"Why not? Objectively, I'm nice."

She doesn't say anything for a moment, so in lieu of continuing this conversation, I head to the area closest to the cookie station and drag one of the folded up tables out. I unlock it and spread it out gently in the middle of the cafeteria, right next to the cookie station.

"You're welcome to tell me I'm a nice person, if that would make you feel better," I joke, as I take a seat on one side.

For that, I get a reluctant smile and an eye roll. "You are," she says, her eyes flitting to mine and quickly away as she takes the seat across from me. I grin, and she points her finger at me. "But don't get gloaty about it."

"Nice people don't gloat," I say, shooting her a little wink that I realize after the fact is entirely too flirty for this situation.

Goddamnit. Noelle does something to me.

She's quiet for a second, her eyes on mine and a slight smile on her face.

I look away, filling this moment by dumping our food out onto the table.

She raises her eyebrows when she sees the spread I got us.

Because *fine*, I was kind of thinking of this as a healing thing for her.

I mean, I'm supposed to do *something* with this girl for another forty-some hours. There's not enough community service in this building to actually fill up that much time. I'm going to have to get creative, and like I said, is it not community service if someone from the community–even if she refuses to accept she's from here–benefits from it?

"Salad for you," I say, nudging the plastic container toward her with a fork. "As well as any candy, chips, energy drinks, or sweets you might like."

She snorts. "Yeah, if I eat that, my whole body is going to break out."

"What? From one piece of candy?"

She rips her salad open. "Yeah," she says, her eyes scanning the array in front of her. "But I can have some chips." She grins and bites her lip. "And the hot Cheetos. Oh lord, I love me some hot Cheetos."

I laugh. "Well, I'm glad I got you something you like."

She purses her lips, looking out over everything else. "I like candy a lot. I just can't really eat it." She's quiet for a second. "I have eczema. It used to be really bad when I was a kid, but I figured out my triggers. Sugar is one of them. I can have salty, greasy things, but no sugar if I can avoid it. Fruits are generally fine but I tend to stick to berries to be safe. I can only use one specific laundry detergent. And it always gets worse this time of year, with the season change and the stress of the holidays."

I nod as I gather the candy back into the bag. "Ah, okay. Well, I wouldn't have tried to tempt you into sugar if I knew."

"I don't usually tell people."

I nod. "Well, thank you for telling me."

She shrugs. "Thank you for essentially doing community service with me. I know things could have gone a lot worse for me."

I shoot her a quick grin. "I'm always happy to help the community."

She rolls her eyes.

"Eat your hot Cheetos, Criminal."

3

NOELLE

Sunday, December 1st

W hy am I suddenly looking forward to community service?

Probably because the guy I'm stuck doing community service *with* has a charming smile. A stupidly nice personality. A trustworthy vibe that has me itching to divulge my high school trauma because something about him tells me he's a black box. A safe space to store those old memories that pop up when you're having an otherwise nice day and crumble that strong facade you've been crafting since they happened.

When I get to the high school, he's sitting at the front desk again, his feet up and crossed on one side and his head in a book. I know before he looks up that he's going to push those glasses up on his head and his hair is going to stick out a little wildly around them. He's going to raise his eyebrows and smile kindly at me, like maybe it's a nice surprise to see me or I'm his regular Sunday morning date.

The thought sends a little jolt down my spine. *His*

Sunday morning date. Like maybe instead of meeting each other at the local high school-slash-prison, I might turn over, pulling the sheets from between us, and nestle my face into his bare chest. Like he might kiss my head while I'm still groggy and read in bed while waiting for me to become a real human.

I find myself wondering if he has chest hair. What color his sheets are. Whether he drinks coffee or wakes up naturally this chipper.

"Good morning," I say, approaching the front desk.

And he does the whole thing. The glasses, the slight smile. His feet drop to the floor and he stands, stretching in a way that highlights his pecs through that stupid Snow Falls High School T-shirt he's wearing. *God, does he have* any *other clothing?*

"Good morning, Noelle."

Every time he grins, it reaches his eyes, and it seems so genuine. Like he doesn't give smiles without a good reason, but he *always* has a good reason.

I take a deep breath to calm the butterflies rioting in my stomach.

"I have something fun for us today," he says, watching my face as we walk the halls.

"That makes me nervous," I say.

"Why?"

"I don't know. I feel like teachers don't know what fun is. Like, every time a teacher has *ever* said that to me, I think I've had possibly the *opposite* of fun. God, group projects? Pop quizzes? That time Mr. Carmichael brought a tarantula into school? Not fun. Nope. Do I need a doctor's note?"

Nick laughs. "To be fair, I think in most cases when a teacher says that to their class, they mean it's going to be fun for *them.*"

"Ah, there's the context I've been missing." He stops in front of a very familiar door, and I raise my eyebrows. "What do you have up your sleeve?"

He pulls a key out of his pocket and opens the door, holding it so I can go in first.

And to be fair, this is one of the few places I *don't* have bad memories.

It still smells the same. Old books with a hint of something a little bit stale. I swear, I can *smell* that old-lady perfume Mrs. Nguyen uses, like maybe she actually does sleep under her desk.

"So I talked to Mrs. Nguyen, who remembers you fondly by the way," he says. My face heats, because for some reason this arbitrary judgment from my high school librarian turns me back into that validation-seeking teenager I once was. "And she was thrilled to learn that despite your criminal tendencies, you're doing well. And she said that if we were searching for a community service project to take part in, she could really use some help in updating the software on the computers. And if we wanted to sort out the holds for the week and shelve some returns while we were here, that would be a great help."

"I can't believe you're going around telling my old high school librarian that I'm a criminal."

He shrugs. "To be fair, she said your dad deserved to be egged."

A disbelieving snort jumps from my throat. "Oh."

"I guess you're not the only one who's done with his bullshit."

That feels kind of good. Vindicating, really.

My dad's the kind of person who can charm people easily. Always grinning or laughing. Usually drinking. It's a special kind of torture to have someone look at you in confusion when you mention your dad has trouble showing up to holidays or school events. To have people discount your experience of your own family based on their own arbitrary interactions with them.

All that to say, it feels good that Mrs. Nguyen saw right through that. Like she's on my side.

A little drop of optimism blooms in my chest. Maybe she always *was* on my side.

I shake the thought away as Nick leads us to the bank of computers set up in a semi-circle in the middle of the library. Around us are rows and rows of books, filling up the first floor, with several stacks stuffed into the balcony above us.

I've always loved how libraries are set up. Endless words and information at your fingertips surrounding you like a threat but whispering with invitation. The ability to learn or read almost anything. Stories and characters you'd never otherwise experience. Hobbies that are completely foreign to you until you flip through a few pages of a book.

We sit side by side at two computers and power them up with the login information Mrs. Nguyen left with Nick.

We could zip through them, bounce from one seat to another as the updates plod through, clicking 'Next' as soon as the button pops up on the screen.

But instead, we sit and wait, angled toward each other like the purpose of the day is *us* and not the computers.

He gives me a soft grin. "So are you ever going to tell me what your dad did to deserve The Great Egging?"

I purse my lips, clicking through another few prompts before turning to him. "He didn't care."

Nick's brow furrows. "What does that mean?"

I let out a long breath. "He never really cared, honestly. When my sister and I were in high school, we found out he had a second family. One that apparently means more to him than his first. He left us to go live with them. Ironically, he had two little girls. Two new ones. Shinier and brighter than me and Christina."

"Wow, that's messed up."

"Yeah. Not exactly a fun holiday season, that one. Luckily, it was my sister's senior year so she was leaving anyway. A year later, I followed her. Got my GED while living in her spare bedroom. I think we all needed that space, honestly. My sister and I needed to be away from him, and I think my mom needed some alone time to grieve her relationship and pull herself together. He was never there for her much, but I think there was a part of her that never gave up on having her big, happy family."

Nick nods. "I feel for her. That must have been hard."

"It was. I still don't know why she stays in this town. The last thing I need is to run into my dad or his new family. And I can only imagine it's worse for her."

"You don't talk to him at all now? Or... them?"

I shake my head. "Nope. I met them once when I was in high school. But otherwise, I don't come back here. I don't talk to him or them at all."

He nods. "Well, I guess I can understand the egging."

"Oh, that's not why he got egged." I sigh. "My sister is kind of my opposite. God, I love her to death, but she keeps trying to be a family with him. Like, always forgiving him for what he's done. And if that's what she wants to do, that's fine. But after Thanksgiving this year, she went over to his house to bring him a pie. She wanted him to feel like she was included. Turned out, they weren't home at the time. I think they were visiting the harlot's parents–"

Nick's eyebrows jump up.

"Sorry, that's what we've always called her. She's actually

a very nice woman and we eventually found out that she was as oblivious as we were to the whole arrangement, but you know, the nickname stuck."

I take a deep breath, clicking into the next screen. "So they weren't home when my sister went over, and she figured she would leave the pie on the doorstep. No biggie, right? Well, when she left, she slipped on a patch of ice in the driveway and went down *hard*. Called my mom to come get her and take her to the ER because she heard a snap and, sure enough, she had broken her leg."

"Ah," Nick says. "It all comes together."

"I was still at my mom's because I refused to take part in bringing him a pie. He can suck my dick, you know? So my mom and I went over to get her together, picked her up and took her to the hospital. She got a cast and everything, and she's looking at a full recovery so no big deal."

"And that's why you egged his house? Because she tripped?"

I shake my head. "No. Not at all. I mean, ice happens, you know? I egged his house because she called him first. My sister called our dad for help, and he said he couldn't leave right away. They were in the middle of Thanksgiving dessert."

Nick presses his lips together. "Oh."

"I don't think I've ever been so angry with someone in my life. You can disrespect me. You can tell me you don't care about me in as many ways as you want. But you do *not* fuck with my sister."

He rubs a hand over his chest, shaking his head. "I didn't expect to be so angry when you finished that story."

I laugh. "What, you didn't think I'd have a good enough reason to egg my own father's house?"

He shrugs. "I don't know what I expected. But I have to say, if I were you, I wouldn't be sorry either."

I nod. "I don't regret it. Even if that means I'm back here in this stupid town in this hellhole of a school, it was all worth it. Honestly, I wish I would have done worse."

"*Two* dozen eggs?"

"Exactly."

BY THE TIME we're done updating the computers, we're only about halfway through our day, so I take some time to run a defrag while we're there. If I had to take a guess, these old computers haven't had a bit of optimization since they were installed years ago, and I show Nick quickly how to do the same so we can do two at a time.

"And she's a computer whiz, too," he comments, as I show him the last button he needs to click and the computer goes through its process. "This won't hurt the computers, will it? You're not setting me up to take the fall when all of the computers are wiped and the kids turn them on to find only a video of you cackling maniacally, are you?"

I snort. "No. If I wanted to do that, I'd at least start in the rooms where there aren't cameras."

He raises his eyebrows. "That answer came to you entirely too quickly, and it's starting to make me wonder whether I should be alone with you."

"Always be on your toes, Mr. Monroe." I shoot him a quick grin. "No, this won't hurt the computers. All it does is move pieces of the hard drive closer together so things run a little faster. You might not even notice it, but my hunch is that these computers will be here until they don't work anymore. This might preserve their life a little bit."

He grins. "Look at you helping the kids."

I glare at him. "I'm helping the *computers*."

He snorts, rolling his eyes. "Okay, computer genius. How'd you learn to defrag a hard drive?"

"Google?"

"Oh." He's quiet for a second. "Well, I guess that makes sense. You had a slow computer, I take it?"

I shrug. "One of my employees did, actually."

He cocks his head to the side. "Your employees?"

I swallow. "I run a little web design business. It's a small thing. But one of my people was having a lot of trouble with an old machine–I started out with a group of freelancers who originally worked off their own equipment–and that was one of many things I tried to help her with before I ended up buying her a computer."

He nods, digesting this. "So you're the kind of smart that gets bullied in high school and ends up being everybody's boss later in life?"

I shake my head. "No. I never intended for this to happen. I just... I guess after college, I realized I had a talent that I really enjoyed. So I figured out how to talk to people and sold, sold, sold, until I realized I had too much business to conceivably do myself. So, I had to hire people. And now, I guess I own my own little boutique web design business."

He stands, moving to the next computer down to start another defrag. He clicks through the prompts quickly as I take the next computer after his, doing the same.

"That's really cool," he says, turning to face me. "You could probably teach me a thing or two, huh?"

"I don't know about that."

He cocks his head to the side. "Why aren't you more proud of yourself?"

I let out a breath. "It feels a little bit like too little, too late. Like I struggled and failed in high school, did moderately okay in college, and afterward it was like everything clicked into place, and sometimes I don't really believe it's real."

He nods. "So you know not to take it for granted. You can still be proud of all the work you've done."

"I guess. I just... it's not something I talk about much and it's not something I bring back to this town with me. My life in the city is my life. And I don't let anyone screw with that. Especially considering the person I shrink into when I'm in this town, I just... need to keep things separate."

His brow furrows as he nods.

The word vomit comes too easily. "I've done a whole lot of making myself smaller so other people can feel big, and that started here. And I'm not really interested in boosting lackluster egos anymore."

"Ah," he says, as if every piece is clicking into place. "The dudes can't handle it."

I shrug. "A lot of people can't really handle a young woman doing her own thing. But I'm good at this. And it's taken me a long time to trust myself in spite of everyone else."

He raises his eyebrows. "How big *is* this company of yours?"

"How big *is* this dick of yours?"

He nods. "Touche. You leave it in the city." He's quiet for a few moments. "But for what it's worth, anyone whose first inclination isn't to respect the hell out of what you did and what you continue to do is a complete and utter jerk." He shakes his head. "And I really hope you never shrink yourself again. You're too cool for that."

I raise my eyebrows. "The math teacher thinks I'm cool?"

He shrugs. "I mean, you're alright."

"The math teacher thinks I'm cool," I say, in a singsong voice.

He rolls his eyes. "Alright, forget I said anything."

I grin. If I knew him better, I'd take his face in my hands and plant a big old kiss on his cheek.

That is, if he's the sort of person who can put his money where his mouth is. There have been far too many guys who have given me a similar speech but haven't been able to back up their words with actions.

We spend the rest of the day hopping between computers, filling our silence with easygoing chatter as we knock out one computer after another. When we're finally done, Nick signs my timecard with a flourish as we walk out of school together.

Although I'm excited to be back home with my sister, there's a part of me that's dreading leaving. I tell myself it's the three-hour drive home.

"So, I meant to tell you earlier. Next weekend the theater kids are going to be in school for dress rehearsals for the winter play. I didn't know if that would bother you, but I wanted to give you the option to switch up days if it does."

I purse my lips, debating this.

It doesn't exactly sound like my idea of fun.

But maybe it wouldn't be the worst thing to actually have a few days off. As much as I appreciate Nick being willing to work with my weekend schedule, I'm realizing that doing this *and* signing in for work over the next five days is a little rough.

I let out a long breath. "Do you want to do a week of nights, maybe? And if there's no one here the weekend after, we can try for that?"

He nods. "Sure. That works for me." He leans against the side of my car as I fish my keys out of my purse. "I'll have to dream up some fun weeknight community service activities we can get into."

I laugh, mirroring his pose and leaning against my car. "Whose definition of fun are you using?"

He winks at me again, and my throat goes dry. "That's for me to know and you to find out."

I find myself wishing for the kind of fun we could have without any clothes on. The kind where his stubble scrapes against my skin and his fingers dig into the flesh of my ass.

"So you'll text me what sort of schedule works for you?" he asks.

I nod, knowing I should be opening my car door and slipping inside right about now.

But this moment feels like the end of a first date. That nervous dance when you're trying to figure out if the other person wants to kiss you or not. He's standing close enough that I can smell him—that smoky s'more scent that has my mouth watering.

He clears his throat, and something about the way he takes a very intentional step back from me tells me that he feels this tension, too.

"Well, drive safe," he says, patting the roof of my car.

"Yeah, I will."

He nods, turning on his heel and heading straight for the only other car in the parking lot.

4

NICK

Monday, December 2nd

I sit at my desk, running my hands over my face as the bell rings and my post-lunch seniors filter in. This class is particularly rowdy this year. Usually after lunch, the kids get a little sleepy and slow, but this year I somehow got the perfect storm in this class. A group of friends who eat lunch together and get themselves all riled up before having to settle down for math.

My energy is running low, mostly because I was up half of last night thinking about a certain criminal in a very inappropriate way.

The look she gave me before she finally got in her car was loaded. Her pink lips were slightly parted, her eyes wide and her breathing heavy. We've gotten to know each other just enough to have rosy views of each other.

I try to be the sort of person who gives the benefit of the doubt, mostly because I work with kids and a lot of times assuming good intentions gets you further than brandishing sharp punishments for the sake of keeping up your authority.

But something about the way Noelle spoke about her family inspired this understanding of her. Like I *get* her a little bit now.

This town gave her a hard time. Her dad gave her a hard time.

And now, her sister is her safe space. And she will do anything to protect her.

Including turning herself into a criminal.

That fierce defensiveness was something I didn't necessarily expect from her. I knew her dad must have wronged her in some way for her to so vehemently insist that she didn't regret a thing, but to hear that it wasn't a wrong against her, but someone she loved, and she still didn't regret it one bit?

I like her. More than I should.

And I have to somehow squash that, because it's inappropriate for me to be having feelings for someone whose timecard I'm signing.

Even if the whole thing is pretty much a sham.

I don't know how I'm going to do it. She has a good forty hours left, and if I'm reading her correctly, she's into me too.

How the hell am I supposed to spend another forty hours alone with Noelle without completely derailing my boundaries?

I consider asking Hank to chaperone, though I have a feeling that any explanation I give him would encourage him to deny me. He'd probably find the whole thing entertaining, and I don't doubt for a moment that he would relish the opportunity to make fun of me for crushing on the criminal.

I could plan activities for us that are public only. Maybe clean stuff up in the town square, not that it's particularly dirty, or maybe hand out fliers for the Christmas parade or the concert.

But considering the look on her face when she heard the kids would be taking over the school next weekend, I'm not sure she would love *that* either.

A boisterous laugh fills the room as one of my favorite and least favorite students enters. One of my troublemakers who has a heart of gold but a difficult family life. He acts out because it's the only thing that gets him attention, unfortunately both at home and at school, and considering I have twenty other kids to teach at the same time, I can't give him the individual attention he's craving.

He's overweight and gets bullied because of it, and I can see the way he shrinks into himself when he thinks no one is looking. He sits in the back of the class whenever he has a chance, and although he plays along with the bullies, making fun of himself, I see the way his shoulders drop when they finally turn their attention elsewhere.

He's on another level today. Laughing the loudest, snickering even when the others have stopped. He stands at the front of the room, a bottle of Coke in his hand.

"Hey, hey, want to see what I learned in science class today?" he asks his friends, holding the bottle out in front of him.

"Robbie," I bark. He turns his attention to me. "Sit down."

"I'm showing them a trick," he says, his eyes wide like he thinks he's going to get one past me.

I stand from my chair. *I don't fucking need this today.* "Robbie. I know the trick, and you're not doing it here. Sit down."

And then he takes a mentos from his pocket and swiftly drops it in the soda.

Coke sprays all over my classroom, soaking me, the kids in the front row, and Robbie.

It's like a faucet.

Kids are screaming, Robbie is laughing, and all I can really do is take the bottle from him and try my hardest to screw the cap on top.

When I finally do, I struggle to control my breath.

My eyes dip to the floor beneath us, now completely covered in soda. To the girls who were sitting in the front row who are now completely doused and screaming. To the kids in back who are only snickering, wide-eyed.

I am surrounded by chaos, and the only thing I can do is point to the door. "Hallway. Now."

As I follow Robbie out, I can already feel the sugar on my skin. My clothes are soaked, as are Robbie's, and in the few steps it takes to leave the room, my shoes start squelching with the stickiness.

Fucking Robbie.

Mrs. Harper next door pokes her head out of her room as we step into the hallway, eyebrows raised. "Everything okay?"

I shake my head. "Any chance you can watch my class for a few minutes? Somebody"–I nod to Robbie–"thought it was a good idea to show the class what he learned in science class today."

She nods, turning back to her class. "Five minutes to finish your reading," she calls out, and then quickly scutters toward my classroom, where the noise level is only growing in my absence and spurred on by the chaos everyone witnessed.

Thank god Mrs. Harper's first post-lunch class is one of the quiet ones.

"Alright!" she shouts, closing the door behind her. "Settle down! Take your seats! I need everyone quiet so I can call the janitor."

I turn to Robbie, who has the decency to look sheepish.

"Robbie," I say, throwing my hands out in front of me. "What was that?"

He shrugs. "I thought it would be cool. It wasn't that messy in science class."

I nod. "I'm more miffed about you not listening to me. I told you not to do the trick and you did it anyway."

He shrugs again, his eyes glued to the floor.

I bite my lip, a mixture of emotions warring inside my brain.

And then a thought occurs to me. A way to kill two birds with one stone, so to speak.

I let out a long breath. "Well, I'm going to have to give you detention for that."

I'VE FOUND us a volunteer gig for the Christmas festival that gets set up in the town square every year. They need people to help build the little vendor huts that line the walkways, and although I'm not thrilled about the prospect of manual labor, I'm relieved we have a bigger purpose to support. And a solid itinerary.

When I asked Robbie if he was okay with the change—helping build huts instead of sitting bored in detention—he nodded enthusiastically. He's spent enough time in detention to know being *anywhere else* is preferable.

We're meeting at the school before walking over together, and I take my usual spot at the front desk once the teacher on bus duty clears out.

Robbie shows up first, raising his eyebrows in lieu of a greeting.

"We're waiting on one other person," I explain.

He nods, leaning against the far side of the desk.

And fifteen minutes later–what seems to be Noelle's usual–she wanders through the front doors toward the desk.

She smiles, nodding quickly to Robbie before turning toward me. "Hi."

"Look who made it," I say as I stand.

She glares at me. "Sorry I'm late."

"Noelle, this is Robbie," I say, gesturing to him. "Robbie, Noelle."

She gives a small wave. "Hi."

"Hi."

And then there's silence.

This is going to be an interesting walk.

"Shall we?" I ask, grabbing my coat from the back of my chair and pulling it on.

I gesture for Noelle to lead the way, and Robbie falls into step behind her. She pushes through the front doors, holding one open for Robbie, who then holds it open for me.

"Do you go here?" Robbie asks, as we step down the stairs to the sidewalk. Noelle is in the middle as we turn, following the path that will eventually take us past the football field to the town square on the other side.

Noelle scoffs. "Not anymore. Thank god."

"Noelle is fulfilling a community service requirement," I explain.

"Oh."

And the only sound is that of our feet on the pavement.

"So what did you do?" Robbie asks.

She crinkles her nose. "I threw eggs at my dad's house."

Robbie's laugh is boisterous–as it always is–and Noelle can't seem to resist laughing along with him.

"Why?" he asks.

She shrugs. "He didn't show up for my sister when he really should have. And I got mad and needed to do something, and I went in the fridge for a drink and came out with a carton of eggs instead."

Robbie chuckles again, eyes wide with delight.

"Don't get any ideas," I tell him.

"I mean, it was pretty cathartic to be honest," Noelle says.

I turn to her, giving her my best stern teacher face because the *worst* possible outcome of this pseudo-punishment would be further trouble.

"But a bad idea," she finishes, her eyes on mine. "A very bad idea. Because now I'm a criminal."

I nod my approval.

"Hmm," he says. "I don't know. Might be worth it to do once."

"No," I say. "It's not."

Noelle waves me off. "Well, wait. Whose house would you egg? Maybe we can get creative. I mean, they might *deserve* an egging, but we might have options for vengeance that don't land you in community service."

"Hey," I say, drawing their attention to me. "No egging. No vengeance." I pause, making sure my words hit. I'm suddenly worried this was the *worst* idea I could have concocted. "Today is about undoing past wrongs by contributing positively to the community."

Noelle rolls her eyes. "Okay, what are you, an after-school special?"

Robbie's laughter fills the air once more, and the glare she's giving me crumbles into a smile.

"Can the two of you do me a favor and just behave for the next two hours?" I ask.

Robbie shrugs. Noelle rolls her eyes.

And silence descends upon us once more.

"So in theory, if there was a kid in Snow Falls who was going to egg somebody's house, whose house do you think he would egg? Speaking as a totally objective third-party observer who understands that egging houses and enacting vengeance is wrong."

I throw my hands out in front of me, turning my attention to Noelle.

She brushes her hair behind her ear, her attention on Robbie, and–

She's flipping me off. She's brushing her hair behind her ear with her middle finger, lingering a second longer than she really needs to.

And when she glances back at me, she only grins.

What have I gotten myself into?

Robbie shrugs. "As an objective third-party observer, I would say that a kid in Snow Falls who is definitely not me would probably egg his own house."

I crinkle my eyebrows. Noelle glances at me again. "Why?"

"Because his mom is an asshole who can't even show up to the principal's office when he was waiting for hours to go home and he had to call one of his friends to pick him up instead because by the time everyone realized she wasn't coming, the busses had already left."

I bite my lip. *Yeah, she's an asshole.*

"Wow, she really *is* an asshole."

"I agree with the sentiment," I say. "But can we watch the language?"

Noelle turns to me. "What the hell is the matter with you?"

"I'm a teacher. I literally *have* to give a detention if I hear cursing on school grounds."

She shakes her head and glances over her shoulder.

"We're not on school grounds anymore. And is 'asshole' even really a curse? I mean, it's not like he called her a fuck-face or something."

I run my hand over my face. "Noelle. Seriously?"

"What are you going to do, give me detention?"

The dare in her voice has a slew of unsavory thoughts running through my mind.

"So your mom is an asshole," Noelle says, turning back to Robbie. "I'm sorry to hear that."

He shrugs. "I'm used to it at this point. I'm just counting down the days until I graduate so I can get out of this stupid town."

She nods. "I hear you. That's what I did. My sister went to college in the city and I followed her. Got my GED and went right to college."

He blinks, quiet for a moment. "How do you get your GED?"

"It's just a test. I think you might be able to take it online now and you can get a diploma from the state."

Goddamnit, Noelle.

"But it's really not the same as getting a high school diploma," I say. "You should stick it out, Robbie."

He nods, seemingly absorbing this.

"I did fine," Noelle insists. "I was able to take classes at the community college and roll them into my degree when I started at Temple."

"That's a different situation," I say, trying desperately to find a middle ground here. "Stay in school, Robbie. You've only got a few months left. I know it sucks now, but it'll be worth it in the end, to graduate with your class and have that diploma that you *deserve*."

He nods, stuffing his hands into his pockets.

"There's nothing wrong with knowing your options," Noelle says, as we cross the street to the town square.

"Absolutely nothing wrong with knowing your options, but without a reason to leave high school early, I don't think it's the right way to go. If you have college or technical training for a job, that might be a different story. But don't leave just because you don't like school."

He shrugs noncommittally as we join the group of volunteers congregating by the pagoda. "I don't know what I'm going to do yet," he says.

An irrational discomfort sits in my gut.

The *only* thing I want right now is for Robbie to say he'll stay in school.

At the front of the group are a few people dressed in neon orange shirts who are picking off small groups and leading them to different areas around the town square. There are a number of groups ahead of us, chatting casually as they wait their turn.

"Hey Robbie, do you mind checking us in when the volunteers get to us?" I ask.

He nods. "Sure."

Noelle raises her eyebrows, and I nod to the street behind us. Thankfully, she follows me without protest.

When we're a good fifty feet from the volunteers, I turn back to her.

"You need to chill with the GED stuff. Don't encourage him to egg houses. And for the love of god, can you please stop cursing in front of him?"

She rolls her eyes. "I had a feeling I was about to get in trouble. You realize he needed to tell someone about his issues with his mom, right? *That's* what that was about. He's not going to egg his own house. And you do realize that he probably has the mouth of a sailor around his friends.

Nothing I'm saying is new to him. And honestly, why is it so bad to get your GED? It's an alternative diploma."

"Noelle"–I make sure she's not going to start spewing words again–"I am his *teacher*. If you want to be buddy-buddy with him, that's fine. But I can't condone certain behaviors when you're around and then do the opposite in school. Sure, you can make excuses and explain that we were outside school, but that doesn't mean it's not confusing."

She shakes her head. "I don't understand why you're keeping up this farce. It feels so inauthentic."

"I know. I agree." I pause, hoping this lands. "But I'm his *teacher*. The farce is part of my job."

She's quiet for a second, and then relents. "Okay. I will encourage the kid to stay in school even though in some cases, it's probably more damaging. I will act suitably remorseful about egging my father's house and drone on about how *terrible* community service is with the stick-up-the-butt math teacher. And I will even censor myself for you. But know that when we're alone, I'm going to let out a string of pent up expletives so long you're going to wonder whether I'm a construction worker or having an orgasm."

I raise an eyebrow. So she's trying to get a reaction out of me.

Too bad for her, I'm plenty experienced at keeping a straight face.

"I've never *wondered* whether a woman is orgasming before."

Her mouth pops open and she blinks.

"So that's how I get you to stop talking? Good to know."

"I–"

"Come on," I say, nodding behind her to where Robbie is

now talking to one of the people in orange shirts. "Looks like we're up."

I turn and head back, Noelle following a moment later.

And while the volunteer walks us along the path and explains that all the directions we should need are in these little packets he hands us, I wonder how the hell I'm going to keep *my own* mouth shut.

That comment was incredibly inappropriate.

In my defense, she started it.

But I'm supposed to be impervious to little comments like that.

I'm supposed to be a *professional*, goddamnit.

And instead I'm latching onto her bait and playing into the palm of her pretty little manicured hand.

WE FINISH our hut well within our allotted two hours, mostly because Robbie McGuire is apparently a tank.

There were a few times Noelle and I glanced at each other when he would pick up a piece that was very obviously meant for two people and hoist it above his head like it was nothing. He somehow managed to memorize the directions within a few minutes, and rather than double-checking or trying to figure out what we should do next, Noelle and I both very quickly snapped into waiting mode, letting Robbie direct us.

He seemed excited, almost. Like he got to be the boss and tell everybody else what to do for once.

It was kind of awesome to watch.

As we clear up and get our hut checked over by one of the orange-shirted volunteers, I realize this form of punishment might have actually been *perfect* for Robbie. Sure, it wasn't the way he planned on spending his night, but he clicked into something he was really good at, and it certainly didn't *seem* like he hated it.

"I bet you're the kind of kid who likes building Ikea furniture," I say.

He shrugs. "Sometimes my friends ask me to help build stuff and I don't mind it."

"You're a fucking badass," Noelle spouts, a big grin on her face. And then she starts, covering her mouth with her hand. "Oh, shoot. Sorry. But I think that if I get one more accidental expletive for the night, that one is worth it."

Robbie shrugs, the corners of his mouth tugging into a smile.

I roll my eyes. "You did well," I say. "I agree with Noelle's sentiment despite her potty mouth."

She shrugs, grinning again. "I wonder if there's a job that's, like, doing that, but bigger."

"Foreman," Robbie says.

I raise my eyebrows. "Is that what you want to be?"

He shrugs. "I don't know."

"Because I think you'd be good at it."

He glances up at me but doesn't say anything else.

And then the orange-shirted volunteer speaks. "You guys are looking good. Thanks for helping us out today."

"Thanks for having us," I say, nodding.

We gather up our things and the three of us walk back to the school together. Robbie is quiet but he doesn't seem upset. Introspective, maybe. Noelle yawns and stretches, rubbing at a spot on her arm that she knocked when trying to drill one side of the hut together.

She's cute when she's exhausted.

I knock that thought from my head as quickly as it enters.

Robbie calls a friend for a ride as we walk, and when we get back to the school, Noelle and I wait on the stairs out front for his ride to arrive. He stands on the curb, looking out over the parking lot like his vigilance might inspire his friend to drive faster.

"So, same time tomorrow?" I ask Noelle, leaning against the concrete side of the staircase.

She lets out a long breath. "Same time tomorrow," she agrees.

A car careens into the parking lot, music blaring, and comes to a stop in front of Robbie. With a quick wave behind him, he clambers inside and zips off with his buddy.

Noelle stands once he's gone, stifling a yawn in her elbow as she heads toward her car.

As I've taken to doing, I walk with her. I don't know why–this school is a safe place, even at night, but when I think about waving to her over my shoulder and diverting off to my own car, something about it feels completely wrong. Like I'm shirking my duty to make sure everybody here gets to their transportation in one piece.

It must be the teacher in me.

I sigh as we walk, both relieved and nervous about finally being alone with her. She hands me her timecard, and I scribble incoherently across it like I've done every other day.

When I hand it back to her, she gives me a dainty smile with eyes full of warning.

"Fuckity fucking shit stain dickhole twat waffle," she says, catching my eye and grinning.

I blink. Points for creativity. "So that's really been building up, huh?"

She shrugs. "So what's your determination: orgasming or not?"

I purse my lips because I *want* to laugh.

But I know she's baiting me again.

"Goodnight, Criminal."

She rolls her eyes as she tugs her car door open and slips inside. "Goodnight, Saint Nick."

I wait until all feet and elbows are safely within the car, and close the door on her. She blinks up at me from the other side of the window for a moment, the hint of a smile on her face before she turns the car on.

I take a step back, grasping my hands behind my back while she puts it into gear and slowly drives away, waving over her shoulder as she heads for the road.

Man, I am in over my head with this one.

5

NOELLE

Wednesday, December 4th

Another day, another two hours of community service.

Nick is reading again when I arrive, his feet propped up on the desk like usual. He grins when he sees me, and for a second, I mirror that grin right back at him.

And then something comes over his face, like he remembers he's not supposed to be happy to see *his criminal,* and his smile fades.

He checks the time on his phone as he stands. "Look who's almost on time today," he remarks.

I roll my eyes. "I finished work earlier than usual. Thought I would grace you with a few extra minutes of my presence."

"I'm honored," he deadpans, slipping his phone into his pocket. "Did the hut-building work for you yesterday?"

I shrug. "Sure. What else are we going to do for *community service?*"

"Again, clapping erasers out back is always an option."

I roll my eyes. "Come on, Mr. Monroe. Let's go build some huts."

He nods and follows me out the front doors of the school.

Where we run smack dab into Robbie.

"Am I late?" he asks. "Sorry, I needed to find a ride."

I look at Nick. *How many detentions did he give the poor kid?*

"For hut-building?" Nick asks.

"Yeah."

Nick glances at me. "You did your detention yesterday. You didn't have to come back again," he says.

Robbie shrugs but doesn't say anything further.

"Unless you *want* to build huts?"

He shrugs again.

"To be clear, you're welcome to come with us, but you're under no obligation to help."

He shrugs again, glancing at me.

"Oh my god, Nick. Let the kid build a hut if he wants to build a hut."

Nick throws his hands up at me. "God Noelle, it's like zero to sixty with you. I'm making sure he knows he's fulfilled his duty."

I gesture to him. "I think he knows he's fulfilled his duty. Right, Robbie?"

He nods, and then opens his mouth like he's going to speak and decides against it. Nick and I both naturally wait, seeing if he's going to speak. "I liked building the hut yesterday."

I nod. "Well, thank god you'll be there because I don't think I can lift some of those pieces on my own and lord knows old Mr. Monroe can't do it himself."

"Hey! I'm not old."

"You're the oldest one here," I parry back, noting the small smile on Robbie's lips as we turn and head in the direction of the town square.

"Well, somebody around here has to be an adult," he says, knocking my arm.

"It's called having fun. You should try it sometime."

He shrugs. "I have plenty of fun outside school."

And when I glance at him, he winks.

He *winks*.

What on earth is this man implying?

And why do I so desperately want to be a part of it?

I won't lie—I was poking the bear a little bit yesterday. Talking about swearing while coming and all that bullshit.

But I can't get a read on whether he's into it or not. Warmth trailed down my spine when he implied he *knows* when a woman is orgasming.

Every time he walks me to my car, I feel like the natural closure of our night should involve a good, old-fashioned kiss at the car. Maybe a little groping with some tongue action. Hell, throw a little grinding in there too.

I never got to be the fun girl in high school. I had one relationship that ended with the sharing of a picture that really *did not* need to be shared.

And thanks to that picture, no one ever wanted to touch me.

And now I keep getting funny warm feelings in my core when he looks in my direction. When he gives me those hidden smiles that Robbie doesn't see or those *winks* that— I'll be honest—make me salivate.

"Yeah, I bet you have fun outside school by, like, calculating an exact twenty percent tip anytime you eat out."

Oh god. And now I'm thinking about him eating me out.

And taking twenty percent of his tip.

To start, at least.

"I do find it very rewarding to be able to do mental math quickly when I need it," he says. "Though to be fair, recently I've been giving closer to twenty-five percent and rounding to the nearest dollar. I'm really into integers lately."

I look at Robbie and make a gagging face. "Are you hearing this? Really into *integers*?"

"And what are you into, sans serif fonts?"

I snort. "Okay, I'm a web designer. I literally *have* to have an opinion on fonts as part of my job."

"I'm a math teacher. I should enjoy math. I don't think it's all that wild."

I eye him. "You have one of those shirts that says, like, *I heart math* or something like that, don't you?"

He narrows his eyes. "If I catch you snooping through my drawers, I'm going to put you in detention again," he tells me.

I raise an eyebrow. "Is that a threat or a promise?"

"Jesus Christ, get a room already," Robbie mutters, walking ahead of us to check in with the orange-shirted volunteers.

Nick stands beside me as we wait for Robbie to return, and when he speaks, his voice is low. "Keep it in your pants, Noelle. You're making Robbie uncomfortable."

I turn to him, ready to spit fire, when Robbie calls us over and beckons for us to follow him and the volunteer to our hut's location.

I keep my voice low when I turn to him. "If you catch me in your *drawers*? That was all you, Mr. Monroe. Are you trying to invite me into your pants? Because that's certainly what that sounded like."

"*Dresser* drawers," he says.

"You're not denying it," I say, coming to a stop as the volunteer gives us the same spiel he gave us yesterday.

He gives me that stern look he whips out every once in a while when I poke him enough. "Why don't you get your head out of the gutter and focus on helping Robbie build his hut?"

I point at him as I drop my bag off on the far end of the hut, which, if yesterday was any indication, should be out of our way. "You started it."

And when the volunteer leaves and it's the three of us, Robbie rolls up his sleeves. Nick and I click into our roles easily, letting Robbie run the show and tell us where to go, what to do, how to build.

He and Nick lift the heavy pieces, and I dart around underneath and between them with the drill, screwing bits and pieces in as Robbie directs me. At some point, the two of them are holding up a large piece of particle board, and as I position myself underneath and screw it into place, I can't help noticing that Nick's sweatshirt has gotten caught on the edge, tugging it up enough to see a smattering of hair dusting his skin above his jeans.

My mouth goes *dry*.

And I accidentally hit the power button on the screw-driver, drawing attention to myself.

Nick ducks underneath the edge of the board with a furrowed brow.

"You okay?" he asks, as his shirt drops back down and disappointment settles in my stomach.

"Yep," I say, clicking the power button again and holding it up. "Just trying to screw you." When his eyebrows pop up, I realize what I said. "Just trying to say 'screw you'!"

The damage is already done.

He laughs, and I think I detect a hint of pink in his cheeks. "Inappropriate, Noelle."

I shut my eyes in embarrassment as he turns his attention back to the board he's holding up.

Fuck me. Leave it to me to try to have an attitude and instead attempt to–well, screw him.

I need to get my thoughts under control.

I step up to the edge of the board and screw the pieces in according to Robbie's directions.

And for the rest of the day, every time I use the drill, he raises one eyebrow at me, because apparently we *both* know what I'm thinking.

That I desperately want to screw the math teacher.

TODAY GOES TWICE AS FAST as yesterday, and we finish with a significant amount of time to spare. Robbie wanted to stay and see if we could build another in our allotted time frame, but the volunteers in charge were concerned about having people out too late.

So instead, we wander back to the high school. And like last night, Robbie calls his buddy for a ride as we're walking home.

Nick and I wait on the stairs outside the high school until the same car appears and Robbie excitedly clambers in.

And then it's just the two of us.

"Anything else I can help with?" I ask, checking the time on my phone. I can't get a read on whether Nick is the type to give me a free pass for the extra hour I was going to get tonight if Robbie hadn't been such a quick builder.

He shakes his head. "No," he says, and throws me a quick

grin as he starts across the parking lot toward my car. "But don't worry, I'll still give you the full time."

I follow him, somewhat reluctantly. "I'm surprised you're not making me bang erasers together."

"If I'm being totally honest, I think it would take an hour for me to track down enough erasers to make it worth your while. I'm one of the few teachers who still has a chalkboard, and I use a rag instead of an eraser."

I raise my eyebrows, leaning against my car as I dig through my bag for my keys. "Whose Cheerios did you piss in to get that deal?"

His brow furrows. "I requested the chalkboard."

"You did? But it's so messy. And you know, chalky. You like having that texture on your hands all day?"

He shrugs, mirroring my lean and resting one elbow on top of my car. "I think there's something charming about it," he says. "When I was a kid we only had chalkboards at school. So when I decided to become a teacher, I kind of thought of that as part of the deal."

I nod. "You've romanticized your chalkboard." I hum. "I think you have Stockholm Syndrome, sir."

He laughs, turning to face the parking lot. "It's not like my chalkboard is holding me hostage."

"It's sure keeping you in the past."

He gives me a look, one eyebrow raised. "You can tear my chalkboard out of my cold, dead fingers. I don't care what you think about it. I like the chalk on my hands."

"To each their own. Personally, I prefer knives in my eyes."

He shakes his head while he laughs. "You really have a response for everything, don't you?"

"Not everything," I say, the viscerally remembering that

cocky comment he made about never *wondering* when a woman comes.

I didn't have much to say to *that*.

Other than *Bet*.

I tug my timecard out of my bag and hand it to him. He signs quickly, copying one row down to the next, and hands it back to me. "There you go, Criminal."

"Thank you," I say, replacing it in my bag and letting out a long breath as I look up at him. I swallow, because I swear he's giving me *kiss me* eyes.

Or maybe it's me giving him *kiss me* eyes.

He moves forward a smidge, and for a second I think he might.

But he only pats the top of my car and reaches for the driver's side handle. He pulls it open and gestures for me to get in.

"Get home safe," he says.

"Thanks."

And he closes the door on me.

WHEN I GET BACK to my mom's house, she has Christmas music on full blast and an array of presents scattered across the living room floor. She's wearing a Santa hat and drinking something out of a tea cup that's likely alcoholic, considering the way she flails when I walk in the door. Her frizzy brown hair is pulled into a long braid that falls over one shoulder as she moves.

"Noelle!" she screeches. "You weren't supposed to be home yet! Close your eyes!"

"Sorry," I say, holding a hand in front of my face as I move through the living room to my old bedroom.

The sound of crinkling paper almost drowns out the tune of *Jingle Bell Rock* playing through the speakers. She stacks all of the presents I wasn't supposed to see underneath the coffee table and covers it with a red and white striped blanket.

Her house is a small bungalow with an open floor plan and high ceilings. The kitchen and living rooms are separated only by a plushy gray couch, and off to one side, a staircase brings you to the bedrooms upstairs.

I head for the stairs, doing my best to avoid the shrine to my sister and me that covers the wall.

"Wait, honey!" my mom calls, scrambling to her feet and following me. "How was community service? Were you with the math teacher again?"

I nod. "Yeah, I'll probably be with him for at least the near future," I say.

My mom crosses her arms over her chest and leans against the wall before her. She gives me a sly grin that tells me the small town gossip chain is alive and well. "Hank said the two of you are getting along well."

"We're getting along fine," I say.

She smiles, waiting for me to continue, but when I don't, she says, "Well, that's great, honey! It's nice that you have a friend in town that you can hang out with."

I narrow my eyes. "He's not my friend, and we're not hanging out. It's community service."

She waves that off. "It's *Hank* community service. I'm happy you're not hating it."

I shrug. "It's a lot better than I thought it would be," I admit.

She grins. "I hear he's cute," she says.

I turn on my heel and continue up the stairs. "Goodnight, Mom!"

"I take it you agree!"

I shake my head as I close myself in my childhood bedroom. A moment later, I hear her moving around downstairs, the ripping of tape as she wraps presents and her low hum as she sings along to her Christmas songs.

And I throw my dirty clothes into a pile by the door, shower, and change into a silky sleep set that I bring whenever I have to stay at my mom's because it gives me a smidge of adulthood in a place that is otherwise filled with memories of my parents' divorce, of uncomfortable high school years, of never feeling *right* in my own skin.

IT's our last day of community service for the week. I have my dirty clothes packed up in a bag in the trunk of my car, as well as my sheets, which I have to cart back and forth so I can wash them in my special detergent. My mom bought the same kind and does her best, but I think her normal detergent gets stuck and mixed in somehow, because I always end up itchy after my mom's house, no matter what.

A niggling feeling in the back of my mind tells me it's not the detergent, but the stress of being in a place I never fit in.

But that, I can't change. So I do what I can with my sheets and pretend like I won't spend the next few days itchy.

When I walk into the school, I'm in a chipper mood. Just a few more hours of watching Robbie slipping into the skin of a confident, proud kid, and then I get to go home and see my sister.

I give Nick a big grin as I push through the doors, and he smiles right back at me.

"Someone is in a good mood today," he observes, standing and tucking his hands into his pockets as he rocks back on his feet.

I shrug. "I'm happy to be going home soon."

"Ah. You got that Friday feeling," he says knowingly. "I think Robbie had himself a Friday feeling today, too. He was all sorts of chatty during class today–apparently he has a date with some girl he likes. Why do I feel like the two of you are going to give me a run for my money tonight?"

"Better watch out," I tell him.

He grins, and we step out to the front of the school to wait for Robbie to show.

"So, what are you up to this weekend? Hanging out with your sister?" he asks.

I nod. "Yeah. Knowing her, she's going to want to watch some Christmas movie and cut snowflakes or something."

"Your sister is a Christmas person, too?"

"Yeah. Not as bad as my mom, but she definitely enjoys the holiday. Add you into the mix and it's like I'm surrounded from every angle with people who *love* Christmas."

He shrugs. "Is that the worst thing in the world?"

I roll my eyes, letting out a long breath. "Is it the worst thing in the world? No. Is it a little tiring sometimes? Yes."

"Tiring?"

I bite my lip, wondering how much of this I should divulge to him. The divorce that manages to derail every single Christmas season in some way or another. My sister's leg, this year.

"My family always seems to have had a rough time during Christmas. And I don't know why, but when I was growing up, it was almost like they tried even harder at Christmas to even out the shit we were dealing with. I remember wondering why everyone was trying so hard. Like my dad has a second family, this Christmas is going to suck. So can we all accept that and tap out this year?"

He's quiet for a moment. "I guess I can understand why Christmas might not be your favorite time."

"I don't have a problem with it now. But it does feel a little disingenuous sometimes. Like, we're adults. We don't believe in Santa. We work and buy ourselves something if we want it. So it seems like a whole lot of fanfare for... nothing. And you kind of have to pretend like it's this magical time of year."

He nods. "I think a lot of people feel like that around the holidays. I think you should think of Christmas in whatever way it works for you. If it's a chance to spend time with loved ones, maybe that's all it has to be. They can do their silly little traditions, and you can enjoy spending time with them."

He leans against the concrete wall along one edge of the stairs, his hands still in his pockets. He looks so easygoing, with a light breeze ruffling his hair.

"Is that what you do?" I ask. "Use it as an excuse to spend time with your family?"

He clears his throat, one hand running through his hair and his eyes darting away from mine.

And at that moment, a car careens into the parking lot, music blasting. It pulls up right next to us, and Robbie stumbles out, giving us a tense smile in lieu of a greeting. He waves over his shoulder as the car drives away.

"Hey, Robbie," Nick says.

Robbie only nods, and Nick's head cocks to the side so subtly that I doubt I would have noticed it if I hadn't been studying the curve of his jaw.

"Ready?" Nick asks, his eyes snapping to each of us in turn.

"Ready," I confirm.

Robbie nods and turns to lead us over to the town square.

I catch Nick's eye as he follows, and he gives me a look that I can't quite decipher.

I tug on his arm, leaning close. "I thought you said Robbie was having a *good* day," I say, not at all immune to the rock hard forearm in my palm. I have to stop myself from squeezing it, from wrapping both hands around it and rubbing.

Because the man has some *sexy* forearms. Strong, with a few nice veins running through. A dusting of the right amount of hair along the top.

"He *was*. I hope everything is alright," he mutters, his eyes glued to Robbie.

I let out a breath. "I guess we'll see."

NICK

Friday, December 6th

I'm not a fan of moody Robbie.

Mostly because he's prone to outbursts if he's upset, because no one in his life will let him vent. He's been taught that the way to deal with big feelings is by keeping them balled up inside until they get so big they spew out in every direction and all anyone can really do is run for cover.

Not that his outbursts are all that bad. The other day when he decided to spew Coke all over my classroom was an outburst—one that I never got to the bottom of because I have twenty other kids to take care of, too.

But I wouldn't be surprised if it was related.

Noelle picks up on the shift in mood immediately. Something tells me she identifies with Robbie a little more than I might.

I had my share of rough times in high school, as anyone does, but Noelle left because she was bullied.

"So how was school today?" Noelle asks. When I glance over at her, she only shrugs.

"Fine," he huffs. He's leading the way to the town square, his shoulders hunched against the cold.

"You seemed like you were having a pretty good day after lunch," I say.

He shrugs. "Things change."

I don't mean to catch Noelle's eye, but I do. Her brow furrows.

"What changed?" she asks.

He shakes his head. "Nothing."

She purses her lips, letting out a long breath through her nose. "Okay."

We cross the street to the town square in silence and check in with the volunteers. They lead us down the row of huts that are now set up, to the very end, where there is only a pile of pieces waiting to be put together.

Robbie gets straight to work, opting to pull pieces out of the pile and boss us around rather than chatting.

I have a bad feeling we're going to get moody Robbie until we figure out a way to get him talking.

Fortunately–or unfortunately, depending on your view– for me, I have a feeling the change in mood has something to do with the date he was looking forward to.

"You excited for your date with Catherine?" I ask, praying I got her name right, as we begin arranging the boards around the designated space.

He scoffs, and it's confirmation I hit the nail on the head.

Noelle raises an eyebrow at me when Robbie doesn't offer any further explanation.

"Who's Catherine?" she asks.

He shakes his head. "Nobody."

"It sounded like you were pretty excited to go to the fair with her earlier," I say, doing my best to tread lightly.

Robbie lets out a quick puff of air, lifting a board in front of his face and gesturing for Noelle to come over with the drill. "Apparently she doesn't appreciate being called a chubby chaser."

Noelle pauses halfway there, her mouth hanging open as she looks at me. "Did she say that to you?"

"No," Robbie says. "Fucking Tommy Rothwell called her that in front of me and when he asked if she's still planning on going with *the chub*, she said no and walked away."

I can hardly control the anger that bubbles up in my chest. Mostly because Robbie and Tommy are like two peas in a pod–until Robbie has something Tommy wants. Then suddenly Robbie exists to serve *him*. "I hope you know Tommy Rothwell is a two-faced jerk who couldn't tie his own shoes until fifth grade. He said that because he saw that Catherine likes you and wanted to one-up you. That has nothing to do with you, but him."

"Wow, fighting words from Mr. Monroe," Noelle says, her eyes flashing with delight. She aligns the drill with the pieces Robbie's waiting for her to screw together. "Honestly, it sounds like Tommy Rothwell is a piece of shit who needs a good egging and Catherine... well, to be honest, she sounds like a twat. Because if she really liked you, she wouldn't be convinced out of it by somebody calling her a chubby chaser. You're better off."

"Can we please stop with the egging stuff?" I ask her.

She shrugs. "I'm not *suggesting* we go egg Tommy Roth-well, but I *am* suggesting we clap when someone else does." She peeks over the board Robbie is holding and points at him with the drill. "Don't go egging. But he's going to get what's coming to him one day and I hope you extract every ounce of pleasure from it when that happens."

Robbie shrugs, looking away from her.

Her voice is lower when she speaks, and I notice she doesn't look away from Robbie in the same way that he's looking away from her. "I hope you know that's seriously not cool for someone to comment on your body like that," she says. "It's out of line."

He shrugs, rolling his eyes. "I *am* fat," he says. "No need to lie about it."

"Robbie," she scolds, "do you see what you're doing right now?" She takes a step back, gesturing to the boards he's holding together. "You are literally holding up, what, almost a hundred pounds of wood right now? And you're not even breaking a sweat. Robbie, you are *strong*."

He shakes his head. "Doesn't mean I'm not fat."

Noelle takes a deep breath. "Nobody is happy with their bodies, Robbie. I mean, fuck, I've gone *months* of my life covering up my skin because of severe eczema. I put my life on hold so many times because I didn't want to be seen, but one day I realized I was forgoing my own happiness in order to cover up something I was embarrassed about. And you know what? I focused on something else. I have a rash all over my thighs? Cool, cool. But god, my hair looks fantastic today. I have scarring over my elbows from years of scratching? So be it—my new glute workout is giving me an ass worth eating."

If I had a drink in my mouth, I would have spit it. Judging from the wide-eyed look Robbie is giving me, he feels the same way.

"All I'm saying is there comes a point in life where you have to accept your body as it is. There is nothing wrong with changing your body if that's something that *you* want, but don't do it because someone else called you a mean name. That has everything to do with who they are as a person on the *inside* and very little to do with who you are *at all.*"

Robbie glances at me, and I hesitantly nod. I'm not sure I have anything to add to that.

But I hope this can be another healing moment for Noelle. The fire in her eyes as she spoke gave me the impression that she *feels* Robbie's struggle. In a way that I probably never could.

It might not be the healing that she wants or needs, but I hope there's a little part of her that's talking to her high school self and smoothing over that old wound.

Robbie purses his lips, shrugging. "I was thinking about going to the gym," he admits.

"As long as you're doing it for you," she says. She rests the drill on the ground and puts her hands on her hips. "And do me a favor: go to a boxing gym or something so you can learn how to knock Tommy Rothwell the fuck out."

"Noelle!" I scold, and she stomps her foot.

Just when I thought she was doing so damn good.

But if anything, I find her even more charming. That underlying ferocity that oozes from her. I've always thought there's something special about a person who doesn't try to inflict their pain on others, but does everything in their power to stop it from taking down someone else.

She might be a troublemaker and the cutest damn criminal I've ever seen, but she has a kind soul, too.

"I'm sorry! I'm mad. Don't actually do that," she says. "But god, I can't believe kids are still this mean!"

"Yeah. High school sucks," I say, and they both whip toward me.

"What? I'm not immune to it. There's only so much I can do."

Noelle glares at me. "I bet you were cool in school."

I shake my head. "I really wasn't."

"I bet you were valedictorian or something," she says.

"Nope."

"You were at least, like, a sports dude."

I raise an eyebrow. "Why do you say that?"

She gestures to me. "You're built like a tank. Surely you were on some sort of team."

I bite my lip, wondering how much of my high school experience I should tell her. It wasn't exactly typical, and bullying was the least of my concerns after my mom's death. "I was a mathlete, and I was in debate club."

She snorts, and a second later, Robbie is laughing along with her.

"And before you ask, yes, I got made fun of for both."

WHEN WE FINISH our hut and head back to the high school, Robbie is in better spirits. He's not his normal, boisterous self, but he does seem a little more comfortable in his own skin.

Sometimes all it takes is the validation that someone agrees your experience is shit, too.

Noelle and I wait on the stairs until Robbie's ride arrives, and he waves over his shoulder as he slips inside.

I wait until the car starts moving before turning to Noelle. "An ass worth eating?" I ask. "Really?

She shrugs sheepishly. "If I'm being totally honest, that's how I got over it. You can spend your whole life fighting with something that can't be fixed, or you can embrace it and make the best of the rest."

"So, ass worth eating," I say.

"Hey, if eczema is going to make my skin look like shit, at least the rest of me is edible." She shrugs. "I don't know. I guess it was powerful for me to work on other parts of myself. I got my skin under control over time, once I stopped having to go to swim class and once I figured out that I have to use only the Downy sensitive stuff. But it wasn't an easy process, and it was kind of nice that when my skin mostly cleared up, it wasn't like I was picking out the next worst thing to work on. I kind of realized, one day, that my skin looked better. And that I was... borderline happy with the way I looked."

"Only borderline?" I ask, and I realize only after the words leave my mouth that my reaction is based purely on *my* view of her.

Which is that she's a way-too-cute little brunette–yes–with an ass worth eating.

"Like I said, no one is ever totally happy with themselves. But I think it's really powerful when you get to a point where you can accept yourself as you are. If there's stuff you want to change, sure, do it. But unless you can find a way to accept yourself *now*, you can make all the improvements in the world and it'll never make a difference."

I nod. "Well, I'm glad you were able to accept yourself," I say, but the words don't quite feel like enough.

She shrugs. "It was a long process, but I got there eventually." She shakes her head. "To think I left this place because of it. My whole high school experience, it seems, was derailed by my fucking skin."

"How so?"

She bites her lip, her eyes dipping to the pavement

between us, and lets out a long breath. "I had a really bad outbreak in high school. I kind of ended up tearing up my legs because I couldn't stop scratching. And my stupid high school boyfriend Louis Prince snapped a picture and sent it to his buddies asking if I had an STD."

I bite my tongue to avoid letting out a string of expletives that I've worked very hard to train myself out of. At least on school grounds.

"That's terrible," I say.

She shrugs. "And that's why I got my GED. Because after that, he left me for fucking Stacy Mann and apparently the one thing he kept telling her was, 'don't worry, I never fucked her.'"

I grimace. "Yikes."

"So, you know. Fuck high school."

"Fuck Louis Prince."

She raises an eyebrow. "Is that the first time I've heard you curse?"

I shrug. "Some situations call for it."

She laughs. "Wow, look at me. Once the high school virgin, and now I'm the bad girl who makes the goodie two-shoes math teacher curse."

"Goodie two-shoes?" *Oh, the things I would do to her to prove her wrong.*

"Yeah," she says. "I mean, in a cool math teacher way. But you've definitely got a bit of a goodie two-shoes thing going on."

"So I'm a *cool* goodie two-shoes math teacher? That's your determination?"

She pauses, eyeing me. "I can't tell whether you're offended by that or not."

"It's interesting." *Interesting considering I've been thinking about eating your ass for the past half hour.*

"I don't know what you mean by 'interesting,'" she says.

I laugh. "Noelle, it doesn't have to mean anything."

She raises her eyebrows. Then narrows her eyes. "I can't get a read. I can't tell if you think I'm nuts or charming or funny or psycho."

I give her a little smile. "Yes."

She pauses, and then grins. "You answer 'or' questions like a math teacher."

"Am I supposed to be offended by that?"

She raises an eyebrow at me. "Is that something they teach you in teacher school? To answer questions with questions?"

"No, that comes naturally."

She laughs, and I realize, standing in the light from the entryway of the high school, that I could probably stand here all night, bantering back and forth with her. Giving her non-answers and extracting little bits of Noelle piece by piece.

"Come on, I'll walk you to your car," I say, nodding out to the parking lot.

Her face drops, like she had been thinking the same thing I was. That *right here* is where we want to be. Despite the chill in the air and the empty school looming above us.

"Well, thank you," she says, as we step around to the driver's side. She pops the door open and stands in the opening, turning to face me. I lean an elbow on the top of her car, as I've been doing whenever I walk her out like this. She mirrors my pose, one elbow on the roof and the other resting on her open door.

She looks so open to me. So ready to be kissed. Like her waist is calling out to my hands. The skin of her neck thirsting to be nuzzled. She takes a step toward me, and I recognize that this moment can go one of two ways.

I can throw an arm around her shoulders and hug her. A weird thing to do if I'm supposed to be helping her with community service, but probably better than the alternative.

Which is to weave an arm around her waist and tug her close. Turn us so she's pressed against her car. So I can step between her legs and hoist her up. Dip my hands underneath the hem of that little shirt she's wearing and feel the warm skin underneath. Press my lips against hers and taste that smart mouth.

She licks her lips, staring up at me. *Begging me to kiss her.*

I step away.

No. I will not be that guy.

I nod to her, nearly running toward my own car.

"Goodnight, Noelle," I call over my shoulder, my heart thumping.

She huffs, her brow crinkled.

She sounds unsure when she speaks. "Goodnight?"

I close myself in my car, taking a deep breath as I stare at the wheel in front of me.

What the fuck have I gotten myself into?

A moment later, she slips into her car, turning it on and waiting a moment as if to see if whatever freakout I had is passing.

I lock my doors, staring straight ahead, and wait for her to leave first.

7

NOELLE

Tuesday, December 10th

"She's back!" Christina exclaims as I walk into our apartment. "Have you suitably repented for your sins?"

She's sitting on the couch in front of the Christmas tree, knitting a scarf that will no doubt end up in either my mom's or my pile on Christmas morning. Her blonde hair is tied up in a bun on the top of her head, and she's wearing one of her many Christmas sweaters. A Pentatonix CD plays through the sound bar, a glass of wine on the table in front of her.

"I have suitably repented for my sins," I tell her. "Although I have probably one more week before I can get all my hours in."

She throws her arms around me when I lean down to kiss her cheek. "And then you get to hang out with me until Christmas!"

I laugh. "Yes, then I get to hang out with you until Christmas." I nod to the leg she has propped up on a stack of pillows on one side of the couch. "How's your leg? You need anything?"

She shakes her head. "No, I'm fine. Thank you, though."

I move to grab her computer from where it's propped on the couch next to her, and she closes it quickly, moving it to the coffee table before I can.

I grab myself a glass of wine in the kitchen and join her on the couch, taking the place of the pillows underneath her cast.

She eyes me as I sit. "So Mom told me the math teacher you're doing community service with is hot."

I bite my lip. "I mean, he's fine."

She's quiet for a moment. "Only fine?"

"Okay, he's attractive."

She takes a sip of her wine, gesturing for me to continue. "So? Did you do it?"

I throw my hands out in front of me. "Um, no! He's helping me with community service."

She cocks her head to the side. "But it's fake community service."

Of course that's what my sister would get from that.

I huff. "I know. And honestly, I thought I might get some tongue action tonight at least, but no dice."

I realize what I said when her eyes light up. "Oh really? Like on his desk?"

"No! I meant, like, a kiss."

"Oh. That's boring."

I shake my head, taking another sip of wine. "Okay, well I'm sorry I didn't immediately spread my legs for the math teacher."

She sighs, picking up her knitting again. "Man, all I wanted was a spicy little Christmas story."

"Sorry, Chris."

She huffs. "Maybe next year."

"Maybe once I finish my community service."

"You think?" she asks.

I shrug. "I don't know. I mean, it's not like anything could really come from it. Like, he seems like he would be fun, you know? Like he gets all stoic and quiet sometimes and I feel like in his head maybe we're doing naughty stuff. But if it's the community service that's the problem, it seems almost... moot."

"Moot?"

"Yeah, like if nothing happens until I'm done, then what? One wild night and then we promptly forget all about it? I mean, I'm not going back to that town unless I need to."

She rolls her eyes. "Oh, it's not that bad," she says. "And honestly, why *not* have one wild night with him? I mean, have yourself a holiday season. You deserve it, after all the community service you're doing."

"I *would* be serving the community."

She throws her head back cackling.

"And after all the manual labor he has me doing, I really should get at least *one* orgasm out of the deal."

Christina nods her agreement. "Absolutely. He owes you."

"He has us building those Christmas huts they have for the fair every year–"

"Oh really?" she exclaims, turning toward me and grabbing my arm. "Oh, that doesn't sound like community service! That sounds like so much fun!"

"I mean, it's not the worst thing in–"

"Because you're staring at math teacher eye candy."

I press my lips together. "Because it's not like I have to sit and take a remedial class on what I did wrong or pick up trash from the side of the highway or something. One of his students has been helping out. He got detention one day and then just kept coming back afterward because he liked it, and it's honestly kind of sweet to watch his confidence grow, you know?"

Christina eyes me. "Are you becoming a sap?"

"No. It's *nice*."

"I think the math teacher put you under a little Christmas spell."

"Christina!"

"Do you have a picture? Mom said he looks like Henry Cavill with glasses."

I blink. "That's not inaccurate."

She sticks her tongue out, panting at me. "Oh, we are *so* going to the fair this weekend."

"What? No. Don't you want to do normal weekend things? Claw your eyes out with rusty hooks?"

"More like get wine drunk with you and listen to you complain about how you hate Christmas while I make you your special extra dark chocolate-covered berries that you devour with a scowl on your face."

I rear back. "That happened once."

"It happens every year, Noelle."

I glare at her. "You can't even walk."

She waves me off. "I'll bring my scooter, I'll be fine. I want to look at the hot math teacher who looks like Superman. And I want to go to the Christmas fair! Maybe I'll let you buy me a hot chocolate and we can take bets on when Hank's going to finally ask Mom out."

"Ugh. Mom can do better. You realize he was the one who gave me community service, right?"

Christina nods, raising her eyebrows like I'm missing

something. "Um, yeah. Because he has a gigantic crush on Mom."

"So why wouldn't he let me off?"

"Because, Noelle, literally *nobody* wants you throwing eggs at Dad's house. Even Mom."

I take a sip of wine and cross my arms. "I don't regret it."

She leans forward and pats my arm. "And this is why you're the wildcard of the family."

WHEN I HEAD into the high school the next day, the very first thing I notice is the T-shirt Nick is wearing.

"You have to be fucking kidding me," I say, and his head snaps up, his eyes meeting mine above his book.

He grins. "We're in school, Noelle."

"Tell me you didn't buy that shirt for me."

He closes his book, coming to his feet in front of me and throwing it on the desk. "I did not, in fact, buy this shirt for you." He tugs on it, straightening out the *I heart math* across his chest. "It might surprise you to know that other people in the world also assume that math teachers love math, believe it or not."

I raise an eyebrow, trying to decipher whether he's screwing with me or not. "I guess the better question is, how many *I heart math* T-shirts do you own?"

He crinkles his nose, his grin widening. "More than I'm willing to admit."

"Oh my god, I bet you have an entire closet dedicated to *I heart math* shirts."

He shrugs. "None that I bought myself. But yes, more than enough to keep me clothed for the rest of my life."

"Pity," I say, and then catch myself. He blinks, and I start talking too fast to cover up my slip. "That's kind of adorable in a really nerdy way."

God, that's not much better.

He bites his lip. "Well, if you like them so much maybe I'll give you one as a present once you're done with your community service."

"And there I go thinking I'd get one of those T-shirts that says like, 'I went all the way to Snow Falls and all I got was debilitating high school trauma.'"

He pauses before he speaks. "I don't think you need a T-shirt to tell people that."

My jaw drops. "Saint Nick, are you busting my balls right now?"

He grins and holds up two fingers. "Maybe a little bit."

"Wow, I kind of like this side of you. There's a little zing under those glasses, huh?"

"Keep it quiet. I don't need my kids finding out I'm funny."

I snort. "Hey, now. Nobody said anything about funny."

He raises his eyebrows. "What is 'zing' if not funny?"

I falter. *Drop dead sexiness hidden behind Clark Kent glasses. Nice boy in the streets and dirty-talking lover in the sheets.*

"I don't know. What is this, English class? I'm bad at English, don't test my vocabulary please."

He laughs. "Don't worry. Turns out I'm the math teacher," he says, pointing to his chest.

"Ah," I say, nodding. "Of course. How could I ever forget?"

He rounds the desk, stuffing his hands into his pockets as he gestures down the hallway to the garage. "The kids finished decorating the float yesterday. I figured, if it's cool with you, we can go ahead and use today to clean up the mess they left."

I raise my eyebrows. "Is it really that bad?"

He shakes his head. "No. But the huts are all done so I had to get creative when I was thinking things up for us to do today."

"So cleaning it is," I say.

He shrugs. "Unless you can think of something better to do?"

I nearly scoff at the very obvious answer.

But I press my lips together and shake my head instead.

Something tells me he wouldn't be amused if I asked him whether boinking the math teacher could count toward my hours.

THE GARAGE IS NOT PARTICULARLY messy, and I get the feeling that Nick is really scraping the bottom of the barrel when I see that 'the mess' he was referring to can be taken care of with a quick sweep of a broom.

I blink as I take in the bits of tinsel on the ground. The few plastic wrappings that once held ornaments that are now affixed to the sides of the float. I pick one piece up, turning to face Nick with a grin, and walk it very slowly toward the trash can.

"So can I ask what other options were brewing in your head for tonight?" I ask, as I head toward the wall that holds the cleaning equipment. A broom stacked against the wall, a mop that we likely won't need for this project.

He sighs, straightening a bit of tinsel on the float, and leans back against it.

"Well, I asked Mrs. Nguyen if she had anything we could do in the library," he starts, watching as I drag the broom toward him. "She had nothing but praise for our computer

updates, but unfortunately nothing to add to our to-do list."
I stop in front of him, resting my hands on the top of the
broom and leaning against the float like he is. "I asked Hank
if he had any troubled youths we could corral into a game
night."

I grimace. Forcing teenagers to play board games sounds
horrible. "You did?"

He nods. "And Hank made a very similar face. Said if I
wanted to herd cats and do experiments on them, he has a
few strays hiding out in his barn."

I snort. "Thank god. That sounded horrible."

"I even *looked* for kids who were misbehaving during
school so I could give out a detention."

I cock my head to the side. "How would that have given
us something to do? Then there would be *three* of us
cleaning up this tiny mess."

He clears his throat, pushing his glasses up onto his
head and running his hands over his face. "Ah, you're right. I
guess I was looking for any sort of distraction. Or inspiration, I guess I should say."

He shakes his head.

I narrow my eyes. "Distraction?"

"You know, because we'd have to do something."

I bite my lip, watching his eyes as they follow the movement. "Like clean up this very tiny mess?"

He nods, his eyes on mine, and after a few seconds of
heated eye contact, he shakes his head. "You know what? All
this is pretty silly anyway. I can sign your little timecard and
you can head home. It's fake community service anyway,
right?"

I shrug. "I don't mind. I mean, I told Hank I would go
through with it. Told my mom I'd be around a little more
this Christmas. I might as well fulfill my promises, right?"

"Well, we're not *doing* anything, right?"

I push the broom back and forth across the floor. He raises an eyebrow.

"I'm doing something," I say.

He's quiet for a moment. "Why?"

Because I want you to kiss me. "Because this is my duty."

"Which I'm releasing you of. Seriously, I'll mark down the full two hours. I mean, god, I'll go ahead and give the rest to you. I don't even know how I got in this position. One day, Hank waves me down while I'm on a run and the next he has his friend's daughter showing up waving a fake time-card at me. Like, take your hours and go. You've served the community."

He takes a deep breath, crossing his arms over his chest.

"I bother you," I say.

He shakes his head. "You don't bother me at all. Really. It just... this whole thing is a little ridiculous."

"No, I mean I bother you in a different sort of way."

He's quiet, his breathing heavy.

I lean the broom against the float and take a step toward him. "I do, don't I?"

He's staring at me, his arms crossed tight over his chest, and I feel the intense urge to slip my hands underneath his shirt and feel the muscles underneath. Stand on my toes and press my lips against the bit of skin above the neckline of his T-shirt.

When he doesn't move away, I take another step forward, resting my hand on his thick bicep.

He looks down at it, his eyes glued to my hand like they might start solving whatever math problem is causing that little wrinkle in his brow.

"Noelle," he says, my name low and gruff from his lips. His eyes lift, meeting mine. "I'm a professional."

"You don't have to be, with me."

He bites his lip, his eyes darting all across my face, and takes a step back.

"I do."

8

NICK

Wednesday, December 11th

I'll give it to Noelle, she doesn't act rejected when I move away from her. On the contrary, she puts all of her efforts into her cleaning. She sweeps away every last bit of trash on the floor, and when that's all gone, she focuses her attention on the float.

The kids have decorated it like a candy cane this year, all red and white stripes. There are a few pieces that have fallen out of place, and she does a circle around the float, putting fresh glue wherever it's needed.

I busy myself cleaning the floor she painted that's already covered in dirt from the kids' shoes. I fill the mop bucket, even though it's overkill for the job I'm doing, and clean slowly, trying my hardest to pay attention to anything but her.

She's acting totally normal, like nothing ever happened, but every time she turns away from me I get this tight feeling in my chest like she's upset with me.

And I can't help but wonder *why* I was so ready to sign

her timecard and be done with her. As much as I hate to admit it, I kind of enjoyed our time cleaning and building huts. As much as I wouldn't necessarily categorize those things as *fun,* they felt like Christmas activities. The same way that cleaning up the wrapping paper on Christmas morning isn't a fun job, but it's one that has to be done.

And the joy that comes with it is worth the chore.

I also wouldn't have to be so *professional* anymore, if I just gave her the rest of her hours.

But that sounds like a dangerous game to play.

Sure, I could tug her into my chest and kiss her in the way I've been imagining, but she could also choose to walk away and never see me again.

And as much as I don't want to admit that I'm scarred from past experiences, it doesn't take a genius to see the lasting effects Emily had on me. The fact that everything *I* had ever wanted was never good enough for *her.* The way I excused her behavior so quickly because I thought she might be the person I was looking for.

Noelle would be fun, no doubt, if the way she wields that tongue of her is any indication of what her hips can do.

But I'm not in a place where I'm looking for mindless sex. And I'm not sure I can dive headfirst into something more, right now. I'm stuck in the in-between–I *want* something more than sex, but I'm not sure I can handle it.

I don't think I realized it until recently, but ever since my mom died, I've been searching for a family of my own. Someone to spend this time of year with other than my students or fellow teachers who invite me out for the occasional beer.

As much as I'd love to bend Noelle over the side of that float, I'm not here for random sex.

And unfortunately for me, she's not here for much longer.

When we finish our cleaning and head back to the front entrance, she's quiet. I surreptitiously glance over at her only to see her chewing at her bottom lip, her eyes following the ground in front of us carefully.

I push open the front door for her to walk through and she nods to me in thanks.

I follow her to her car, like I do every night.

But when she turns to me, she takes a deep breath, her shoulders rising and falling as she lets it go. "Look, I'm sorry," she says, throwing her hands in the air. "What I said was really inappropriate, and you know, I got that vibe from you. The professional vibe. And I feel so bad that I pushed it."

I shake my head, leaning against the side of her car in the hopes that the casual movement might portray that I'm not, in fact, curling up in the fetal position on the inside. "Really no issue, Noelle."

Her nose crinkles. "I must have read the room totally wrong, and I'm really, sincerely sorry. And please, can we forget all of that ever happened?"

Her eyes are on mine, desperately waiting to be released from whatever turmoil is going on inside her head.

And now I have to choose between maintaining that boundary I set and giving her her confidence back.

"Look, you didn't read the room wrong," I tell her.

She eyes me. "I didn't?"

I press my lips together. "I'm trying to be professional, Noelle."

She nods. "Okay." She pulls open her car door. "You're trying to be professional, but it's difficult?"

"What?"

She shakes her head. "Never mind. Sorry, that was an inappropriate question, too."

I squeeze my eyes shut, and when I open them again, I take the outside handle of her door.

"Yes," I say, and then I close her in before she can say anything else.

I catch her eye through the window before turning on my heel and heading back to my car.

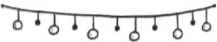

IT's the first day of the fair, and I've been assigned to hot chocolate duty with a number of my students. Mostly mathletes, who decided they wanted to participate in this year's fair to raise money for letter jackets for this year's competition.

Because apparently math nerds have style now. They convinced me into joining by offering me one.

The high school kid in me couldn't resist.

Plus... I didn't really want to go to the fair alone. I'll go for a few laps through the town square through the night–it's not like the mathletes actually need me anyway–but it's nice to have a reason to be here. Like all the parents walking around while the kids go off with their friends.

Otherwise, I'm just some teacher who goes to town events alone.

Once the kids have gotten into a good groove, serving people and thanking them for contributing to their jacket fund, I step out of our hut, warm cup of hot chocolate in my hand. I take a right on the pavement and head around in a big circle, exploring what this year's winter festival has brought us.

Mrs. Smith's scarf booth, piled to the ceiling with warm

weather clothing. Mr. Bellman's rare coin and train booth. Mrs. Pontsky's cookies–I stop for a packet of warm ones because I have dreams about them all year. Various Christmas ornaments and peppermint snacks and ugly sweaters and every Christmas treat under the sun.

People of all ages swarm along the pavement ahead of and behind me. There's laughter and Christmas music and someone ringing bells above the crowd.

I finish up my loop, saying hello to the multitude of former students and parents that I've gotten to know over the past few years, and head back toward the hot chocolate booth. I'm pleased to see a long line out front and the kids running the booth hustling to fulfill orders. They work quickly and without getting flustered.

I make my way toward them, weaving through the crowd gathered out front.

And as I'm about to slip behind the table, a manicured hand grabs my arm.

I turn to see Delia Wilson grinning at me, her fingers squeezing my arm through the fabric of my jacket.

"Nick," she says, her smile too white and her eyes too bright. "So nice to see you."

As much as I wanted to like her, Delia was a problem parent. Her daughter graduated last year, but before that, she was up my ass almost every day asking what sort of extra credit her daughter could do to get an A in my class. About what sort of extra credit *she* could do to ensure that happened.

Her daughter got an A because she deserved it. She was a hardworking kid, and I was happy to write her a reference letter for college. But her mother rubs me all sorts of the wrong way.

Mostly because she always looks at me with that wide smile and a look in her eye like we *know* each other.

We don't. I don't want to know her like that. She bothers me–not in a good way–and I have no inclination to hang out with her. I can't tell what's going on in her head because she always wears the same delighted expression on her face, and while I could see that others might find it welcoming, I find it jarring. No one is *always* that happy, and it gives me that same uncomfortable feeling you'd get seeing someone walking around the Christmas fair in a hockey mask.

Maybe it's because I'm one of the few who knows it's all a manipulation. Just a sneaky way to get what she wants from people. I've seen it work a number of times–on other teachers, on the principal, even on other parents. She says what she wants and then she smiles at you until you bend to her will.

"Delia," I say in greeting, doing my best to not let it show how little I want to talk to her.

"How have you been?" she asks, her hand still on my arm.

I give her a terse smile. "Fine, and yourself? How is Hattie doing at college?"

"Oh, she's doing so well. Really flourishing," she says, shaking her head. "I'm so relieved to see she's doing well. You know how much support she always needed."

I blink. "I think Hattie always had a good handle on things."

She grins, waving me off like this is a compliment. "Oh, that's so sweet of you to say. We both know she needed a little outside help from time to time."

I let out a long breath. I know exactly what she's implying, and it drives me insane that she thinks all of those times she's hit on me is the reason her daughter did so well in school.

Hattie did well *despite* her.

"She certainly needed no outside help from me," I tell her, pressing my lips together to avoid telling her that all she did was make a fool of herself. "Hattie earned every good grade she ever got on her own."

Delia nods exuberantly. "Oh, right, right. Of course, yes. Hattie earned every good grade she ever got."

And then she winks at me.

I'm momentarily stunned to silence. Delia really just believes what she wants to believe.

"You know, I was thinking. Now that Hattie's off at school, it might be nice if we got together for a drink sometime."

I shrug away from her, glancing at the crowd around us waiting for hot chocolate. "Look, I'm supposed to be helping out with this booth. I should probably get back to it," I say, turning and ducking around another few people until I'm safely surrounded by mathletes.

I take a long breath, running my hands over my face as I step out of the way of one of my students who's balancing three cups of hot chocolate in his hands. He raises his eyebrows at me as he passes, as if to ask what I'm doing standing around, and I take a step toward the front of the line to take the next customer.

"Oh for–"

I stop myself before an expletive slips out.

First Delia, now Noelle. Two opposites of the same spectrum.

Delia, who I refuse to touch with a ten-foot pole, and Noelle, who I can only barely manage to *not* touch despite putting every barrier I can think of between us.

She raises her eyebrows, pressing her hands against the table between us and leaning toward me. "Did I nearly catch Mr. Monroe dropping an f-bomb?"

"No," I tell her flatly, eyeing an older woman with frizzy brown hair and nearly identical facial features behind her, and a blonde woman balanced on a scooter that looks closer to Noelle's age. Mom and sister, if I had to guess.

"Oh, is this the math teacher?" the blonde woman asks, scooting forward and nudging Noelle out of the way. "I'm Christina!" she says, holding her hand out to greet me. I shake it gently while one of the mathletes drops off a few cups of hot chocolate between us. "Noelle's told me so much about you!"

I raise my eyebrows as Noelle's cheeks turn pink. "Have you, now?"

"I mean, only the basics," she says, rolling her eyes. "Like, the fact that you're a math teacher. And I do community service with you."

"And that you look like Superman," Christina says.

"*I* did not say that," Noelle bites back. "*Mom* said that."

The older woman shrugs, taking a step forward to shake my hand too. "I'm Helen. Nice to meet you."

"Nice to meet you too," I say.

And then fucking *Delia* pops up again.

"Nicky, honey, can you grab me two hot chocolates?"

My jaw ticks as I watch Noelle's face. Her eyes flash wide, and one eyebrow pops up as she turns to get a glimpse of the woman who took it upon herself to call me *Nicky*.

Excuse me while I barf.

"Nicky?" Noelle asks, her voice low.

"You call me that, I'll make sure you have enough community service that you can never leave this—what do you call it?–godforsaken town," I mutter to her, and her mouth pops open, a grin spreading across her face.

I ignore Delia, instead turning to the people waiting on Noelle's *other* side and passing out one cup after another.

"You *hate* her," Noelle says under her breath, leaning across the table between us.

I press my lips together, and that seems to be all the confirmation Noelle needs.

I hand her a cup of hot chocolate that she passes to her mom. "Oh, I can't wait to hear this story."

I shake my head. "No story."

I pass along the second cup, which she hands to her sister, and another for her, but she waves me off. "I can't. Too much sugar." And she raises an eyebrow as I pass it off to someone else in line. "Come on, tell me the story."

"There really isn't one."

She nods. "Well, I'm not sure she's gotten the memo."

"Despite my best efforts."

"Want me to spill a hot chocolate on her?"

I pause, my brow crinkling. "Are you kidding me? I think you'd get a lot worse than community service for that."

She shrugs. "Honestly, I was trying to get a gauge on *how much* you don't like her. Want me to egg her house? That's right in my wheelhouse." She pauses. "Although you'd probably end up stuck with me for another installment of community service."

She eyes me like she's baiting me to react.

"As much as I love the torture, maybe it's best to refrain."

She nods, her eyes narrowed. "Well, you let me know."

"I'll keep your number in my phone in case I ever need a professional egg-thrower."

She grins. "I always knew I had a higher calling."

She holds my gaze for a moment, until her sister taps her shoulder. "Noelle! Dad!"

Christina is off like a rocket, scooting along across the pavement as her mom follows after her.

Noelle's face instantly drains of all color. She glances over her shoulder to where a man stands between two teenage girls, a wide smile on his face as Christina scoots toward him and envelops him in a big hug. Helen stands a respectful distance away, opting to nod while greeting the two teenagers next to him.

When I turn back to Noelle, she's...

Gone.

My brow crinkles, wondering where she could have disappeared to in the two seconds I was focused on her family.

And then I notice the edge of the table cloth is being tugged strangely. As if someone slipped underneath it and is doing their best to hide.

"Nicky? Those hot chocolates?"

I grab one of my mathletes as they zip past, and gesture to Delia. He gives me a firm nod, and while Delia's focused on the crowd around her, I take the opportunity to slip underneath the table, readjusting the table cloth as I come face to face with Noelle.

Her eyes are wide as I take a seat on the pavement across from her, nearly knocking my head on one of the table's supporting bars. Her arms are wrapped around her knees, making her look small. I, on the other hand, feel like a giant as I try to fold my limbs in any sort of comfortable way.

"This is *my* hiding spot," she tells me sternly.

"Well, this is *my* booth," I remind her.

"It's your mathletes' booth."

I purse my lips. She has a point there.

"Noelle, can you please share your hiding spot with me until she goes away?"

As if on cue, Delia calls for me. "Nicky?" she asks, the confusion clear in her voice.

Noelle grins. "What's up with the 'Nicky' business?"

I shake my head and lower my voice when I speak. "She's one of *those* parents. The kind that takes pride in being a thorn in your side because it's *helping* their child. She didn't help her daughter one bit. Only made the teachers dread her call. Hit on me endlessly, thinking it would get her daughter a better grade. And her daughter was *smart*—all she needed was for her mom to get out of her way."

She nods. "Sounds like she deserves an egging."

"Noelle!"

She scooches closer, her smile still wide across her face. She smells like roses and chocolate, and it makes me want to move closer, to stick my nose right in the corner of her neck and breathe her in.

"Really, I'd be happy to extend my services," she says.

I pause, wondering how serious she is. "Alright, sure. Why don't you go egg her house?"

She rears back. "What?"

Bluff called. "That's what I thought."

"Well–"

I shake my head. "I don't trust you to be a serious egg-thrower now. You faltered. I have no more faith in your egg-throwing abilities."

She huffs, but she can't stop the laughter jumping from her throat. "Nick!"

I shrug. "Confidence is the name of the game when throwing eggs, and I don't think you've got it."

She scrambles to her knees so she can crawl toward me and whacks me lightly on the shoulder. "Maybe I'll egg *you*," she says. "From this distance, I bet I could get you right on the nose." She reaches out and pokes it.

I ignore the zip of heat that runs down my spine with the contact.

"With what eggs?" I press. "Unprepared." I make a tsking noise with my tongue while shaking my head. "Sorry, Noelle, I can no longer recommend your services to the rest of the neighborhood."

She laughs again, shaking her head. "Don't *egg* me on. I can figure out where you live."

I raise my eyebrows. "Wow, the threats are getting real now. Do I need to call Hank to arrest the criminal again?"

She purses her lips as she glares at me. "Maybe I'll give you a pass this time."

And then we hear it again. "Nicky?" from somewhere above us.

I shake my head, pushing my glasses up into my hair so I can run my hands over my face. "God, what is *wrong* with this woman?"

When I put my glasses back on, Noelle is staring at me, her eyes wide and her mouth slightly open. "You okay?"

She blinks and averts her gaze. "Yeah."

I sigh. "I guess I'm going to have to face her at some point."

"She really annoys you, doesn't she?" Noelle asks.

I nod. "And it really fucking sucks because she hides behind these big smiles and nice words and has everybody fooled. And if I don't like the former president of the PTA, *I'm* the asshole. God forbid I tell anyone she shamelessly threw herself at me last year in a completely unneeded attempt to get her daughter's grade raised. I can only imagine how that would turn out."

Noelle purses her lips. "I'm sorry."

I shrug and shake my head. "I'm overreacting. I don't have to see her anymore aside from town events. It's a non-issue."

Noelle reaches out, resting one hand on my arm to stop me from scrambling out from under the table yet. "Maybe we can make her think you're no longer available."

I raise my eyebrows. "What does that mean?"

She bites her lip as she reaches for my hair, running her fingers through it. She pushes on one side of my glasses so they're lopsided.

"Can I touch you?" she asks.

My blood freezes in my veins. Because *fuck yes* but *no no no.*

"Like, put my arm around your waist?" she clarifies.

I clear my throat, desperately trying to will away the images that flew through my mind when she asked if she could *touch me.* "Yeah."

She musses her own hair, pinches her cheeks, and scratches at part of her neck.

"What are you doing?"

She shrugs. "Beard burn," she explains.

My mouth goes dry at the thought. Some sort of caveman instinct flows through me, and I suddenly have no thoughts in my head other than tearing her hand away from her neck and making that *real.*

She reaches for me and pinches my cheeks, and I feel the urge to grab her by the hips, tug her legs around me, and kiss her.

No one can see us right now.

She lets out a quick breath. "Ready?"

No. I nod.

"You go first and pull me up," I say.

"What?"

"Just go," she says, picking up the tablecloth with a flourish and grabbing onto my hand when I propel out of there.

I pull her up behind me, and we nearly bowl over a mathlete with a cup of hot chocolate who only raises an eyebrow but thankfully doesn't comment.

When I turn back to the line out front, Delia is still there. She has a cup of hot chocolate in her hand, so I can only assume she was just waiting for me to turn up again.

Noelle slips her arm around my waist, delicate but strong, and when I glance down at her, she's grinning at me like she got away with egging somebody's house. "Oopsie," she says, giggling as she leans in close to me. She rests her chin on my shoulder, turning slightly away from Delia and lowering her voice. "You know, this would be a good time to pretend you like me."

I swallow, clicking back into the plan, and clamp my arm tight around her. She nods subtly, like she approves, and I take the opportunity to run my other hand through her hair.

Her eyes widen as she leans into the touch.

And I think I might be addicted to it.

I let my hand fall to her neck, resting in the crook there while she looks up at me. I brush my thumb along the line of her jaw as her lips part slightly.

It feels like I should kiss her.

"I think it worked," she murmurs, breaking our spell.

When I glance back at the line, Delia is gone.

But I don't want to remove my hand from Noelle's neck. Or the arm from around her shoulders.

She reaches up, her hand covering mine, and squeezes.

When she sighs, I feel it deep in my abdomen.

It takes every ounce of willpower to remove my hands from this woman.

When I do, it's like her skin has seared me. My thigh, where her hip pressed against me. My waist where she tugged on me. The skin of her neck on my hands.

Every part of me where she was is now on fire.

And she only smiles as she tugs on my hand, pulling me out of the booth.

9

NOELLE

Thursday, December 12th

I s it a bad idea to hang onto Nick so that I don't have to see my dad for the first time since I egged his house? Maybe.

But he desperately needed a way out of that booth, and I desperately needed some way to ensure my mom and sister didn't come and force me into a conversation with him.

He's here with his *new* family. He doesn't want anything to do with the old one.

So I tug Nick along, spying the parent who so shamelessly threw herself at him and beelining in the opposite direction.

"I probably should help the mathletes. It's kind of busy," he says, glancing over his shoulder.

"You were more in their way than you were helping them," I say, waving him off.

His brow crinkles. "That's not true. And they do technically need a faculty member present to call it a school fundraiser."

I raise my eyebrows at him. "Nick, they're a bunch of mathletes. They're not going to get in trouble. Besides, while you were standing there talking to *me*, I caught at least three of them giving you dirty looks because you were holding up the line."

"Really? Oh man, I didn't realize I was in the way."

I slip my hand into his elbow, patting his arm. "It's okay, Mr. Monroe. One day we all become obsolete. You had a good run, but now you have to let your mathletes carry on without you."

He rolls his eyes. "I'm not that overbearing."

I shrug. "Wasn't saying you were."

He's quiet for a second, and I look up at him. His eyes catch mine, and I get that flustered feeling you get when somebody looks at you a little deeper than surface level. Like by looking into your eyes, they can see everything that's going on in your mind.

"Thanks for saving me," he says.

I squeeze his elbow, the closest I can get to hugging him without actually hugging him. "You're welcome." I let out a long breath. "To be fair, you saved me too."

"Still not talking to your dad?"

I shake my head.

"I'm honestly kind of surprised you're not rubbing it in his face. Like, 'look what I did because you're such a jerk, Dad,'" he mocks.

I roll my eyes. "I don't know. I feel like it's not worth it. Christina forgives him for anything because she has some insane notion that being family means you always forgive each other. My mom goes along with it to make her happy, even though I know he makes her stomach churn. But me? I spent high school in hell and I don't feel like going back there. I don't spend a single moment of my life dealing with anyone who makes me feel less than. If Christina wants to give and give and give, and that makes her happy, then I will support her. But I'll do so from a distance." I shrug. "And if I'm being totally honest, I can count on one hand the times he's made a real effort. And I don't forgive that quickly."

Nick nods, squeezing my hand in his elbow. "Good for you," he says, giving me a quick nod. Not encouraging me to include him in family events because *it's Christmas*, like my sister. Not telling me it's water under the bridge. Not pointing out that he's learned his lesson–look how good a dad he is to his two *new* little girls.

"Thanks for not pushing me to ignore my feelings for the sake of the holiday," I say.

He shrugs. "Thanks for telling me." He's quiet for a second. "Maybe you should tell him, too."

I look up at him, desperate to know what's going on behind those brown eyes. He hasn't shrugged away from my touch or insisted on going back to his booth. He's walking with me... like a friend. One that I kind of want to see naked.

"Tell my dad that he's a big jerk face?"

"Maybe not in those exact words, but... it might be healing for you. I know you said the egg-throwing was a result of finally breaking, but maybe by *not* talking about things, you're holding tension that you can let go of in perhaps a less criminal way?"

"Is this your attempt to guard against recidivism?"

He rolls his eyes, laughing. "No. I'm just thinking about that little story you told me about eating lunch in the library. Talking about it didn't change the experience, but I got the feeling you were able to find some peace with it. Maybe telling your dad what's what, instead of egging his house, can do the same thing."

I purse my lips. "Maybe. But then I'd have to *talk* to him."

He nods. "Yes, you would have to talk to him. But some-times speaking your truth can give you some relief. No need to hide under tables anymore because talking to him no longer equates to hiding your feelings. And who knows, maybe some accountability would be good for him."

I scoff. "Yeah, I don't think he's listened to a word I've said in my life."

Nick hums. "Sounds like a great way to raise a daughter who thinks egg-throwing solves problems faster than communicating."

I turn to look at him, my best glare plastered across my face.

"I'm going to shut up now." He pauses. "But I'm also going to rest easy because I've said my piece, and if you don't want to listen, that's fine."

I raise an eyebrow at him.

He takes a deep breath, letting out an overdramatic *ahh*. "What a beautiful night to have freed myself from the stress of holding onto something I should have just said."

I can't help the laugh that escapes me. "Point taken. I'll think about it."

"Think about it or don't, it's up to you. I'm just very happy to have said it."

I roll my eyes. "Very subtle."

When I look up at him, he's grinning again.

And as much as I don't want to think about all of the wonderful childhood trauma that causes me to throw eggs at my dad's house instead of speaking my truth, I just... can't help but smile right back at him.

"How'd you learn to be such a good communicator, Saint Nick?"

He shrugs. "I wouldn't say I'm *always* good at communi-cating. I mean, sometimes I really suck at it."

I cock my head to the side. "How so?"

He shakes his head. "I've been told I'm emotionless at times. Which isn't true. But I can see how the way I work sometimes gives that impression. I'll say something before I let myself get truly upset about it. And when someone tells me they're upset, I don't really react. I just try to figure out a solution. *Everyone* has emotions, but some people show them very differently."

I nod, detecting a hint of defensiveness in his words. "I see your emotions."

He raises his eyebrows. "You see my emotions?" he asks, deadpan.

I nod. "Yeah. In the way you push your glasses onto your head and run your hand over your face. When you grin, sometimes it reaches your eyes and they go all squinty, but sometimes you kind of raise an eyebrow a little bit. Just the littlest bit, and it's somewhere between happy and–"

He looks at me, making that exact face like he's daring me to say it. That *that* face is something different. An intense focus, coupled with something like fascination.

I shrug, swallowing my words. "I don't know. It's an emotion that feels uniquely you."

He nods. "Guess I should restrain myself a bit, huh?"

I laugh. Because yes, he is on the stoic side. But there's no doubt in my head he's full of all sorts of emotions. I see them running so subtly across his face.

I shake my head. "Don't you do that. You're perfect just as you are."

He laughs, and this grin reaches his eyes. "Okay, well, no need to lie to me."

"What? I'm serious. Sometimes I feel big emotions and I go too far. Sometimes you feel big emotions and others still have to search them out. Both are okay."

He gives me a quick nod. "As long as the former doesn't result in any egging."

I roll my eyes, knocking him on the shoulder, and decide this is probably enough emotion talk for the day. Or else I'm going to end up pantsless and pawing at him because there is something about the way this man insists that he has emotions that makes my heart swell.

Fuck whoever made him feel self-conscious about that.

If I only had an egg...

"So I take it you don't have much family drama around the holidays, Saint Nick?"

He shakes his head, looking out over the crowd as we weave between people. "Nah, I don't."

"Not even a little? Nothing you have to talk very calmly about?" I ask, and as we skirt around a group of kids creating a bottleneck in foot traffic, we turn toward each other to squeeze by. Our coats swish past each other, but I swear I can feel his heat through the fabric.

"I don't really have much family."

"Oh." I keep my hand on his elbow as the walkway opens up. Some part of me feels like I need to hold onto him, keep him close. "So there's not much *opportunity* for drama, huh?"

He shakes his head. "Nope. Pretty much zero possibility," he says.

He smiles when I glance up at him, and I can't help but overanalyze his words. Is he telling me he has *no* family?

"What do you normally do for the holidays?"

He shrugs. "Depends on the year. Usually... this."

I raise my eyebrows. "This, as in wander the Christmas fair with your community service gremlin on your arm?"

A laugh bursts out of him, and he shakes his head. "For the record, when I call you my community service gremlin, know that it's entirely your fault."

My laugh sneaks out despite my best attempt to suppress it. "Okay, that's fair."

He sighs, turning his attention out to the crowd again. "I usually do community stuff around the holidays. Participate in the fair or help the school with the winter play or the winter concert. I'm not picky," he says. He takes a long breath, and I stamp down every part of me that wants to start talking again because I can *feel* he's about to tell me something important. "My mom loved Christmas."

Loved.

I bite my tongue to stop the words from spilling out.

"And it makes me feel close to her, this time of the year, when I go out and do Christmas-y things around town. I technically have a dad somewhere, but he was never in my life, so it was always just me and my mom. When I was little, she would cart me around to any and all Christmas events she could find. She didn't always have the money to give us really big Christmases, but she always made sure we had some way to celebrate together. So now, this is how I celebrate with her."

A lump builds in my throat that I desperately try to swallow over. My lip trembles, and I bite it in an attempt to stop it.

My mom loves Christmas. *My* mom carted us around to all of the Christmas events. *My* mom still takes it upon herself to wrap a multitude of fruits and household items for Christmas morning because it was me and Christina's favorite thing to just rip the damn wrapping paper on Christmas morning.

He glances down at me, his brow furrowed, and starts laughing. "Careful, Noelle. You know what happens when gremlins get wet."

A laugh tumbles out of me at the same time as one little

tear leaks out. I wipe it away before he notices. "I'm sorry. That's a really beautiful sentiment and now I feel bad about making fun of you for liking Christmas."

He shrugs. "You can still make fun of me. I deal with high schoolers all day–believe me, there's nothing you can say to me that I haven't heard before. Or heard worse."

I nod. "Well, I'm not going to make fun of you for liking Christmas anymore. I'll stick to the nerdy math teacher jokes."

He grins. "Now what sort of sob story can I come up with to make you feel bad about *that?*"

"Oh!" I knock into him lightly, and when he corrects course, he squeezes my hand in his elbow. As if to tell me he likes having it there.

And there go the butterflies, knocking around inside me again.

As we turn a corner to another long row of huts–several of which we set up–I spy someone I was really hoping I'd never have to see again.

I tense up, trying to turn and accidentally walking straight into Nick instead.

"You okay?" he asks, placing his hands on my shoulders.

"Louis Prince and Stacy Mann are apparently still together," I say under my breath, turning my head so they can't see me.

But then I hear his voice. "Noelle? Is that you?"

I press my eyes shut quickly, and when I open them, Nick is staring down at me, his eyes soft. He loops a bit of my hair around his thumb and lets it go as his fingers dig into my shoulders. "Test run, Noelle. Tell him how you feel," he says softly.

My words run on repeat in my head. All of the nights I've been up late, thinking about things I *could* have said to

Louis Prince. All of the ways I wanted to put him in his place.

They all consisted of saying something different at the time, in that little alcove in the high school where we last spoke.

But I guess *late* is better than *never*.

I glance up at Nick as if he's some sort of safety net. He squeezes my shoulders. "He deserves to know that what he did had lasting effects. And even if he doesn't listen, you deserve to say it."

"I don't know."

"Don't feel pressured," he says, his fingers moving in small circles on my shoulders in the most distracting way. "But I think it might be cathartic for you."

He glances at them and then back at me.

"Do you want to pretend?" he asks, his hands moving down to my upper arms and squeezing.

I bite my lip. *No, I don't want to pretend—I want it to be real.* "Yeah."

He nods, taking a moment to run his fingers through my hair. His eyes follow the movement, his thumb brushing against my temple and continuing down until the strands fall flat against my coat. Goosebumps pop up along my skin that are thankfully hidden by my coat.

I think I could probably stay in this moment forever, his eyes on mine and his hands in my hair.

But he turns, throwing an arm around my shoulders, and tugs me into his side, that now familiar scent of s'mores infiltrating my senses.

I wrap my arm around his waist, and a second later, his lips brush against the side of my head.

The contact makes my breath catch, and I freeze in place, wishing he would stay right there, just like that.

But by the time I glance up at him, his attention has moved elsewhere. To the couple now standing in front of us, wide grins on their faces.

"Noelle, so nice to see you," Stacy says, and I begrudgingly look at her.

"Nice to see you, too," I say, even though the only thing I *want* to see is Nick's hands on me. His arm around my shoulder. I wish I could have a bird's eye view of this moment so I could see what we look like together. If this comfort I feel right now is visible from the outside. If we fit as well as it feels like we do.

"Glad to see you're doing well," Louis says, and I don't miss the way he throws an arm around Stacy's shoulder. Like he's mirroring us.

"Very well," I say. My eyes drift up to Nick's, and my heart stutters when he grins down at me.

I know it's all for show, but there's a little part of me that warms to this. Like maybe it doesn't *have* to be so fake.

"I don't think I've seen you since your last day of school," Louis says.

The last day of school where he met me in the alcove between lockers because he didn't want to risk our goodbye getting around to Stacy. Even though our goodbye amounted to no more than him, brow furrowed, telling me he was sad I was leaving but hoped we could remain on good terms.

As if he wasn't the reason I was leaving.

I, being the dumb high schooler I was, didn't chew him out the way I should have.

"Yeah. After you started spreading rumors that I had an STD, high school wasn't a very fun place anymore."

Nick snorts. Stacy's mouth drops open. Louis's face turns a truly delightful shade of crimson.

"I hope you know I didn't mean for that to happen. And I mean, it was so long ago..."

I stare at him, swallowing down every inclination in me that's telling me to run and find somewhere to hide. To take back my words or laugh them off with a joke.

"It was just a picture," he says.

I wait a moment before speaking. "Well, what was to you a picture, was the end of high school for me." I glance at Stacy. "I'm happy you're happy together." I turn back to Louis. "But I'm more happy that I learned who you are before I ended up stuck with you."

I glance at Nick, who nods subtly at me. Like he's proud of me.

And I beam back at him.

I *want* him to be proud of me. I want him to look at me like this, all the time.

He knows the story, but he doesn't truly know what I've been through. But he still looks at me like this moment has lit up his day.

It has me all sorts of gooey on the inside.

Nick tugs me closer, leaving a kiss on my forehead that has me jumping out of my skin.

He turns to Louis. "I hope one day you learn how to take accountability for your actions."

And if I know Nick as well as I think I do, that was his version of egging Louis Prince's house.

He nods once, quickly, and then steers us around the suddenly silent couple. Ahead of us is only a parking lot–Stacy and Louis must have just arrived–but we continue regardless.

We walk a few paces before his arm tightens around me, surrounded by only cars and the distant sound of Christmas music playing through the town square speakers.

"How did that feel?" he asks, his voice low in my ear as our pace slows. I recognize Nick's car as we stop and he leans casually against one side. He makes no move to get in, and I find myself wondering if we were both just looking for a quieter place to exist with one another, where children aren't screaming all around us and Christmas music isn't on blast.

I turn to him, a grin spreading across my face. "To be totally honest, I have this feeling in my gut like I went too far. I get that, sometimes, when I stand up for myself. But my life was impacted significantly because of something he did, and yes, it was many years ago, but it felt good to say it. To put the onus on him for being the asshole, instead of myself for keeping quiet and pretending like it doesn't still hurt sometimes."

Nick puts his hands on my shoulders again, his fingers running through my hair. "You did good, Noelle."

"Yeah?"

He nods, and I can't fight the pull to him anymore. I crash into his chest, wrapping my arms around him and squeezing him tight. His arms wrap around my neck a moment later.

"I'm glad you were finally able to tell off the dickhead."

I laugh into his chest, nuzzling into him where his coat is unzipped.

He tightens around me, swaying slightly, and when I look up at him, he only stares me down, a slight smile on his face as his fingers drift through my hair.

And something about the way he's holding me, looking at me so gently, makes me stand on my toes, my lips brushing hesitantly across his jaw. I pause afterward, gauging his reaction, but he seems almost stunned.

His eyes search my face, his fingers still moving through

my hair in a way that sends little tingles flying across my scalp.

And then he leans down and kisses me so lightly that I might actually start drifting through the air and fly away.

I grab at him, fisting his shirt in my hand and pressing my lips against his. A moan escapes me, betraying the warmth building in my abdomen. I press myself against him as his fingers move up higher in my hair, resting on the back of my head and pulling me closer. His other hand dips beneath my coat, his fingers impossibly warm on the small of my back.

A strangled sound escapes him as he twists us, pressing me up against the car. His lips move against mine, our delicate touch morphing into something more primal. He licks at the seam of my lips and his tongue enters my mouth, tangling with mine in a way that has me two seconds from dropping to my knees and freeing him from his jeans. My leg lifts, my heel finding the back of his leg and tugging him closer.

I'm desperate to feel him.

"Noelle," he mutters against my lips, his kiss slowing our frenzy.

"Nick," I say, and it comes out sounding like a moan.

"Noelle," he repeats, his mouth moving to my cheek, his lips brushing against the skin of my neck. "We can't."

I nod. "Right," I say, grabbing hold of his chin and pulling his mouth back to mine. "We can't."

He kisses me forcefully. Intentionally. He has me pinned against the car, his lips moving against mine as my hips search for friction. He makes a guttural noise deep in his throat as I dig my fingers into his neck, keeping him close.

"Noelle," he says, his voice sharp as he pulls away. He takes a step back, but rests his hands on the car on either side of me. His hair is all sorts of wild, his glasses askew. The dim light emanating from the fair casts one side of his face in shadow, like a hint of the caveman underneath the math teacher persona is showing through.

Because of me. I'm pulling out the man underneath it all. His weakness or his poison, I'm not sure.

But I love this side of him.

I run my hands along his strong chest, my hands dipping beneath his coat.

"Community service is fake anyway," I say, brushing my lips along the edge of his jaw.

"You're taking it seriously," he says.

I shrug. "I told my mom I'd go through with it. That's not really *taking it seriously*."

He gives me a flat look. "Hank is taking it seriously."

"Because he's in my mom's pocket. Or she's in his."

"If everyone else is taking it seriously, I need to take it seriously, too."

He seems resolute. And as much as I want to think I can change his mind, I kind of like that when he makes a commitment, he follows through with it.

"What about after?" I ask.

His head drops as he rests one hand on my hip, his eyes following the motion as his fingers dip beneath my coat.

His thumb rubs a small circle into my skin and every particle of my being focuses on that contact.

He looks up at me, his eyes finding mine. "After would be okay."

I nod, my hands trailing along his jaw, his neck, the thick muscles underneath his shirt that I'm desperate to kiss. I press my lips against his jaw. "And maybe one more to hold us over?"

His hand shoots to the back of my neck, holding me in

place as he kisses me harshly. His tongue winds into my mouth, his breath running warm across my cheeks as he holds me against him.

When we break apart, he tugs my head into the crook of his neck, his arms strong around me. "How many hours do you have left?"

I laugh as his hands roam my body, groping at my ass and finding my waist underneath my coat. "Who's being tortured more here, me or you?"

His laugh is deep, more of a grumble than a laugh. "Seriously, Noelle. How long do I have to wait?"

His words send a rush of heat through my body as I imagine what it would feel like to truly be *touched* by him. He's an unassuming math teacher on the outside, complete with his little Clark Kent glasses, but the way he grabbed me was rough. Like he knows how to touch a woman.

"I think I have twenty hours left. Ish."

"Are you here for the weekend?" he asks, his lips brushing against the skin of my neck in a way that has each of my muscles taut, ready to pounce on him.

I nod.

"So in theory, you could be done Sunday."

"I mean, if you think you can come up with enough community service activities to fill up twenty hours over *one weekend*, sure. But that's a lot. And you were already running out of ideas."

He shrugs, nipping lightly at the skin of my neck. "Maybe I'll have you sit there for twenty hours so I can stare at you."

"That doesn't sound like it serves the community."

"It serves me," he offers, and something about that sounds deliciously naughty.

"Just say the word," I say, my hand running through his hair as his lips leave goosebumps along my skin.

He groans. "You can't say things like that, Noelle."

He steps away from me, taking his glasses off with one hand and running his other through his hair. He looks disheveled, a little tortured.

All because of me.

"Sorry," I say.

"Twenty hours," he says, putting his glasses back on.

I nod in agreement. "Twenty hours."

He gives me one last kiss, his fingers digging into my skin and a groan slipping from his throat.

10

NICK

Saturday, December 14th

I *have to keep my hands off of Noelle.*

That's what I tell myself when I see her car turn into the high school parking lot and slowly head in my direction.

I spent most of my night trying to figure out ways we can actually help the community that don't leave us alone together. Because as tempting as it is to pull something out of my ass–mop the cafeteria, clean the bleachers, prepare pamphlets for the school play–I know that the second it's the two of us, every single one of my thoughts will be focused on the feel of her skin beneath my fingers. The way she moaned into my mouth when we kissed and hiked her knee up around my waist.

And I'm not sure I'll survive twenty hours of that.

She has a scarf high around her neck when she steps out of her car, an army green jacket covering her torso. She zips it up against the cold as she walks toward me, giving me a small wave as she starts up the stairs. I lean against the railing, my hands in my pockets so they don't magnetically attach to her hips.

"Good morning, Saint Nick," she says, a knowing smile skirting her face with the nickname.

There's no hiding what she does to me now.

"Criminal," I greet her, biting back my matching grin.

"So what delightful activity do you have planned for us today?" she asks. I detect a hint of subtext in her words, like she's just daring me to say the naughty activities we could be doing if she wasn't my criminal.

I smile, despite every muscle in my body itching to touch her. "We're heading back to the fair."

She raises her eyebrows and then narrows her eyes. "You seem too happy about this for it to be a fun thing."

My smile ticks wider. "Well, since I know how *excited* you are to serve your community, I asked around to see if anyone needed help with their booths this weekend."

She purses her lips, waiting for the catch.

"And Hank said he could use a few volunteers to help hand out fliers."

Her face drops. "Nick!" She stomps. "You have to be kidding me."

A grin spreads across my face now. "And you're going to love the fliers we're handing out."

She presses her lips together, her jaw ticking. "What are the fliers?"

"It's an after-school program held at the police station for troubled youths."

Her eyes bore into mine. "Nick."

"And I thought, who better to hand them out than our very own town criminal?"

I eye her, searching for signs of steam coming out of her ears or boiling skin.

"Is this your own personal brand of torture?" she asks.

"I'm so glad you're looking forward to it. I think this program is really going to bring positive change to our community."

She throws her hands out in front of her. "This town doesn't *have* troubled youths! Who the fuck is Hank trying to recruit?"

I shrug. "Honestly, I don't know. Hank is going to do what Hank is going to do. He seemed like he was at a bit of a loss when I asked him for suggestions for what to do with you."

She lets out a long breath as she takes a step closer to me, the front of her coat brushing against mine. "I could give you some other ideas of what you could do with me." She raises an eyebrow. "Or *to* me."

Fuuuuuck. My dick twitches. I know I should take a step back, stop her from getting any closer with that devilish tongue of hers.

But I like the proximity. I like that she wants me as badly as I want her.

It's intoxicating.

"Like what?" I ask, feigning innocence and cocking my head to the side. I keep my hands tucked in my pockets to stop myself from touching her.

She shrugs. "You could kiss me like you did last night. And then maybe just... see what happens after that."

"See what happens?"

She nods, biting her lip. "I think that might be a good use of our time. And I mean, teachers do so much for this little community of ours." She rests her hand on the front of my coat and I'm simultaneously angry and relieved that I can't feel her fingers on my chest. "It feels only right that we give a little something back. Make *them* feel good, too."

I nod, falling into her trap for only a moment. My job *is* hard. And sometimes it wears me down to the point where I wonder if I can keep it up forever.

And when I have dainty little brunettes smiling up at me like they want to rip my clothes off, I wonder whether a little bit of indulgence is really *that* terrible. This palpable tension between us could probably be solved with an afternoon between the sheets. I could throw her around a little bit, make her come on my face and again on my dick.

I've had what I thought was love, and losing it ripped out a piece of me.

And now Noelle has me thinking all sorts of inappropriate thoughts about her. While I tell myself it doesn't have to be a long term thing–that we can have some fun and continue on with our lives–I know that Noelle would stick in my mind and worm her way into my heart.

She hates this town. Wants nothing more than to be done with community service. And the second that happens, she'll be gone.

But maybe I'm getting ahead of myself here. I'm already reeling over my future heartbreak when the reality is, we'd have to explore something first to even *get* to the heartbreak.

All I have to go on is what I feel right now, and that is mind-bogglingly attracted to someone who really shouldn't inspire these sorts of feelings in me. I ultimately want someone to spend my life with–to spend this time of year with–but having Noelle standing one step below me, her hand on my chest and that snarky little grin on her face, makes me want to throw all of that out the window and show this woman a good time.

We just have to get through this weekend. And then... well, maybe something will happen between us.

Or maybe she'll run back to her little apartment with her

sister that's three hours away and never come to this town again.

The thought inspires an ache in my chest that I brush away with a quick shake of my head.

"You don't want me to make you feel good?" she asks, her eyebrows crinkling.

I shut my eyes, resting my hand on top of hers and gently removing it from my chest. "Noelle, there is plenty that I want but can't have."

She purses her lips, quiet for a moment. "You can have me."

I take my glasses off–partially to obscure my view of her, pink cheeks and playful smile–and run my hand over my face.

"Noelle," I say, my voice cracking in a way that probably tells her *exactly* what I'm thinking about doing to her at this moment.

"Nick," she parries.

"Behave."

She bites her lip, a grin spreading across her face. "And what if I don't?"

"I will sign you up for more community service with Hank, handing out fliers that only get more and more cringeworthy."

Her nostrils flare. "Well, that's no fun." She crosses her arms over her chest. "I was thinking more along the lines of spanking. Maybe a little bit of edging. Those seem like appropriate punishments."

"It's not a punishment if you enjoy it."

She shrugs. "I promise I'll play my part well. 'Oh, Mr. Monroe, *please* don't leave chalk hand prints on my ass! Oh, Mr. Monroe, it's *so* uncomfortable to be bent over your desk like this,'" she mocks, clasping her hands over her chest.

What I wouldn't give for a stick of chalk right now.

Her eyebrows raise when I place my hands on her shoulders, but her face falls when I twist her and direct her toward the fair. "Hank is waiting for you."

THE FAIR IS as crowded today as it was yesterday, and as we weave through the crowds of people, I find myself nodding and smiling to a slew of parents and kids I've taught over the past few years. Noelle walks with her arms crossed over her chest, glancing up at me every once in a while with an eye roll when I greet yet another person.

"Are you the town sweetheart or something?" she asks me, when I finally spot Hank's booth in the distance, a banner attached to the front with Snow Falls' district number on it. "How the hell do you know *everyone?*"

"I taught everyone's kids. That's how."

She scoffs. "I bet they all loved you, too."

"As long as they don't love me like Delia."

She crinkles her nose. "Yeah, that was gross."

"You know, I meant to ask you," she says, turning to me. "You were going on and on about speaking your truth the other day, yet you were hiding under the table right there with me. What's the deal? Why don't you speak your truth to Delia?"

I eye Hank's booth in the distance–he's happily talking to someone across the table from him and doesn't seem pressed for help.

So I turn to Noelle and let out a long breath. "Delia is unique. She was president of the PTA and you either love her or you hate her. And I just... honestly, don't want to get mixed up in any of that. I don't want to take sides and I don't want to make enemies with someone so involved in my job."

"Didn't her daughter graduate?"

"Yes. And she's *still* everywhere I turn."

Noelle nods. "Have you told her you're not interested?"

"Yes, Noelle. I do practice what I preach." I shrug. "She does this thing where if you say something she doesn't like, she just kind of smiles at you. Like, she waits with this big grin on her face until you feel uncomfortable and then backtrack. So help me god, I know it's coming. I expect it. Yet she still gets me every time."

"So. She's a psychopath."

I laugh. "I don't know about that, but if you want to go ahead and get her committed somewhere, that'll be a great start."

"Maybe I can frame her for an egging."

I shake my head. "Noelle, you're just going to get yourself in trouble again."

She shrugs. "Maybe I'll just smile real big at Hank until he lets me go."

"Hey, if that works, go right ahead." I nod to the booth in the distance. "Come on, he's waiting for us."

She sighs and turns to follow me, pausing when she sees the booth in front of us. "Oh, for fuck's sake," she mutters. "Can you write 'Criminal' on my forehead and call it a day? This is downright–I don't know–*ostentatious*."

I can't help the laugh that escapes me. "*Ostentatious?*"

"Ostentatious," she confirms.

I shrug. "Sorry, already told Hank we'd help him out. Better put on that orange jumpsuit of yours and show up for the troubled youths of your hometown."

She grumbles, crossing her arms. I rest my hand on the back of her neck, gently guiding her forward. She shivers at the touch. "It's one day, Noelle. Besides, it'll make Hank really happy."

She lets out a long breath. "I hate Hank."

"You're annoyed with Hank but you begrudgingly like Hank."

She shoots me a glare. "No, I hate Hank."

"Okay."

I drop my hand from her neck, and she turns, grabbing at it to put it back where it was. "No, keep your hand there. I can live off that for the next hour."

A surprised laugh escapes me. "Wow, if a hand gets you through an hour, imagine what the rest of me could do."

Her eyes widen as her jaw drops, a grin spreading across her face. "Saint Nick."

"Yeah, that one slipped out a bit," I confess, running a hand through my hair.

"What I wouldn't give to see the thoughts running through your head right now."

I shake my head, knowing we're entering dangerous territory again. "I can guarantee you they'd have you blushing."

Her eyes flash. "Tell me! Please. And if you could make it last ten hours."

"Don't know whether I can last ten hours but for you, I'll give it my best."

A surprised laugh tumbles from her mouth.

Keep it the fuck together, Nick.

Hank is in front of us, and I head toward him like he's the lifeboat I need to survive. I can stop paddling for my life now that he's here to save me, and even though I'm taking small gulps of water, I know I won't drown.

"Hank!" I bark, nudging her forward with my hand on

the small of her back. "I brought you a criminal to serve as an example to the troubled youths of this town."

"There she is!" Hank says with a grin as he stands from his chair behind the table. He runs a hand over his short, graying hair that contrasts his dark skin. On the table in front of him, he has a number of pamphlets lined up, ranging from general info, to community events, to summer programs for kids. "Nice to see you, Noelle."

She gives him about the fakest grin I've ever seen, and he takes it in stride.

"Nice to see you, too, Hank," she says through clenched teeth.

He rounds the table, clapping a hand on my shoulder. "Nick says you've been doing well with the community service. Really putting your all into it. I really appreciate it, Noelle. As does the town. I think everyone enjoys seeing one of our own come back successful and investing into the community. Though I have to tell you, I'm surprised you haven't found a way to bring your business into it."

"My business is *mine*, Hank," she bites. "You know that."

He holds his hands up. "I know, kid. But god, you're so smart. The kids around here could use that, especially the ones who have less-than-stellar high school experiences. And I mean, I think your mom certainly wouldn't hate having you around a little more."

I narrow my eyes. *Okay, so Hank and Noelle know each other better than I thought.*

"I get to choose what I bring back to this town and what I take from it," she says. "My business is *mine*, and it stays at home with me. Just like my dad and every other asshole in this town is the town's, and I get to leave them here when I'm done."

He rolls his eyes, waving her off. "Alright, alright. Whatever suits you, Noelle." He turns to me. "We've really got our hands full with this one, huh?" He nudges her arm lightly and she gives him a tight-lipped smile.

"That's an understatement," I agree, earning me another glare.

"So," Hank says, turning back to the table and gesturing to the array of pamphlets. "I'm so delighted that you wanted to help out with the sheriff's booth this year. It's an easy job. All you have to do is man the booth and answer the occasional question when someone comes around. It might help to do a quick read-through of the pamphlets–most questions are answered in there, and I'll be here if you need help."

She rolls her eyes. "Great. Wonderful. I can't wait to help troubled youths by shouting at their parents that they're troubled."

Hank gives her a look before turning to me. "Make sure she behaves, will you?"

The grin she gives me over his shoulder is nothing short of devilish.

I struggle to keep my laughter at bay as I nod. "I'll do my best."

NOELLE, despite being unenthused about today's community service, takes her job seriously. She hands out pamphlets and speaks kindly to anyone who stops by to say hello, though most of them are here to chat with Hank and move on. She calls after anyone who leaves the booth without a small stack of pamphlets and makes sure they get one of each, shooting Hank and me dirty looks every time she catches one of us looking at her.

Which... is hard *not* to do. Whenever someone walks up to the table, she leans forward to greet them and the only thing I can think about is how she would look with my chalky handprint on her ass.

As we get close to lunch, Hank asks us what we want and heads down the street to pick it up for us. It's on him, he insists, because we've been so gracious with our time.

Even though I'm not doing much other than ogling Noelle. It's not like our booth is getting bombarded with people–it's the sheriff's booth, for Christ's sake, and most people are more interested in Christmas presents and snacks than they are with us.

So I greet any townspeople I know and do my best to make myself useful, but mostly I imagine all the ways I could make Noelle come. If I had been smarter, I would have brought a book to read during those moments when no one is around. Anything to distract me from her ass and the toned legs underneath.

There's a part of me that wonders whether she's doing this on purpose. Every once in a while she turns around to look at me, and I can't tell whether it's amusement or annoyance in her eyes.

While Hank is gone to get food, I get my answer. She twists to look at me, wiggling her ass in my direction. "Getting a good look, Mr. Monroe?" she asks, catching me staring shamelessly at her backside. She's leaning across the table in front of her, and when she catches my attention, she arches her back ever so slightly.

"You're trying to make this as hard as possible, aren't you?"

She grins. "Is it working?" Her eyes dip and I swallow, pushing my glasses onto my head so I can't see her anymore, and run a hand over my face.

I mean, I can see a very sexy blob in front of me, but the detail is gone.

"Yes," I say gruffly, as I reposition my glasses in front of my eyes.

She grins. "Good. Because I'm sure as hell not going to be the only one tortured this holiday season."

I shake my head as I laugh, tipping my head back and staring at the ceiling of the hut for a few moments before turning my attention back to her.

And that's the moment Hank returns, bag of food in his hand, and sets it down on the little fold-up table in the back of the tent. "Sandwich for you, sir," he says, as someone stops by the booth. Noelle speaks easily to them, handing over pamphlet after pamphlet with a smile on her face as if she's actually *happy* to be doing this. "Noelle, when you're done, I have your salad here for you."

"Thanks," she calls over her shoulder, returning her attention to the family she's talking to.

My eyes linger on her a second longer than I should, caught on the way her hair flows down her back, the way her body is all smooth curves.

I shake my head in an attempt to focus my brain.

And when I turn my attention to the food in front of me, I catch only Hank's grin.

"You gonna ask her out or what?"

I swallow. "What?"

"You've spent all morning staring at the girl. You might as well make a real go of it."

My heart thumps. *Does this mean I have Hank's blessing?*

Not that I *need* it. But we've already entered dangerous territory.

But if Hank's not upset, maybe I shouldn't try so hard to fight this thing between us.

"Hank, I sign her timecard."

His laugh is boisterous enough that Noelle turns to see what the commotion is. I shrug, hoping she's not listening too closely to our conversation. "I found that timecard online and printed it out on card stock so it looked border-line legitimate."

I snort. "If everyone else is taking it seriously, I feel like I should take it seriously."

Hank shrugs. "Well, whatever. Just don't sit around with your thumb up your butt too long because that girl is going to go running away from here the second her hours are done."

"You think?" I carefully unwrap my sandwich with one eye on Noelle.

He nods. "Her mother's been trying to get her to come back for ages. Won't stay longer than a holiday unless she's forced to, and when she does, it's nothing but temper tantrums. Like that egg-throwing incident." He sighs, pulling the plastic from around his wrap. "I get it. I really do. High school is tough for a lot of kids. But she's not in high school anymore, and she's got family here who want her around. I mean, once her sister moves back here, she's going to be alone and essentially shunning everyone who cares about her."

I pause, my sandwich halfway to my mouth. "Her sister is moving back here?"

I don't recall Noelle telling me this, and something tells me it's not the sort of thing she'd keep under wraps. It seems like the sort of thing she'd be screaming about.

Hank nods, taking a bite of his wrap. "Christina got a job closer to home. She was always a little townie. Homecoming queen in high school, always participated in the play and the parade and all the town stuff. As much as Noelle hates this town, Christina misses it."

I nod, watching Noelle from the corner of my eye. "Does she know that?"

Hank shrugs. "I would guess so. The two of them live together."

I lick my lips. "Yeah, I don't think Noelle knows."

His brow furrows as he rests his sandwich on the table in front of him, eyeing me. "No?"

I shake my head. "I know I don't know her all that well, but I think she'd be upset."

Hank lets out a long breath. "Well, that's not going to go over very well, is it?"

"Should we tell her?"

He crinkles his nose. "No. I think if Christina hasn't told her yet, she has a good reason."

"Reason being to avoid Noelle going nuclear?"

Hank cringes. "I don't know." He pauses, shaking his head. "Next time I see Helen, I'll ask what I should do. Come to think of it, I'm not sure *I'm* supposed to know that Christina is moving back here, either."

I narrow my eyes. "You're not *supposed* to?"

"I think she told me that in confidence, probably."

I stare at the older man, searching for meaning in his eyes, but he won't look at me.

And I get the distinct feeling that Hank is sleeping with Noelle's mom.

11

NOELLE

Saturday, December 14th

While handing out pamphlets for the sheriff's office is not my idea of *fun*, I'm enjoying the way Nick's eyes are glued to me. Every time I turn around, there he is, watching me.

If he's trying to hide it, he's not doing very well.

I bend over a little further as I talk to people wandering by the booth. Give him a little treat to get him through the day in the hopes that he returns the favor later. Maybe he'll rest his hand on my neck like he did this morning. Grab my ass like he did last night. Shove his tongue down my throat and tug us close.

He was quiet during lunch, but I wouldn't be surprised if that was because of Hank, who seemed to be particularly talkative today. That, and I'm also trying my hardest to obscure our burgeoning connection. Because Hank will tell my mom, who will tell my sister, and before I know it I'll be completely surrounded by people making fun of me for it.

After lunch, I pick right back up where I left off. Smiling

despite my annoyance with the situation. Hank and Nick talk in low voices behind me, every once in a while standing behind me to greet whoever it is I'm talking to. For Nick, they're former students and parents. For Hank, they're townspeople.

I don't really *hate* Hank. He bothers me, and I hate that *he's* the one who caught me throwing eggs at my dad's house, considering he's buddy-buddy with my mom, but I don't *hate* him.

While Hank is pulled into another conversation off to the side, Nick stands to talk to someone he recognizes. And I'm left between the two of them, a fake smile plastered on my face, as I hand out yet another little pile of pamphlets.

And then Nick's hand lands in the small of my back. A simple touch that ultimately holds very little meaning, but it sends another little zip of heat down my spine. No one can see the way he's touching me, and judging from the genuine smile he's shooting at the people we're talking to, I can't help but wonder if he's even doing it on purpose.

Like maybe his hand is magnetically drawn to my back in the same way my vagina feels magnetically drawn to his dick.

I move a little closer, and his fingers move gently across my coat. I smell him all around me, that smoky sweet firewood scent that infiltrates my brain like a drug that makes me want *more more more*.

And as we wave goodbye to the people whose names I've already forgotten, I spot a familiar face in the crowd, just as he's spotting me.

"Fuck," I say, taking a step behind Nick, breaking that contact that had me distracted enough to not notice my dad was skulking around nearby.

"You okay?" Nick asks, holding his hands out on either

side of me as if he's waiting for me to jump into his arms. Which, to be fair, doesn't seem like the worst idea in the world. If anything, it would at least make everyone else feel as awkward as I do when my dad is around.

"My dad," I say, crouching so that he won't be able to spot me.

Nick glances over his shoulder and gives me what looks like a pained smile. "I think it might be too late to hide, Noelle."

I grimace. "Fuck fuck fuck," I whisper.

"What's the matter?" Hank asks, his attention turning to me as he rests his hands on his hips and takes a step closer.

"Nothing," I say, because having everyone's attention on me really only makes things worse. "It's nothing."

"Her dad," Nick explains, and I throw my hands out in front of me in response. "What? Are you going to sit here and pretend he's not the reason you're hiding when he's about to be here in five seconds?"

"Maybe!"

He raises an eyebrow, and I put my hands over my face, leaning forward and resting my forehead against Nick's chest. A second later, he hesitantly hugs me, strong arms squeezing me against him. He lowers his voice so only I can hear. "Do you want me to ask him to leave?"

"No," I say, and it comes out a little breathy. "I guess I have to talk to him eventually."

"I can," he says, and when I pull away from him, he keeps his arm around my shoulders. Like a protective little box where no one can get me. His fingers are in my hair again, and all I want is for him to lean forward and kiss me. "Really, you don't have to talk to him if you don't want to. You know I will always be the first to suggest talking rather than stewing, but you don't have to do anything you don't want to do."

My eyes snag on his as I wonder when the change happened and I started trusting him. Not that I ever explicitly *didn't*.

But more than anyone I've known before, I feel like he's on my side. Like he sees my struggle and while he wants me to work through it in a healthy way, he's not going to force me into anything.

I do think he would get involved if I started looking for another carton of eggs, though.

Hank huffs as I take a hesitant step away from Nick. "Better you talk to him than me."

I turn to him, struggling to figure out what *that* means.

Hank shrugs. "I'm just saying, if there's one man in this town who deserves some scrambled eggs on his door, it's him." He shakes his head, taking a step toward the back of the hut as I cock my head to one side. "And just so you know, I do not condone that behavior." He takes a seat in his chair and nods to me. "But I'm glad you did it."

A surprised laugh escapes me, and when I turn back to Nick, he's grinning. He shrugs and takes a step to the side.

And I come face to face with my dad. And my two half-sisters, I guess you'd call them. If I remember correctly, the second one started high school this year.

"Hey, kid," my dad says, his voice happier than I'd expect, considering the last time I saw him, I was in the back of Hank's cruiser. "How are you?"

I force a smile onto my face. "I'm doing well. And yourself?"

I don't mean to sound so formal when I speak to him. It just comes out that way when I'm nervous. I didn't have this side of me in high school or else I would have used it a lot more often. Once I figured out I had some sort of talent designing websites and it was something I actually enjoyed doing, I went full speed ahead finding clients. I spoke to executives I had no business talking to, with only my professional voice and a false sense of confidence.

In the halls of my high school, I turn into sad Noelle with no friends. But in the real world, I can deal with hard questions from clients. I can deal with losing the occasional contract–not that it happens often, but such is life. And I'm going to deal with my dad in the same way I would a business deal. Confidently and without emotion.

If he wants emotion, he can refer to Appendix A: The Egg Splattered Across His Door.

"Doing okay, kid. I miss you. The girls miss you."

I clench my teeth to avoid scoffing. "Miss you, too."

Nick's hand brushes across my lower back, and a second later, he's holding his hand out to my dad to shake. "Nick Monroe," he says, and my dad tentatively shakes it, his eyes darting back and forth between the two of us. There's no doubt in my mind he's wondering what's going on here. "I teach math at the high school."

To start, he knows Hank and I aren't the best of friends. And he knows I wouldn't be caught dead in this town participating in community events.

That, and the math teacher. Why the hell is the math teacher touching his daughter?

Or at least, the woman who used to be his daughter.

My dad spies Hank in the back of the hut. "Hank, nice to see you."

Hank grunts, and I turn to give him the most confused look I can muster while fixing my face for when I turn back to my dad.

My dad clears his throat, running a hand over his hair as he puts an arm around his closest daughter, who is much more interested in her phone than she is in our conversation.

I don't blame her.

In the few seconds of silence between us, my dad decides to speak. "Hey, uh," he starts, "I wanted to say I'm sorry about Thanksgiving. I didn't know Christina was coming over, and I didn't realize when she called me that her leg was broken. I thought she was... I don't know, just upset."

I *know* this conversation has the potential to derail me. I'm betting Hank and Nick know it, too.

I clench my jaw, trying my best to remain level-headed. "Don't you think it's worth showing up even if your daughter is *just upset*?"

He blinks. "Well, of course. I just meant that I didn't realize how serious it was."

"So to be clear, you're teaching your two replacement daughters that you're not going to show up for them unless they have a broken leg to prove that something is wrong?"

The small one blinks up at me, her eyes finding mine. I'm struck for a moment how much she looks like me. There's no more of that little kid playfulness–she has that discerning teenager eye now that tells me she's sizing me up right now as much as I'm skewering our shared sperm donor.

"No one is replacing anyone," he says, holding a hand up to stop me. "I was trying to teach them that I'd be there for them during the holidays. No matter what. And I was."

And I go off the deep end. Dad: 1, Calm Noelle: 0.

"Ugh, that's such bullshit. A holiday means nothing if you don't show up otherwise. It's a stupid day where everyone decides to shove pie up their asses and pretend they're one big happy family. Yet the family that actually *needed* you to show up was left lying on black ice in your driveway."

The taller one raises her eyebrows. I get the feeling she didn't know how Christina's leg was broken.

My dad shakes his head. "Alright, I'm not getting through to you," he says. He wraps an arm around each of the girls' shoulders. "I'm not trying to be an asshole. I was trying to apologize."

"Apologize by proving you can show up when you need to."

He turns, tugging the girls along with him. I shout after them. "And by the way, you two small fries," I call, because of course I'm blanking on their goddamn names. They turn, despite my dad's best efforts to face them forward. "Just because he doesn't show up at the right times, doesn't mean that you don't deserve someone who does!" I'm fully aware I'm making a fool of myself, but along with the anger my dad is inspiring, I feel a certain amount of kinship with these girls.

When you don't have someone to teach you what you deserve, you end up looking for validation in all the wrong places. My sister and I figured it out, thanks in large part to my mom swiftly kicking my dad to the curb when she found out about his second family.

But if you don't have anyone to correct your course–to listen when you need an ear or *plain show up* when you need them–it's a recipe for disaster.

I don't want them to have to claw their way back the way I did.

Before I can stop myself, I'm screaming over the crowd of people closing in between us. "And if you're ever upset and you need somebody to talk to who will *listen*, you come find me! I'll listen to you!"

The small one's eyes catch on mine, and I nod as if to reaffirm this, before she's tugged away by my dad and disappears into the crowd.

Nick's hand moves against my back. "You okay?"

I blink, reorienting myself to the space around me. "Yeah. Sorry." I cringe. "Oh god, I think I need to get into the fetal position for a while. Jesus Christ, I can't believe some of the things that come out of my mouth sometimes."

Nick laughs, his hand pressing into my back a little harder through my coat, like he can sense I need that comforting touch.

"Good for you, Noelle," he says as the blood rises in my cheeks.

He doesn't move his hands as I spin slowly toward him, and they come to rest on my hips. His eyes are on mine, his eyebrows raised as if he's waiting for me to combust or derail or otherwise spin out of control.

All I *want* to do is press my face into his chest, feel his warm hand on the back of my neck and his breath darting across my face. I want to feel his hands in my hair and hear the way his voice dips when he's speaking only to me.

"It feels like I'm warring with myself," I say, rubbing my hand over my chest. "I feel like I'm fighting for my life to retain who I've become while simultaneously trying to stand up for who I used to be." I let out a long breath. "Honestly, I just hope he can get his shit together for those girls. Do better for them than he did for me and Christina."

Hank grunts. "Deserves a lot worse than a talking to if you ask me, but unfortunately, I'm the sheriff."

I crinkle my brow, cocking my head to the side. "Hank, if I didn't know any better, I'd think you're *asking* me to egg his house."

He points a finger at me, his eyes connecting to mine.

"Listen to me, Noelle. If I catch you throwing eggs at his house again, I'm not letting you off easy with community service with the new math teacher that has all the ladies in town fanning themselves."

Nick's eyebrows rise. "Excuse me?"

I can't help the laugh that tumbles from my throat. "Hank, you think this was letting me off easy? Look what he has me doing. He might be a looker, but he's certainly not easy."

His cheeks go pink. "If everybody else is taking this seriously, I feel like I should take it seriously."

I squeeze Nick's arm and he smiles down at me, one hand still resting on my hip. I step away slowly, heading to the back of the hut and sinking down into the chair across from Hank. "Why do *you* hate my dad so much?"

He eyes me for a moment before shaking his head. "I think he's a worthless piece of shit who treated your mother like she was secondary for so long that she started to believe it. I think you explained it perfectly, what happened to her. She was treated poorly for so long that she started to think she deserved it. Nobody should have to fight their way out of that."

I nod, my conversation with Christina coming swarming back to the forefront of my mind. Hank doesn't just have a crush on our mom—he's down *bad* for her.

I warm to him. Hank—as much as he pisses me off—is a good guy at heart. And the fact that he's getting all puffy and angry over how someone treated my mom—one of my favorite people in the world—has the ice I hold in my heart for him thawing.

"I agree," I say. "She deserves a hell of a lot better."

He nods. "She deserves *the best*."

FOR THE REST of the day, I eye Hank. He hasn't made any further comments about my mom, but every time I think back on his sputtery outburst that she deserves better, my heart swells.

It has me a little giddy and excited because my mom hasn't really dated since my dad. There's been the occasional online date, when Christina or I have forced the issue, but she hasn't really made an effort to get out there. As much as Hank is *Hank*, I think he would treat her well.

And *that* is exciting.

Add to that the way Nick keeps touching me today, and my brain is completely scattered. When I turn around, I think about my mom finally finding love again. And when I turn to Nick, I think about the way he kissed me last night in the dim light of the parking lot.

When the fair dies down, Hank waves us off and promises he can take care of the booth by himself. He tells Nick to mark down an extra hour or two on my timecard before taking my seat behind the table, smiling and waving as people meander by.

As I gather my bag from underneath the folding table in back, Nick's hand falls to my back again. A place it seems drawn to today.

We leave the hut like that, his hand so lightly touching me as we weave through the crowd toward the high school.

When the booths are behind us and the Christmas music slowly blends into the background noise of the night, I slide my arm around his waist. A moment later, his is around my shoulders, tugging me closer.

"So I take it Hank has a soft spot for your mom," Nick

says, as we wander along the pavement back to the high school.

I laugh. "Yeah, Christina was saying something about that last week. But it, uh, seems like more than a soft spot."

"Yeah, I think he flat out loves her," Nick says, squeezing me a little tighter into his side. "That's sweet. Cranky old Hank is in love."

"I wonder if my mom knows."

Nick hums. "You don't think he's told her?"

I shrug. "I don't know. I mean, I don't know if she'd even tell me if he did. She hasn't exactly been prioritizing relationships recently. Makes sense, considering how my dad treated her."

He nods, pressing a kiss to the side of my head that has my stomach doing all sorts of somersaults. "I'm really proud of you for standing up for yourself."

I snort, burying my head in his shoulder. "Stop. That was embarrassing. The whole town probably heard me screaming at him."

Nick shakes his head. "You can always look back and wish you had done something another way. But I think sometimes what matters is that you did it. You said the hard thing." He lets out a deep breath. "What matters is that you stay true to yourself and the people you love. And you do that. Religiously."

I shrug. "I spent a lot of my life accepting the way people have treated me. Now that I'm on my own and doing well, it's hard to come back to a place that holds that feeling so strongly. Makes me feel like a caged animal, ready to lash out."

He nods. "Well, you're ticking them off one by one. Louis Prince and Stacy Mann. Your dad. Who else do we have to take down a peg?"

I laugh into his shoulder. "I don't know. They were the big ones." I let out a long breath. "Maybe it's this town, you know? Just the vestiges of having felt less than for so long in exactly this place that it creeps into my bones whenever I'm here."

We cross the asphalt, heading for my car. "Well, maybe it's time you show the town what's what."

I raise an eyebrow. "What does that mean?"

He shakes his head as I hit the unlock button on my key fob. "I know you're committed to keeping your life now separate from what your life once was. But maybe showing off a little is exactly what you need to do to cancel out the way this town made you feel."

I purse my lips. "I get the sentiment. I don't think that you're *wrong* but couldn't it go either way? I can bring this thing that I've worked so hard for into this community–in any way, shape, or form I want, right? And see how it makes me feel. But doesn't it go the opposite way too? I'm not sure I could have built this thing if I hadn't left and started new. And if that's true, isn't it possible that even running web design classes at the local library could, little by little, chip away at all that I've worked for?"

"That's what he wants you to do? Run classes?"

She nods. "Yeah, he's been trying to get me to do that for a while. And I just... I mean, the classes themselves sound fine." I let out a long breath. "Sometimes I feel like the perfect storm had to happen for my life to turn out as well as it did *despite* the circumstances. And it feels like allowing those circumstances to mix with my new life is a recipe for disaster."

Nick nods, digesting this for a moment. "Isn't it possible that the perfect storm is who you've become? That wherever you are, you'll find success because you've gotten *through* those circumstances?"

I shrug noncommittally. "I guess you can spin it whatever way you want. It feels dangerous to me. There's no reason for me to be back here other than holidays, so why force it, you know?" I bite my lip, realizing I'm dancing around dangerous territory with whatever new thing is happening between me and Nick. "If there is a reason for me to be back here, of course I'll figure out a way to make it work. But until that time, I don't see any harm in keeping a boundary."

Nick nods. He doesn't seem upset, so I can only assume I didn't step in shit. In my head, we're lightly exploring something together–and it seems like he's on the same page.

A moment later, he grins. "Well, it sounds like that jerk Hank thinks you're quite an inspiration."

A blush spreads across my cheeks. "Stop! I already feel bad enough."

He shrugs, standing up straight and pulling me against his chest. "For what it's worth, I think I agree with Hank. And I think you could do a lot for this town, if you ever decide you want to. And who knows, that might be an opportunity to tell them once and for all that Noelle deserves better, damnit."

I roll my eyes, pushing away from him for a moment. "You know me too well already if you're trying to convince me into doing something by telling me it's a rebellion."

He grins down at me with his arms still wrapped around my neck, his fingers playing with my hair.

"Despite your best efforts, I've come to find that side of you quite charming."

I press my lips together to dim my smile as I stand on my toes to kiss his jaw. "How charming?"

His arms drift down, wrapping around my waist as he tips his head down to kiss me. "Very charming," he says, one hand squeezing my ass and causing a surprised gasp to jump from my throat. "But not quite charming enough."

He pulls away from me, a grin on his face.

"Oh, come on!"

"Give me your timecard, Criminal."

I roll my eyes, letting out a quick huff as I fumble around in my bag for the card and a pen. I hand them over, watching as he scribbles on the next line and hands it back.

He lets out a long breath as he tugs me into his arms again, and I can't help but notice he pauses there, like he wants to say something more but stops himself.

"You okay?" I ask.

He nods, his eyes darting to the high school behind me. "Yeah. I'm fine."

"You sure?"

"Yeah, Noelle. I'm good."

He runs his hands through my hair, pausing with a hand on each cheek to kiss my forehead, my nose, my lips.

And then he opens my car door and ushers me inside. "Goodnight, Criminal."

12

NICK

Saturday, December 14th

I wait in my car while Noelle starts hers and slowly drives away, waving through the window as she heads for the road.

I don't know if I made the right decision. It was on the tip of my tongue all day, that Hank said Christina was moving back here. But he told me not to tell, and after that, saying anything at all felt like it might make the whole situation bigger than it needed to be.

Unless it *is* that big for Noelle, in which case, I definitely feel like I fucked up.

I like Hank, but when it comes to Hank or Noelle, my loyalty lies with her.

The thought surprises me, and I shake my head as I start my car and head out of the high school parking lot, making a right where Noelle made a left.

Noelle blustered into my life when I wasn't expecting *or* looking for someone. Yet now, after knowing her for such a short time, I already feel accountable to her. I already feel like I don't particularly care if Hank didn't want me to pass along this news because all that really matters is that I know now, and by extension, Noelle should too.

This feeling is new to me, but it's not uncomfortable. I think I've been searching for someone to click into like this.

Noelle is a handful in the best sort of way. She's clear about what she wants and needs, and she doesn't settle for less than what she deserves. Her communication skills leave a little to be desired, but at least I'll know I fucked up if I hear an egg splattering on my front door.

And I mean, she *is* working on it.

But as I loop around the town square, avoiding the most populated parts, I start to wonder if I'm even capable of being everything she deserves.

I don't have a family. I live on a teacher's salary–as Emily so often reminded me. And I live in the one place she hates more than anything.

A tightness blooms in my chest when I realize I really want something that I might not be able to have.

But the question of Christina still bounces around in my head. If *Christina* is moving back here, Noelle would have to make her peace with that. If *Christina* is moving back here, Noelle would suddenly be living in her apartment alone.

Maybe she wouldn't want to anymore.

Maybe she would see my modest townhouse and think, *hey, this ain't so bad after all.*

I spent a lot of time working toward this place. Toward a high school with a good reputation in a town with nice people.

She's spent her time post-high school running away, and I've spent my time post-high school dreaming of this place.

Do we even have a chance?

When I pull into my parking spot, I push my glasses up

onto my head and run my hands over my face. My house is cute but bereft of personality because I'm never home to give it any. I spend most of my time at the high school or out doing community events. That's why I moved here, after all.

But suddenly I wish I had put more into it.

Suddenly I wish there was someone waiting for me inside who might turn an otherwise empty house into something warm. A place I yearn to be rather than a place I rest my head each night.

I lock my car and head inside, struck by the barren walls and lack of decoration in a way that I haven't been before.

The loneliness of it all.

And I realize, as I sink into a couch that's far too big for one person, that I *have* to tell Noelle her sister is moving to town. Whether it's true or not. No matter where I heard it from.

Because from here on out, I'm going to show Noelle that she can get exactly what she deserves from this town.

From me.

I'M MEETING Noelle bright and early for another day of pamphlet distribution with Hank. She smiles when she sees me, her long dark hair tumbling down over her coat and her cheeks pink in the early morning cold. She shuffles toward my car, a thermos full of coffee in one hand, and presses herself into me, leaving a line of delicate kisses along my jaw.

And god, every time she does that, she wipes away every thought in my head and replaces them with her and only her.

I tug her hips closer, and she sighs into me as I dip my head down to kiss her.

"Good morning, Saint Nick," she says, her words soft against my lips.

"Good morning, Criminal."

She gives me a playful glare in return, her free hand dipping inside my coat and running along my chest in a way that has me very viscerally imagining what her bare skin must feel like in the morning.

I clear my throat, intending to start with the Christina news.

"So, last night I went home and did a little sleuthing," she starts, before I can get the words out.

I pause. "Yeah?"

"And I didn't get much of anything, honestly. *But,*" she says, her eyes flashing. "I did happen to find a note in one of my mom's old yearbooks from a guy who signed his name as *Hanky Panky.*"

A laugh bursts out of me that has Noelle dissolving into her own fit of giggles.

"And I don't even want to think about what that implies, but Nick, what are the chances that Hanky Panky who had heart eyes for my mom in high school, is the same Hanky Panky that is now getting all gruff and defensive over her when he runs into her dickhead ex-husband so many years later?"

I nod. "I feel like those chances are good. We should probably run a test to make sure, though."

Her eyes narrow, her hand coming to a stop on my chest. "A test?"

"Well, we have to see if he answers to Hanky Panky."

She throws her hand over her face as she laughs. "Oh my god, I cannot wait to see his reaction."

"If he is indeed, *the* Hanky Panky, my bet is he's going to turn a deep shade of crimson."

Noelle rocks onto the balls of her feet, her hair bouncing with the movement. "Oh, I can't wait! Come on, come on, we have to go find him!"

She grabs my hand, tugging me along after her, and winds her arm around my waist. I pull her closer, slowing our steps to preserve the time we have alone.

And I mean, I can't tell her about Christina if Hank is around. He told me to keep things quiet.

My insides are at war.

"Do you think they dated in high school?" Noelle asks.

I struggle to catch up with her. "If he's signing her yearbook as Hanky Panky, I'd guess so."

She laughs again, the fair looming ever closer ahead of us. *Now or never, Nick.*

"Oh, that's so sweet. You know, Hank gets on my nerves sometimes, but I will forever respect that man if he treats my mom as well as I think he will."

I tug her closer to me. Sweet and spicy, all in one. "I'm sure he'd treat her very well," I say.

The fair is bustling, even early in the morning, vendors wheeling in new products for the day and a few families already milling about.

When I spot Hank's booth in the distance, my heart thumps.

I grab her hand, pulling her to a stop, and she turns to me, her eyes searching my face.

And then she grins, standing on her toes to press her lips against mine.

I can't resist her.

I pull her into me, one arm around her back and one hand on her neck. She moans lightly as she winds around me, her tongue licking at my lips and slipping into my mouth. She tastes like chocolate peppermint coffee, and it stokes that hunger that's been building in me for her.

When she pulls away from me, she bites her lip, standing on her toes to glance over my shoulder. "I think Hanky Panky is looking for us."

Sure enough, when I turn around, Hank is standing behind his table, hands on his hips and a shit-eating grin on his face.

At least he's not angry. I get the feeling he cares about Noelle in the way that her dad *should* have.

She grabs my hand, tugging me along behind her until we reach his booth and duck inside.

I know I was supposed to tell her something, but after the way she kissed me, my brain is blank aside from thoughts of that chocolate peppermint coffee she's drinking. And the fact that Hank is staring at us like that.

"Good morning, kids," he says, eyeing us both. I take the spare seat in the back of the hut, pulling my glasses off so I don't have to watch him watching me. I clean them on the edge of my shirt and affix them to my face again, only to see Hank standing above me, staring me down.

I think I'm about to get a scolding until Noelle speaks. "Good morning, Hanky Panky," she says, her voice all high and sweet, and Hank and I start laughing as we turn to her.

"Hanky Panky?" he asks. "Where the hell did you get that one?"

She shrugs. "Out of my mom's old yearbook," she says, her gaze trained on him as he nods, doing his best to hide the smile on his face.

"Ah," he says. "I guess I forgot about that."

"Did you date my mom in high school?" she asks.

Hank's eyes slide to mine as if he's looking for an out. But I'm looking for a way out of the scolding he's about to give me, so there's zero chance I'm going to interrupt Noelle's questioning.

"Well, we had a little flirtation, I'd say," he admits, nodding to Noelle.

"Aw, you love her!" she exclaims, as Hank's eyes dip.

She turns to me, eyes wide and bright. "He loves her!" she repeats.

"Noelle!" Hank barks. "Your mom and I are good friends."

She winks at him. "I got you."

"Noelle," he warns.

She only grins back at him.

"I don't need you spreading anything, okay?"

Christina pops into my mind again. *Fuck.* Another thing Hank doesn't want spread.

Unfortunately for him, my loyalty lies elsewhere.

She waves him off. "Oh, Hank, I'm not going to blow up your spot. I'm happy for you guys. Long lost loves coming back together. That's so sweet!"

Hank doesn't seem to know where to put his eyes. "We're not long lost loves. We're good friends."

"Uh huh," Noelle says, dropping her bag underneath the folding table in the back of the hut. "You love her and I think it's adorable. For what it's worth–not that you need it–I fully approve."

Hank shakes his head, turning away from us and out to the fair that's slowly growing more crowded with every passing minute. "I don't know what to do with you, Noelle," he grumbles, but I catch the smile in his voice.

She turns to me, a big grin across her face, as she winds an arm around his back and hugs him.

A second later, he hesitantly wraps one around her shoulders and squeezes.

And I can't take it anymore.

"Hank said your sister is moving back here," I blurt.

He turns to me, throwing his hands out in front of him. "Nick."

She blinks back and forth between the two of us. "What?"

"I'm sorry," I say to Hank. "But your loyalty lies with Helen. Mine lies with Noelle, and I can't keep it secret anymore."

Her brow furrows and she rears back, the hint of a disbelieving smile inching onto her face.

And then I realize what I said.

Fuck me.

Noelle shakes her head. "How long has this been a secret?" she asks.

"I've only known since yesterday," I say quickly, realizing I'm throwing Hank under the bus here but I don't particularly care. This isn't about him.

He sighs, turning toward Noelle. "Keep in mind I'm hearing this secondhand from your mother," he starts. "But Christina found a job close by that she really wanted. She went through the interview process thinking she wasn't going to get it, but when she did, she had to reevaluate things. I think she's planning on telling you once she knows what her plan is."

Noelle points at me. "How did you get all mixed up in this?"

"Hank accidentally told me, thinking you knew."

"And you kept it secret?"

"Hank told me to!"

"Your mother told me to! And I'm assuming Christina told her to!"

She glances between both of us, her expression flitting from one emotion to the next with milliseconds in between.

She lets out a long breath, shaking her head. "I think I have to go talk to my sister."

Hank nods. "I think that's probably best."

She turns to me. "Look, I know this was supposed to be the last day of community service. I just..." She waves her hands in front of her face like she's searching for words.

"I know. Go see your sister."

She nods, grabs her bag from underneath the folding table, and disappears into the crowd.

And then it's just me and Hank, staring at each other.

"I'm sorry," I say, crinkling up my nose.

He shakes his head, waving me off. "It's alright. I should have known better than to trust a lovesick fool to keep a secret anyway."

"I am not a lovesick fool."

He raises his eyebrows. "Your loyalty lies with her?" he asks, throwing my words from earlier back at me.

I squeeze my eyes shut. "Okay, that does sound kind of like lovesick foolery."

13

NOELLE

Sunday, December 15th

I stomp back to the high school parking lot with my bag slung over my shoulder. I don't know what's going on, but the fact that people are hiding things from me makes me very uncomfortable. Especially Christina. She tells me everything.

Since high school, she's been the only person I could truly trust. The only person who saw what high school did to me and loved me regardless. She's never asked me to be anyone but my authentic self, but she also won't hesitate to snap at me and tell me I'm being a growly bitch when I've had enough Christmas and she's just getting started.

She was my best friend when I had friends, and it bothers me to think that she's been scared to tell me about some big development in her life. One that she's obviously excited about, if she's telling our mom about it.

A deep sense of guilt hits me in the gut as it dawns on me that she's probably keeping this a secret because she doesn't want to hurt me. I've been moody about community service, and over the past few weeks I've probably impressed upon her a little too strongly how angry I am about being forced back into this town.

Right when she's gearing up to make a big, exciting change in her life. One that unfortunately will result in me being stuck in this town more frequently. Because as much as I love our apartment in the city, with the sunset view over the river and proximity to all the bars and fun things to do, I think we both know my favorite thing about our apartment is her.

And she's leaving.

By the time I get back to my mom's house, I've worked myself into a frenzy. I'm upset that our sister powwow is ending. That she'll be gone and I won't be able to see her as often as I want to.

But most of all, I'm upset that she didn't feel like she could tell me this. I'm upset that that's who I've become in our relationship.

She has her leg up on a pillow on the couch when I get there, a plate of eggs and bacon in front of her. My mom is in the kitchen, Christmas music playing as she flips a pancake on the stove.

"Noelle!" she says, stepping around the counter to give me a quick hug when I pass by. "Honey, we thought you'd be gone all day!"

I nod, returning her hug quickly but keeping my focus on Christina. She's been eyeing me since I walked in, her plate of food untouched in front of her.

I leave my bag on the barstool next to the counter and head straight for her, dropping into the armchair covered in a fuzzy red and white blanket.

She purses her lips, her eyes dipping before landing on mine again. "So, I take it you know."

I huff, leaning forward in my chair and grabbing her hand from where it rests on the edge of the couch. "I'm sad that you felt like you couldn't just tell me."

She lets out a long breath as my mom sets a pile of pancakes and a smattering of breakfast foods on the coffee table in front of me. "I didn't want to tell you until it was a sure thing, but I never really believed it was a sure thing until it was happening and then it felt too late."

"But you're excited about it, aren't you?"

She nods. "Yeah, really excited. I just... I know this is going to really interrupt your life. And I wasn't sure how to tell you."

I throw my hands in the air as I let out a long breath, leaning back in my chair.

The news winded me, sure. My chest is still tight half an hour after leaving Nick and Hank at the fair.

But I *am* excited for my sister. She doesn't make decisions flippantly, so I can only assume she's analyzed this from every angle already and knows this is the right choice. Not just for her but for all of us.

My chest squeezes when I think about Nick. What it might mean for us, if the distance between us wasn't so great.

I shrug, pressing my lips together as I catch Christina's eye. "I'll deal with it. And I guess I should say I'm sorry, because if you felt like you couldn't tell me, it's probably because I've historically made things difficult when it comes to this town."

She shrugs noncommittally. "You don't always make it easy."

"I know I don't." I sigh, thinking about it for a moment. "I think I have to find a way to get over it."

Christina snorts. "How so?"

"I don't know. I feel like I grabbed onto you after high school because you were my only friend. And it's unfair to you, to be in that position. I'm older and wiser now, and if I'm being totally honest, it has felt really good recently to tell the people who deserve it to shove their assholery right up their butts."

Christina's brow furrows as my mom takes the place of the pillow underneath her leg, patting it as she settles her cast on my mom's lap.

She turns back to me. "This sounds like dangerous territory. Maybe we should keep you out. You can visit for Christmas and birthdays, but otherwise you stay in the city."

"Oh," my mom says, whacking her lightly on the arm before turning to me. "You come visit anytime you want. If you could just refrain from throwing eggs, we can deal with anything else."

"Don't tell her that," Christina says.

"I'm not throwing any more eggs!" I give them both a look. "No, I think I feel begrudgingly better being in this town after having stuck up for myself. Do you remember Louis Prince, who sent that fucking picture asking if I had an STD?"

My mom's jaw clenches. If someone had handed her an egg back then, I'm sure she would have thrown it in his face and taken the community service as happily as I did. "I remember."

"I told him off yesterday. He came up to me all nice, like, asking how I've been, and I told him I was happy I learned who he was before I got stuck. And he got all sputtery and I walked away. I mean, sure, you could argue it was almost ten years ago, but it significantly changed the trajectory of my life, and he doesn't get to wander through life thinking he's hot shit when *he did that* to someone."

Christina nods. "Good for you, Noelle."

"I also might have given Dad a piece of my mind yesterday, too."

Christina's head tips back. "Noelle," she groans.

"I feel justified. He came up to apologize and said that he didn't realize you were hurt when you broke your leg–he thought you were *just upset*–and I'm sorry, but I don't think that's good enough. So I told his daughters that they deserve someone who shows up whether they're hurting on the outside *or* the inside."

"You're his daughter too, you know," she reminds me.

"And I think all six of us deserve better than what we got."

"Six?"

My mom shakes her head. "Do not tell me that man has *another* family."

I laugh. "No. I'm including you and the harlot, too."

She holds a hand over her face. "Oh, Noelle."

"What? Can we all say it? Agree that we deserved better?" I turn to Christina. "If you want a relationship regardless, I will support you. But that doesn't change the fact that we deserved better."

My mom pats Christina's cast. "We did deserve better than that."

"He can't change the past," Christina insists.

"No, he can't. And if you're willing to forgive him for that, I promise I will not stand in your way. But I will not stop standing up for you when he should be showing up and he doesn't."

Christina nods. "I suppose that's fair." She shakes her

head, laughing. "You know, I feel like we've traded places since high school. I used to be the first person screaming and throwing a tantrum the second anyone said a word about you. Now you're the one rushing to my defense when Dad continues to be the same person he's always been."

I shrug. "I've spent a lot of my life accepting what others are willing to give me rather than demanding they treat me well." I swallow. "It's weird and uncomfortable but I think I'd rather that be the case than just swallowing down how I feel." I shake my head. "When I'm in this town, I feel like I have to scream at the world that I'm a different person now. That I'm not the Noelle who deals with bullshit anymore, but the one who's made something of herself."

"You don't have to scream it, you know," Christina tells me, squeezing my hand.

"I feel like I do. Like if I don't scream it, old Noelle is going to kick in again and I *can't* go back. I can't shrink into the shell of a human I once was." My mom and sister look at me with sad smiles on their faces. "I'm happy now. And sometimes being in this place makes me feel like I used to. Like everything I've worked for is so close to crumbling."

"So, I take it you will *not* be moving here with your sister," my mom says.

I shake my head. "I don't think it's good for me to be here too long. Before we know it, I'll be overcorrecting and shouting profanities at people from the town square."

"That guy *did* get arrested," my mom tells me.

"Oh great, so the position is open."

My mom reaches over Christina and rests her hand on top of ours. "I hope you know that you don't have to scream, honey. You don't have to hide out in the city to feel like you'll go unnoticed. This town loves you, whether you love them back or not, and whenever you're here, you can bet your sister and me, and Hank, and maybe even that nice math teacher you've befriended? We'll all come running the second you need us."

I do my best to ignore the math teacher comment. If I think about him a second longer, I'm sure the color will rise in my cheeks. "Thanks, Mom. I'm not sure this is a good place for me. Regardless of all the good people here."

She nods. "Well, I tried my hardest. But my Noelle always does what she has to, to take care of herself."

I sigh. "I have a life that I really like now."

My mom pats my hand. "And I'm happy for you, honey. Truly. As much as I would love to have both my girls close by, the only thing I care about is that you're happy."

"Thanks, Mom."

I lean back in my chair, grabbing a piece of bacon off Christina's plate because she's my big sister and I can. She slaps at my hand.

"Hey, Chris?"

"What?" she asks, reaching forward and taking a piece of bacon off my plate.

"You wanna tell me about your fancy new job?"

"Don't you have community service to do?" she asks.

I shrug. "I decided to play hooky today. So you might as well tell me." I take a pancake from the plate my mom left on the coffee table and hand it to her. "Come on, I want to hear."

Her eyes flash as she smiles. "Fine. But if I'm telling you about my fancy new job, I want to hear about the math teacher."

"Oh, I *knew* there was something going on there!" my mom says, settling into the couch. "Christina, you go first. Then we get math teacher details."

I roll my eyes as Christina grins.

"Well, I'm still doing data science, but this new company is actually a non-profit that does research into childhood cancer. They've made a *ton* of progress over the past ten or so years, and they're on track to improve survival rates for childhood leukemia by twenty percent by the end of the year. Twenty percent!"

Christina has always had a passion for kids, but she never found the right way to use it. She's super smart–probably too smart for her own good–and a lot of the jobs she's had haven't let her stretch her brain in the way she wants to.

I squeeze her hand. "If a perfect job does exist, that's the one for you."

She smiles, nodding. "I'm really excited about it. And honestly, I've been missing home." My mom squeezes her shoulder. "I know how much you hate it here, but every time I come back, it's like a breath of fresh air."

"As it should be. If that's what Snow Falls is to you, I will *not* get in the way of that. I'm really, truly happy for you, Chris."

"Thanks, Noelle." She squeezes my hand back, and we have one of those quiet sister moments where I can only hope she's waxing poetic in her head about her love for me like I'm doing in mine for her.

My mom purses her lips, her eyes darting between the two of us. "Okay, now I want to hear about the spicy math teacher!"

"Ew, Mom!" I shout. "He's not spicy!"

She raises her eyebrows. "Honey, I've been on this Earth long enough to know a spicy man when I see one, and he looks at you like you hung the moon and he's ready to feast on it."

My mouth drops open at the same time Christina's does,

and we can only look at each other in shock before my mom starts squirming under my sister's cast.

"Come on, tell me!" my mom says.

"Why don't you go ahead and tell us about Hanky Panky?" I ask her.

Her cheeks go pink, and I bite my lip to soften my grin.

"Yeah, that's what I thought," I say.

"Hanky Panky?" Christina asks, her eyes wide as she turns her attention to my mom.

"We dated briefly in high school," my mom says.

"Long enough that he signed your yearbook *Hanky Panky*."

She shakes her head. "Well, I don't know what to tell you. He was a very nice young man."

"Are you seeing him again?" I ask.

"We're friends."

I raise an eyebrow. "He got awfully defensive of you yesterday when Dad showed up. Certainly seems like there are still some feelings there."

She gives me a look. "We're friends," she repeats.

A beat of silence passes between us. "Well, *I* am just friends with the math teacher."

Christina snorts.

"You shush."

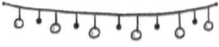

RATHER THAN RETURNING to Hank's booth, I spend the day with my mom and Christina. The two of them overpower me and decide on a number of Christmas movies to watch in turn, my mom squished under Christina's cast and me curled up in the armchair. We order lunch to the house and eventually, my mom moves to the floor where she starts surreptitiously wrapping Christmas presents while barking at us, every single time we stand, to keep our eyes on the ceiling.

When I clean up our empty lunch containers from the coffee table and dump them in the trash, I take a moment to grab my jacket and slip out the door to the front stoop. My mom has a gigantic *Merry Christmas* sign along one side of her door and an array of snowmen in the front garden dressed up in the winter clothes.

I tug my jacket around me and sit on the stoop next to a snowflake with a too-wide smile wrapped in a winter scarf.

It dawned on me, sometime today, what Nick had said when he told me about Christina's job.

That his loyalty lies with me.

I'm not sure he meant it in the way it came off, but there was something so comforting in his words. Like aside from my mom and sister, who have always been my fiercest supporters, there's one other person in this town who truly has my back.

Like it doesn't matter that he and Hank are buddy-buddy, or that he might get in trouble for crushing on the criminal.

All that matters is... me.

And whether he meant it that way or not, it inspired a calmness in me that I don't usually feel when I'm here. Like I can trust him to have my back when I'm not around.

So, I take a deep breath and call him.

He answers in two seconds, almost as if he had been sitting there, waiting for me to call.

"Noelle," he says. I hear the sounds of the fair going on in the background. Christmas music and kids shouting.

"Hey," I say, picking at the hem of my coat. "I wanted to

call and say thank you for telling me about my sister's new job today. I really appreciate that you were in my corner."

He lets out a breath, and I hear the clanging of the folding chair against the table. "Did everything go okay? When you rushed off like that, I worried that maybe I hadn't done the right thing."

"No, you did. I'm sorry. All I knew was that my sister had some big thing going on in her life and I was missing out on it." I shake my head. "I panicked, a little bit."

"Are you okay now?" he asks.

And I can't help but think of my dad, hearing his daughter on the phone asking for his help because yes, she had broken her leg, but she mostly needed the comfort of someone who shows up when they're needed.

And Nick, hours after the fact, doesn't hesitate to ask how I am.

Because his loyalty lies with me.

"Yeah, I'm okay. Thank you for checking in with me."

"Of course. I mean, I feel so terrible that I blurted it out like that, but you and Hank were all jokey with each other and I worried that if I kept it in any longer, it might screw up your relationship with him. Or me, you know?" He pauses, and I wonder if he meant to refer to *us* as a relationship. "Because you're my criminal."

I laugh. "Yes, god forbid you're on bad terms with your criminal."

He lets out another long breath into the microphone. "So you talked to your sister?"

"Yeah. We're fine. She's excited, and I'm excited for her. Bummed that our little powwow is ending, but happy that we had so many years together."

He's quiet for a moment. "Do you ever think of moving

back here? Maybe not with her, but just–I don't know–coming home one day?"

I lick my lips, trying to figure out the right thing to say. I don't want to give him false hope–if we're even at that point yet–but I also don't want to blatantly reject something that... I don't know, might change my mind one day.

"Not really. I'm so uncomfortable here it's really hard to imagine calling this home again."

He hums. "Don't you think if you gave it some time, you'd get used to it here? If you don't come back very often, don't you think you're almost precluding yourself from ever *getting* comfortable?"

I sigh. "I don't know. Every time I'm here I feel like I'm constantly thinking twenty steps ahead in an effort to thwart whoever's going to pop up and try to take me down next."

He's quiet for a second. "I know that that's been your experience, but if you took yourself out of your old bedroom, out of the high school and away from town events where asshole ex-boyfriends crawl out of hiding, don't you think maybe you could breathe easier?"

"What's the point of being here if I have to shun most of the town to feel like I can breathe?"

The silence is deafening.

"I guess you're right," he says, and I realize with that one sentence that I was hoping he might try to convince me.

Like maybe *he* might be a reason to try.

A few more beats of silence pass between us.

"Hey, Noelle?"

"Yeah?"

He lets out a quick breath that makes a *whooshing* sound in the phone.

"Will you help me put up my Christmas tree?"

I blink, wondering where this development came from. I'm sure he doesn't actually need *help*.

And that means he wants to spend time with me.

My chest swells, images of red wine and candy canes floating through my mind.

"Yeah. That would be nice."

14

NICK

Sunday, December 15th

Noelle's knock on my door brings me out of whatever anxious stupor my body devolved into this afternoon after I rushed home from school to clean.

When I asked her to help me put up my tree, I wasn't thinking beyond the possibility of having someone around to put up my tree *with*. It's a little fantasy that's played in my head ever since my mom died, like I'm waiting for someone special in my life to partake in that particular tradition.

But now that that fantasy is becoming a reality, it feels a lot bigger than I thought it was going to. I mean, sure, it's a little date–

I hope *Noelle* thinks this is a date.

Fuck, what if she thinks this counts toward her community service hours?

I pause on the stairs, nearly tripping over myself because my brain is suddenly taking all of my processing power and leaving nothing for extraneous limbs like legs.

When I finally make it to the bottom, I take a deep breath. I make a promise to myself that I won't be upset if she wants this to count toward community service hours. I won't be upset if she doesn't want to make out in front of the tree with me. If I end up alone at the end of the night between sheets I washed three times today for good measure in the Downy sensitive skin stuff that works for her, I'll be fine.

When I open the door, she grins at me. All pink cheeks and white teeth atop an oversize scarf that causes her hair to fan out in every direction.

"Come in, come in," I say, gesturing inside.

When she steps inside, I swear I feel a shift in the house. Like she's meant to be here, all smiles and smelling warm and sweet like chocolate and roses.

"Can I take your coat?" I ask, and she shimmies it off, laying her scarf on top of it as she hands it to me.

"Thank you." She smiles as I open the closet along the wall next to us and hang it.

"You're welcome."

Her eyes dip, one hand moving in a circle to gesture at me. "What is all this?"

I shrug. "It's cold out."

"I have never seen you in a sweater. I thought you only owned *I heart math* shirts and Snow Falls High T-shirts."

I roll my eyes as I turn, motioning for her to follow me down the hall and into the kitchen. "And where's your jumpsuit, Criminal?"

She huffs, and when I turn back to her, her eyes narrow. "What, you don't like my Christmas sweater?"

"I love your Christmas sweater," I tell her, as we round the corner into the kitchen. "Even though it is literally *not* a Christmas sweater."

Her brow furrows. "It is close to Christmas and I am partaking in a Christmas activity. Therefore, the sweater I'm wearing counts as a Christmas sweater."

I lean against the counter. "Are those the rules?"

"Yes," she says, not missing a beat as she steps toward me and presses herself against me, one hand on my abdomen. "And for what it's worth, I like your Christmas sweater too."

She stands on her toes to kiss me, pressing her lips softly against mine. I rest one hand on her hip, drawing her closer, and she sighs into me, her free hand coming to rest on the counter next to me.

"Sweaters must really do it for you, huh?" I ask against her lips, and she laughs.

She takes a step away from me. "What can I say? Every girl has their thing. Although I think the *I heart math* T-shirts are still my favorite."

I raise my eyebrows. "And here I was, thinking you thought I was a total nerd."

She shrugs. "I guess I like nerds."

For a moment, we grin stupidly at each other.

And then I remember that the pretty girl isn't just here to be ogled.

I clear my throat. "Um, I have red and white wine if you want. Or sparkling water." I reach behind me, tugging the plate of extra dark chocolate-covered berries I made earlier closer. "And I wasn't sure exactly what ratios your sister uses for chocolate berries, but I did my best with these."

Her brow furrows as she looks down at them. "You made me my favorite Christmas treat?"

"I mean, like I said, I didn't know the ratios. But I tried, so let me know if I should do something different next time." I almost say *next Christmas* but stop myself.

"Wow," she says, plucking one off the plate and popping it into her mouth. A grin spreads across her face as she chews. "Mm, raspberry. They're my favorite." She stands on her toes to kiss my cheek. "Thank you, Nick. That was so sweet of you."

I nod, a blush spreading across my cheeks. "Of course." I clear my throat. "I mean, I know your favorite Christmas activity is rage-eating chocolate-covered things while other people make Christmas happen, so I figured the least I could do is prepare your favorite snack."

"Nick! I'm not going to come over to help you *put up your tree* and watch *you* do it!"

I shrug. "I don't *need* the help. I just... I guess it never felt right putting up a tree by myself. So if you want to be all growly and eat your treats, go ahead. Just do me a favor and bend over while you do it."

She lets out a surprised laugh. "You're secretly naughty," she says, accusing me with one finger.

"I don't think it's really a secret."

"No?"

I grimace. *That didn't sound great.* "I mean, I put up a bit of a shield at school or around town, you know? I make sure that if there's a kid around to hear or see, I don't do or say anything that I wouldn't want them telling their parents about. It's easier that way."

She nods. "That sounds like it could get a little lonely."

I shrug. "It can, but lonely is a hell of a lot better than having the wrong company."

She's quiet for a moment before she nods. "Yeah, I think I would have to agree with that."

I let out a long breath, shaking my head. "So, you should probably head out," I say, mock seriously.

She knocks my elbow, laughing, and I wrap her up in my

arms again, pressing a kiss to her temple. "Please. You're *so* excited to be putting up your tree with me."

She leans away from me to see my face, and I take the opportunity to nod sincerely. "I really am."

She swallows, quiet for a moment.

"So, can I get you a drink?"

"Red wine?"

I nod, kissing her cheek as I twist her hips to one side so I can grab two glasses from the cabinet above our heads. I pour us each a glass and lead her into the living room.

"Wow, I think this room was made for Christmas," she says, her eyes wandering along the big bay window where I was planning on setting up the tree and the fireplace I lit a few minutes before she got here. With the Christmas music playing low in the background, it *feels* like a holiday in here.

"Yeah, that's kind of what I thought when I bought the place," I tell her, resting my wine on the coffee table in front of the leather couch. She does the same, following me as I round the Christmas tree box I pulled out of the attic earlier today. I pull open one of the flaps as Noelle kneels down next to it.

I pull out the stand and center it below the window. Noelle grabs the tree skirt and wraps it around the base, smiling up at me when she's done.

"Is that how you like it?" she asks, and the words send a jolt of fire right down my spine because I've imagined asking her that same thing in a situation involving much less clothing.

But I only nod, swallowing thickly. "That's perfect."

We attach the main pole to the stand and move slowly in a circle, matching each piece by color to its appropriate spot.

It's surprisingly easy with her. We work well together.

We take breaks for small sips of wine and little kisses

that inspire thoughts that would definitely put me on the naughty list.

"So what made you decide to put up a tree this year, if you normally don't?"

I let out a long breath, shrugging because I might as well tell her the truth if we're here, doing it together.

"You."

She cocks her head to the side, her fingers pausing as her eyes find mine. "Me?"

I nod. "I never wanted to put up a Christmas tree on my own, but when I met you, I thought that I might like to do it with you."

She raises her eyebrows. "That's really sweet."

I shrug, my cheeks heating. I knew that was going to happen. "It's the truth." I press my lips together as I fan out another branch and connect it to the main one. I can feel Noelle's eyes on me, like her focus is branding my skin. "There was a point in my life where I thought all I really wanted was someone to, for lack of a better term, put the tree up with."

She sits cross-legged on the ground, abandoning her branch next to her and reaching for her wine.

"Over time, I think I realized that it's not about *putting up the tree*, per se, but *how* you put up the tree. *Who* you put up the tree *with*."

She bites her lip. "And you wanted to put up your tree with me."

I attach the piece I've been working on and turn to her, feeling sheepish about this roundabout way of telling her I desperately want her. "Yes."

"I love that," she says, resting her wine on the coffee table and crawling over to me. She sits right in front of me, her knee touching mine. "And also, I think that's the absolutely corniest way a man has ever told me he used to be less discerning but has... *found the holiday spirit.*"

I can't help the laugh that escapes me as she tugs on my neck, bringing my face to hers. She presses her lips against mine as I wrap an arm around her back, pulling her against my chest. I lick at the seam of her lips and she parts for me, a small moan escaping her throat that has all of my muscles taut and ready to go full caveman on her.

When she pulls away from me, she's still grinning. She takes a sip of her wine and returns to the branch she had been fluffing, notching it into place.

"So Mr. Monroe, the goodie two-shoes math teacher, isn't a one-night kind of guy," she mocks, her eyes flashing with delight as she pulls another branch out of the box.

I laugh before letting out a sigh. "How did I know saying that would come back to bite me in the ass?"

She cackles, one hand coming up to cover her mouth. "Come on, it's so good. You wear your little *I heart math* shirts around and then invite me over to *put up your tree,*" she says, using air quotes. "You really are a secret naughty boy."

I shoot her a look. "Keep talking like that and I'll show you what it means to be naughty."

Her eyes flash. "Oh, I like this side of the math teacher. Sweet and spicy, all in one."

I shake my head. "Drink your wine and fluff your branch."

She starts laughing again, snickering into her forearm as she works on the branch. "Now all I can think about is every naughty tree euphemism I've ever heard. I mean, 'fluff your branch'? Mr. Monroe, the children!"

I can't help but laugh along with her. "To be fair, every

single time I mention 'putting up the tree' at this point, I have to stop myself from saying 'erecting the tree.'"

She laughs harder, one hand over her chest as her eyes pinch shut.

This is what I want my Christmases to look like. Laughter, red wine, and someone like Noelle fluffing my branch.

It feels so easy.

Once the tree is *erected*, I pull out the ornaments and we move in a slow circle, arranging them one by one, together. It's indulgent, almost, the way we so lazily pick out one ornament and find the exact *right* place for it together. Even though I'm pretty sure neither of us are paying attention to where it goes. I hold the box as she picks them, holding each one gently as if they're all special in their own way.

And I suppose they are. Most of them were my mom's. Some are family heirlooms. Some I don't even recognize but I can tell by the styling that they're at least fifty years old.

"This one is cute," she says, picking up a simple white one with a cartoon image of a woman and her little boy looking out over a field of Christmas trees. "I bet your mom got this one."

"That or it was gifted to her. She wasn't shy about her love for the holiday so she was always easy to buy for. Anything Christmas-themed she would swoon over and you could bet you'd see it again like clockwork the second Thanksgiving was over. Honestly, I think she displayed *every* Christmas item she had *every* year."

Noelle's brow furrows. "That sounds like an awful lot of Christmas."

I nod. "It was suffocating at times, honestly." I shrug. "I ended up throwing out a lot of her Christmas stuff–I couldn't manage all of it and half of it I didn't even recognize. But I kept the stuff that I know she truly loved. And anything that I really liked, of course."

"Of course," Noelle agrees. She places the ornament right in the front of the tree, running her thumb along the bottom of it before turning back to the box and grabbing another. "That's really nice. Precious, almost, these things that you kept."

"It's always bothered me that I don't display them every year. It's nice that I can this year."

She gives me a quick grin. "All because of me. You're welcome, Nick Monroe."

"Thank you, Noelle Adler, for granting me my Christmas wish," I say, shooting her a quick wink.

She plucks another ornament out of the box. "What else are you wishing for this Christmas?"

You, naked.

I shrug. "This is all I really need."

She nods, digesting this. "Me too, I think."

"Yeah?"

She places the ornament near the top, off to the side. "Yeah. This feels really comfortable. Very different from the way my mom and sister do it, which always has this undercurrent of, like, anxiety to it. Like, they try so hard that it kind of takes away the joy of it. I mean, I think *they* enjoy it. But it feels overwhelming to me. And kind of just... fake, I guess. I hate saying it about something they obviously care so much about, but this feels *so good*. To take our time putting up a Christmas tree. There's no checklist or required cookie-making or snowmen *everywhere*. No false pretenses about having one big happy family."

I reach out to straighten a branch that we must have missed. "That bothers you a lot, doesn't it? The forced family time?"

She shrugs. "I wish it didn't. I wish I could show up and go with the flow, but my sister always tries to drag my dad into things but gets upset when he prioritizes his new family. My mom always tries to calm her down, like she's constantly in defense mode to pick up the pieces when she's inevitably disappointed." She laughs. "I guess that's where I get it from, that defensiveness that pushes me to make a problem before a problem even occurs." She shakes her head. "That's literally what happens between my mom and sister, every year. My mom sees the future, acts too soon, and they end up in a fight while my sister goes off to find some disappointment anyway."

I crinkle my nose. "I'm sorry. I get how that could make things difficult around the holidays."

She sighs. "Yeah." She's quiet for a second. "I can see why some people really love the holidays, though." I raise my eyebrows as she arranges another ornament. "*This* kind of holiday, I think I like."

Noelle likes holidays with me. My chest swells, and I take a deep breath to ward off the warm fuzzy feelings that are threatening to take over.

I bite my lip, sure I'm about to get elbowed. "I'm glad I can be your own personal Saint Nick."

She presses her eyes closed, her laughter spilling out despite herself. "Nick!"

"Come on, you teed that one up for me."

She shakes her head, elbowing me lightly so she doesn't knock the box of ornaments in my arms. "You're corny."

I throw her a grin. "You love it."

She purses her lips, doing her best to glare at me before turning back to the tree.

And she plucks one ornament after another, slowly filling in the tree as Christmas music plays in the background. We settle into an easy rhythm, talking and joking as we move in a semi-circle around the tree.

And eventually, another glass of wine later, it's full.

"Do you want to do the honors?" I ask, grabbing the end of the string of lights and holding it out to her.

She raises her eyebrows. "You want me to light your tree?" she asks, a mischievous grin spreading across her face.

I nod as I leave the empty box on the coffee table and grab our wine glasses. "You want a refill?"

"I'll wait until you're back," she says, waving the end of the cord as she kneels on the ground next to the socket.

I head into the kitchen to refill our glasses, and on my way back, I hit the lights in the living room. We can see enough in the dim light from the streetlights outside.

I rest our glasses on the coffee table and sit down in front of it, my back up against the wood.

"Ready?" she asks, eyebrows high.

I nod. "Light me up, Criminal."

She snorts as she turns to the socket, and the room is bathed in the soft white light from the Christmas tree.

She looks up at it for a moment before turning to me with a big grin on her face.

"So?" she asks, crawling toward me.

And fuck, if that's not sensual, I don't know what is.

She sits next to me and I throw an arm around her shoulders, pulling her close. Her cheek hits my shoulder as her arms wind around my middle.

"What do you think?" she asks, her voice soft. She tips her head up to look at me. "Did I do good?"

I nod, my fingers grazing her chin as I tip her face up toward mine. I nod as our lips brush. "You did really fucking good."

Her eyes flash. "Language, Mr. Monroe."

I laugh, kissing her again and tugging on her bottom lip with my teeth. A strangled sound escapes her throat that has me laser-focused on the way her body presses into mine. The way the light from the tree is reflected in her eyes.

She sits up straighter, one hand resting on the back of my neck and tugging me closer.

And I can't help my hands. The one under her chin dips to her ribs, my thumb grazing the edge of her bra through her sweater. The other wraps around her back, my fingers spreading across the fabric and drifting lower.

She inches closer, her leg pressing against mine as she wraps her arms around my neck, the hem of her sweater lifting underneath my palm and exposing warm, smooth skin. I slip my hand underneath, and her back arches to the touch.

So fucking responsive to me.

She lets out a breathy moan that sends a little zip of fire down my spine.

And then I'm wrapping one hand around her knee, tugging her into my lap and taking hold of her ass, placing her just the way I want her. Straddling me, her stomach pressed right up against mine.

She moans again, the sound vibrating all through her body, and I run my hands along her hips, squeezing her tight like I can memorize the curves of her body.

I run my hands up under her sweater again, exploring the delicate taper of her waist. The way she sucks in a breath when my thumbs move against her ribs. Her hips move ever so slightly–almost imperceptibly–and I can't help the grin that spreads across my face.

This girl wants me as much as I want her.

"Nick," she says as she breaks our kiss. Her voice is all

breathy and low and it makes me want to tear her out of her clothes, bend her over and *take her*.

But I don't want to rush this. Noelle is something special. I want to savor this. Savor her.

She lowers her head, her lips brushing against my jaw. She *loves* kissing me there, and it drives me absolutely wild. My muscles bunch and release as I struggle to keep hold of myself. She continues along my neck, and I brush her hair out of her face, relishing in the feel of her lips on me.

I let out a groan as she nips at me, my hands moving down along her back until I have two palms full of ass. I squeeze, and suddenly the gentle movement of her hips against me isn't so gentle anymore.

She moves against me, her hands dipping beneath my sweater and brushing across my chest. She moans, her lips finding mine again as she rocks against me.

"Noelle," I say, keeping one hand on her ass and covering hers with the other.

She hums in response.

"Slow down there, Criminal. You're going to get yourself off before I even get the chance to taste you."

15

NOELLE

Sunday, December 15th

His words send a rush of heat straight into my abdomen. I wasn't intending to hump him wantonly in front of the Christmas tree that very obviously means so much to him.

But here I am.

He has so much more control than I do. While I hopped on his lap and started building myself right up to orgasm, he held me firmly, his hands practiced and controlled.

I'm ready to ditch the clothes and bang one out real quick to relieve some pressure. We can do the slow, meaningful thing later.

Because let's be honest, we've been building up to this moment since the first day of my community service sentence.

This isn't *one night* of Christmas tree decoration. This is weeks of pent up sexual energy begging to be released.

His dick is hard underneath me. It hits me right where I'm so desperate to feel him, and every time my hips move against him, the only thing on my mind is how it would feel to slowly sink down on him, to feel how full he'd make me.

He rests his hand on the back of my neck, his kiss slow and steady as I grab at the hem of his shirt and tug it up over his chest. He raises his arms and I pull it over his head, discarding it on the ground next to us.

And for fuck's sake, he has no business looking like this.

All thick muscle, abs that bunch and release as my hands graze his skin, thick pecs with the lightest dusting of chest hair. I squirm away from him so I can lean down and kiss his bare skin, my hands grabbing at every bit of him they can find.

He tips his head back, releasing a long sigh as he takes his glasses off for a moment and runs his hands over his face.

"That feels so good," he murmurs, as he grabs me by the upper arms and pulls me back to where I was, his erection rubbing at that spot I so desperately want to feel him.

I whimper at the sensation, and he presses on my hips again, mimicking the way I had been grinding on him before. He lets out a low note of approval from his throat. "You really are a live wire, aren't you, Noelle?"

I press my body against his again, my lips returning to his neck, and my tongue flicks out across his skin. "Touch me."

"Fuck," he grumbles, his hands moving deftly from my hips to the hem of my sweater. He pulls it over my head and drops it on top of his.

Before he can slow us down again, I reach behind me and pop the clasp of my bra, letting it fall between us. I grab his hands and press them against my exposed breasts, moaning with the contact.

"Fuck, Noelle," he says, pinching my nipples lightly

between his thumb and forefinger. My hips start moving of their own accord, but before I can find the friction that I'm looking for, he grabs my ass and pulls me up so he can pull one nipple into his mouth.

I cry out with the sensation, my head tipping back as my fingers run through his hair, holding him against me. He sucks lightly at me, releasing my nipple with a lewd pop.

"I love the taste of your skin," he murmurs, his hands still firm on my ass as he kisses his way across my chest to the other one and repeats his delicious torture. He groans into my chest, his teeth lightly grazing my nipple as he releases it. He wraps his arms around my middle, pulling me in close, and I stare down at him.

He grins, and with one hand clamped around my back, he uses the other to tug my leggings down, getting them past my hips before lifting me off of him.

"Stand up. Take your pants off."

I raise my eyebrows. "Bossy math teacher."

"Noelle."

I stand, pausing for a moment to make sure he's focused fully on me, and tug my leggings down the rest of the way. I step out of them, his hands returning to my now bare legs like his skin is magnetically drawn to mine. He tugs on my knee, pulling me back down into his lap.

I feel simultaneously exposed and charged as his fingers run gently along my thighs. His eyes track the movement of his hands as they continue up, dipping underneath the string of my thong. He lets it snap back against my skin, releasing a slow breath as he does.

He touches me slowly, every movement intentional as he drags his hand up along my stomach, squeezing the dip of my waist and continuing up along my ribs. He cups my breast, dragging his thumb lightly over my nipple, and continues until his hand rests on my neck.

He tugs me forward, my stomach pressing against his and my nipples brushing across his chest.

"Do you realize how beautiful you are?"

I swallow. With his hand on my neck, I can't look away from him.

He lets his words linger for a moment before pressing my lips to his.

And god, I'm not sure I can wait any longer.

I writhe against him, my fingers winding between us and searching for the clasp of his jeans.

He grabs my hands before I can free him, and instead wraps one arm around my waist while using the other to hoist us up. A surprised gasp jumps from my throat when he lifts me, and a moment later, he lays me down gently.

On the coffee table.

He kisses me, his tongue winding into my mouth and tangling with mine as my legs jump around his waist. He presses into me for a moment, the thickness hiding in his pants rubbing me in just the right way.

When he pulls away from me, I claw at him. I want to *feel* him.

He presses a hand into my sternum, holding me in place as he kneels before me.

My heart thumps as he kisses my inner thigh, the stubble of his beard scratching along the delicate skin. He rests one hand in the crease of my hip, his thumb trailing so lightly along my underwear. My hips buck up to meet him, yearning for more pressure.

When he presses down on me, a moan emanates from my throat because moving my hips against his hand is getting me *so* close.

"Noelle," he says, drawing my attention to where his cheek is pressed against my inner thigh.

I raise my eyebrows, slowing my movement because I'm getting completely carried away with the way he's touching me.

"I hope you're not planning on riding my *hand* to orgasm."

I groan. "I need *something.*"

A rumble emanates from his chest, low and gruff. "I like you like this," he says, his thumbs slipping beneath the edges of my underwear and slowly pulling them down. I lift my ass as my underwear leaves a trail of wetness along my thigh. "All needy and desperate for me," he says. I groan in response, and he reaches out, running his fingers through the slickness my underwear spread around on my thighs. "So fucking soaked for me."

"Touch me," I tell him, scooting lower on the coffee table.

He grins, turning his face into my thigh and leaving a kiss there. "The more you beg me, the more I want to hold out."

I point at him. "Don't you play that game with me."

"Or what?" he asks, raising an eyebrow as his lips move higher on my thigh. I take a deep breath, struggling to suppress the urge to beg him again. "Hmm?" He presses his lips to the crease of my thigh and my pussy pulses in response. "Noelle?"

He presses the most delicate of kisses right to my clit, and my hips buck up at him.

"Is your pussy going to drown me?" he taunts.

"God, I hope so."

He laughs, his tongue darting out and drawing a long line along my seam.

I let out a long string of expletives as his tongue twirls around my clit.

He lets out another gruff noise from his throat as he runs his hands along my thighs, squeezing every part of me and then resting one hand on my hip, holding me firmly in place. The other, he trails along my thigh, leaving goose-bumps in its wake, until it lands right below his mouth, his thumb running lightly over my entrance.

"Fuck, Nick. Please!"

He presses a finger inside me as my breathing turns ragged. He sucks at me, his mouth pressed solidly against my clit despite the movement of my hips. He adds another finger, pulsing rhythmically as I cry out.

He groans, and it only amplifies his effect on me. My orgasm builds swiftly, and I latch onto his hair, holding him in place as the pressure reaches a breaking point.

"Nick, Nick, Nick!" I scream. His eyes are locked on mine, and his answering grunt tips me over the edge, the vibration of his voice enough to melt me into a puddle.

I throw my head back as I ride out my orgasm, my torso lifting up off the coffee table as the last of the pressure wanes. My legs clamp shut around his face, but he continues licking me until he's sure I'm done.

When he finally releases me, I collapse back into the coffee table, throwing my hand over my face as my breathing slows.

He still has his hands on me, moving gently along my thighs and drawing little circles into my skin.

As I lay there, struggling to catch my breath, he stands, his hands trailing along my stomach until they wind down beneath my back. He latches onto me and lifts me gently and, a second later, sits back on his heels on the ground, holding me against his chest. I wrap my legs around him and rest my head on his shoulder as he leans back on one palm.

"How was that, Criminal?" he asks, the fingers of his free hand running through my hair.

I halfheartedly whack his chest. "I think I might have died and gone to heaven."

He laughs, tugging me closer. "Good. That's what I like to hear."

I lift my head, pointing at him. "You may not curse, but your mouth does incredibly naughty things."

"I literally *do* curse, just not anywhere one of my students can overhear me."

I wave him off. "Your words don't make sense to me right now."

He groans in that deep way that comes from his chest again, and I melt further into him. "Came that good, huh?"

I nod, pressing my face into his shoulder again. He kisses my neck and runs his hands all along my back, sending little shivers down my spine.

And when I finally lift my head to look at him, he kisses me, one hand on the back of my neck to hold me in place. His tongue slips into my mouth, moving indulgently against mine.

He's rock hard underneath me, and I lift up a few inches so I can slip my hand between us, palming him.

He groans into my mouth as I lean forward, letting my nipples graze against his chest. A second later, his hand skirts along my ribs, his thumb flicking at my nipple as the heat builds again in my abdomen.

"Noelle," he says against my lips, his voice low.

"Nick," I counter.

"I think I might die if I'm not inside of you soon," he says, his fingers tightening around my rib cage.

I moan as he kisses me again. "Well, we wouldn't want that," I say, tugging on the clasp of his jeans. His hips move underneath me like he can hardly control the movement. I tug his zipper down and reach into his pants, cupping him.

His head tips back at the sensation, and I move my hand up and down, squeezing him.

"Noelle, please," he says, the fingers around my ribs tightening.

I lean forward, pressing a delicate kiss to his cheek. "Look who's begging now."

He bites his lip as he closes his eyes, his breathing ragged.

I lift up higher, tugging on his jeans. "Lift so we can take these off," I tell him, and he scrambles to comply, helping me push his jeans down his legs. He kicks them off quickly and then lifts me by my hips, putting me right back in his lap.

I trail my fingers from where the spot of precum has darkened his underwear, all down the length of his shaft.

His body vibrates in response.

I tug at the waistband of his underwear to expose him and take him in my hand as a full body shudder passes through him. His eyes are glued to my hand around his cock as I slowly pump him.

"Do you have a condom?" I ask him.

He nods, one hand shooting out to his pants and rifling through his pockets. He pulls out a strand of three.

I raise my eyebrows as I tear one off.

"Prepared, not presumptuous," he clarifies. "I would have been perfectly happy just putting up the tree with you."

I grin, leaning forward and pressing a kiss to his cheek as I tear into the foil. I pinch the tip and slowly roll it down his thick length.

When I lift my head to look at him, he grins at me and places his hand on the back of my neck again, tugging me close for a kiss that is as wild as his body feels.

As his tongue slips into my mouth, I hold his dick in position and slowly sink down onto it.

Our matching moans catch between our lips.

I take my time adjusting to him, letting myself drop slowly until I'm fully seated in his lap. He wraps his arms around my back, every muscle flexing as he tugs on me.

"Jesus fucking Christ," he mutters against the skin of my chest.

"Language, Mr. Monroe."

He groans, kissing my chest and nipping lightly at my skin. "You feel incredible."

I move my hips gently, grinding against him, and the sensation is almost overwhelming.

"Oh god," I mumble, clinging to every part of him I can. My arms are around his neck, my fingers in his hair. My chest presses against his as his hands lower down to my ass, squeezing and lifting me gently.

He presses me back down, his hands coming around to my hips and trailing up my sides until he can play with my nipples.

My hips move of their own accord, his hands winding up into my hair as he kisses me.

"It feels like your body was made for me," he says, pressing kisses all along my neck as his hands drop to my ass again, aiding in my movement.

I moan as the pressure builds in my abdomen, release on the horizon.

"Nick," I pant.

His voice is low when he speaks. "Are you going to come for me, Noelle?" I nod into his shoulder as he kisses my neck. "I can feel you tightening around me." He groans as his fingers weave into my hair, holding me in place. "Yes, take what you need," he mumbles into my neck.

With his words, the dam breaks. I cry out as the pressure releases, as his arms tighten around me and I cling to him. He grunts as he urges my hips through their last few shaky movements before I collapse into his chest.

He kisses my forehead and my cheeks and my neck–anywhere he can press his lips against me.

And then he clamps an arm around my waist and moves us gently so my back is on the floor. "You okay, Noelle?"

I nod as he moves, his hips rolling into me so smoothly. "Oh god yes. I'm really okay. And for Christ's sake, how are you moving your hips like that?"

He laughs, repeating the movement and settling into a rhythm.

"Mm. I'm glad you like it," he says, pumping into me repeatedly as his eyes flutter shut and his head dips into the corner of my neck.

"I really fucking like it," I say, my arms and legs winding around him as he moves.

He grunts, his pace ticking faster as one hand reaches for my ass, tugging on me so he can go deeper.

"Fuck, Noelle," he grumbles as his movements turn jerky. His teeth tug on my earlobe, his breath heavy in my ear as he builds himself up. I kiss his shoulder and his neck, lifting my leg so he can go deeper.

He thrusts into me hard, his muscles going rigid and his fingers digging into my skin as he releases.

"Fuck," he breathes as he stills, his body going heavy on mine.

He lets out a long groan into my neck before pressing up

onto his elbows, his hands weaving underneath my back. He kisses me lightly on the nose.

"I think fucking you might be my new favorite thing," he says.

I can't help the laugh that escapes me, and I hold my hands over my face. "Yeah, I think I get why you like Christmas so much now."

He drops his face back into my chest as he laughs. "Hey, if the presents and the holiday cheer don't do it for you, I'll give you a good dicking for the holiday."

My chest heaves with my laughter. "That sounds like a Christmas movie. 'A dicking for the holiday.'"

"I'm sure there's a porno with that title. You've probably read it," he jokes, and I knock him in the shoulder.

He takes a deep breath, smiling down at me. "So what do you say we have another glass of wine and then head upstairs and do that again a few more times?"

I'm nodding before he's finished his sentence.

I WAKE to sunlight streaming through the window and the erection of a wildly attractive math teacher pressed against my backside. The house is quiet, and as I burrow my face in my pillow, I realize it smells like my fresh laundry from home.

That realization sends a little jolt through my body. *This* feels like home.

I twist, tugging the sheets from between us and pressing myself up against Nick. His eyes are closed, but his arms tighten around me as I nestle into his chest.

"Do you have sensitive skin?" I ask, trailing my fingers along the divot between his pecs.

"It's sensitive to whatever your fingers are doing right now," he says, a little shiver running through his body as his eyes open and he grins at me.

He looks downright edible with morning hair and that stubble running across his face. He squints a little, as he does whenever he's without his glasses, and his eyes dip to my mouth.

"You use Downy sensitive skin," I say.

"Mm. Right," he says, nodding.

"So you *do* have sensitive skin?"

He reaches for me, running a hand through my hair as he tugs my face back into his chest. "No. I have a criminal with sensitive skin."

I push away from him, narrowing my eyes. "Is that another part of being prepared but not presumptuous?"

He nods as his hand slowly moves down my skin and rests on my ass. He pulls me up against him, his dick rubbing right where I want to feel him. "Well, on the off chance you wanted to hop on my dick, I thought having sheets that don't cause your eczema to flare up would increase my chances of getting an encore the morning after."

Lord help me, it does.

I have never had a man so enthusiastically change his laundry detergent. It's hard enough to get them to *wash* their sheets, let alone wash them frequently enough and with the right product.

It's making me swoon. *Hard.*

I throw my leg around his waist and sit up, straddling him.

"Your wish is my command. How do you want me, handsome?"

16

NICK

Thursday, December 19th

Tonight is the town's Christmas parade, and since I've completely run out of ideas to fulfill Noelle's community service, we're going to head down to the high school's float and ensure that candy buckets are distributed to every kid who's supposed to have one. I know before Noelle graces me with that beautiful smile of hers and a quick kiss on the cheek that she is *not* going to be happy with me.

But I also know, thanks to the array of text messages she sent me, that she wants me so badly that she *might* overlook this.

And if not, I'm kind of curious to see what happens. Will she pout and try to hold out on me? I can see how that game will play out. I would kiss her neck and squeeze her ass in the way that makes a little whimper tumble from her lips, and I bet she'd forget all about it. Maybe she'd get annoyed with me and let out all her frustration with a little bit of angry sex.

I bet angry sex with her would be hot.

But I doubt we'd be able to hold onto any negative emotion longer than a few seconds.

I know I certainly wouldn't be able to.

When she pulls up outside my house, I'm waiting at the door.

She grins as she walks in, dropping her duffel bag inside the door and wrapping her arms around my neck to pull me in for a kiss. She's strong for the size she is, and all I can do is hold on as she kicks the door shut behind her and presses her back to the wall, her legs jumping up around my waist.

I'm hard in a matter of seconds, and very thankful that I planned ahead and stuffed another string of condoms into my pocket before she got here.

In case she decided to maul me in the entryway, of course.

I tear her out of her pants and fuck her like my life depends on it, right up against the wall of my entryway. I never noticed the way this area of my house echoes, but I think hearing her moan in surround sound is going to be my new favorite song.

When we've cleaned ourselves up and begrudgingly tugged our clothes back on, I give her one more indulgent kiss, relishing in the way her body bows so easily to mine.

And then I pick up her duffel bag, pleased at the weight of it–she must really be planning on staying a while–and bring it up to my bedroom for her.

When I come back downstairs, she's waiting for me, leaning up against the kitchen island with her phone in her hand.

"So, are you excited for community service today?" I ask.

Her eyes narrow. "I can't tell whether that means you're

going to fuck me again and call it community service or if you have something truly torturous in store for me."

I press my lips together, raising an eyebrow.

"Oh no." She huffs, crossing her arms. "What are we doing?"

I swallow. "We're going to round up all the candy buckets we made and distribute them to the high schoolers when they arrive. Make sure everybody gets one."

Her nose crinkles. "You know, I've really been looking forward to clapping erasers in the schoolyard, and I'm starting to worry that's not going to happen."

"It's your last couple of hours, and handing out the buckets isn't going to take very long. Probably half an hour, if I had to guess, and afterward we can go ahead and enjoy the parade."

She huffs, taking a step toward me and winding her arms around my middle. "Torturing me is your favorite pastime, isn't it?"

I nod, brushing her hair out of the way so I can kiss her forehead. "But afterward we get to enjoy the parade," I say, in a mocking excited tone.

She rolls her eyes. "The harder you work at your Cindy-Lou Who act, the harder I work at Grinching."

I grin at her, holding her cheeks in my hands. "And you do it so well."

I grab her hips and twist her toward the door, smacking her ass as she walks. She jumps with the contact and turns back to me, her fingers digging into my stomach as she presses herself against me in a way that has me *really* wanting to repeat what we just did in my entryway.

"Are you sure you don't want to play hooky?" she asks, her lips against my throat.

I level her with a look. "I actually do want to go to the

parade. And you get a few free hours out of it. I think that's worth it, don't you?"

She lets out a long breath. "For you, I will go."

I kiss her, and when I pull away, she follows, asking for more.

"Maybe I'll even get you to smile a little, too. For me."

She grumbles, rolling her eyes as I push her toward the door. "No. That, I refuse to do."

THE HIGH SCHOOL is packed by the time we get there, and I walk through the halls with Noelle's hand in mine, greeting kids as they weave around us or shout at me.

I've cemented myself as one of the cooler teachers. Not as cool as Mrs. Larson, who sets things on fire in science class every other day—I have her to thank for Robbie's experiment—but I'm not one of the ones who get dirty looks or pointed whispers when I pass by.

And I will admit, Noelle looks *mildly* overwhelmed as we wind through the halls to the garage and we're suddenly bombarded with high schoolers. I tuck her under my arm, gaining a few curious looks from kids who thankfully do not choose this moment to ask when Mr. Monroe stopped being single.

The buckets are stacked along the wall where the float used to be, and we—along with a few kids that I recruit along the way—drag them out the wide doors to the parking lot where the parade starts.

The town fire trucks are parked outside, as well as Hank, who will be leading the parade. Further down into the parking lot, an array of parade participants wait. Decorated

Jeeps, a number of dads on motorcycles, the band and the choir and a local dance team among them.

And as start time draws nearer, kids flock to the float in droves. One of us hands a bucket of candy to each costumed kid as they slowly climb up. Half of them can't see us because of various ridiculous costumes that obscure their faces, and we have to guide their hands to the handles of the buckets.

Halfway through, I hear a kid's voice who sounds vaguely familiar, but I can't quite place it.

"Yo, Mr. Monroe's got himself a girlfriend!"

My eyes snap up to Noelle's as she looks warily toward the float, searching for the voice.

"How'd you manage that, dude? She's way out of your league!"

I can't help the grin that spreads across my face as Noelle's face dissolves into laughter.

I turn to the float, pointing in the general vicinity of where the voice came from. "Whoever that was," I say, hoping I'm actually drawing their attention, "yes. But also, don't let me catch you looking at her."

Several kids burst out laughing as I turn back to Noelle, but I have no idea who actually spoke.

"Looks like you're popular," I tell her, my voice low so only she can hear, and she rolls her eyes, though I detect the hint of a smile.

I can only hope that comment goes to war against her difficult high school experience, even if it is too little, too late.

We hand out bucket after bucket, and as our supply slowly dwindles, a girl dressed as a candy cane stops in front of us, her attention focused on Noelle.

"Hi, Noelle," she says, her voice unsure.

Noelle cocks her head to the side, her brow furrowed, and a moment later, recognition spreads across her features.

"Hey," she says. She clears her throat. "How are you?"

I can only tell the girl shrugs beneath her costume by the way the tip of the candy cane tilts to one side. "I'm okay. Just wanted to say Merry Christmas."

"Oh," Noelle says. "Well, thank you. Merry Christmas to you, too."

The girl nods, the tip of her candy cane pitching forward this time, and accepts the bucket Noelle holds out to her.

"You know her?" I ask, as the girl darts onto the float.

She shrugs noncommittally. "One of my dad's kids." She bites her lip, and then shakes her head. "Fuck, I feel terrible. I can't remember the damn kid's name."

"Ask your sister," I suggest.

She shakes her head. "No. I don't want to give her any reason to think I'm interested in any sort of relationship with my dad."

I nod. "Ah. Well, it seems like she likes you, for what it's worth."

Noelle turns to me, her the space between her eyes creased. "You think?"

I shrug. "In my experience, when a high schooler likes you, they do things like say hello."

She gives me a look. "Is that what all of that experience being a math teacher has taught you?"

"A few other things, too. I've gotten good at two plus two," I say, throwing my arm around her shoulders and tugging her away from the fully-loaded float. "At me plus you," I continue, leaving a kiss on her temple.

She scoffs, but I see the hint of a smile on her face. "Ugh, you're sappy, aren't you?"

I shrug. "Only on occasion."

Once we're out of the crowd, she turns to me, her hands resting on my chest. "For what it's worth, I really like practicing my me plus yous," she says.

I grin, my hand dipping only briefly to her ass now that we're mostly out of the crowd.

"Mm, I like that too," I say, closing my fist around her jacket and tugging her close.

"Maybe we should go practice somewhere," she says. "Like your bedroom."

I kiss her again. "Nice try, Noelle."

She huffs. "Alright, alright." Her hands slip underneath my coat, running across my abs and causing them to bunch in response. "We'll go to the damn parade instead of getting naked and touching each other," she says, standing on her toes to press a kiss to my jaw. "And instead of watching me slowly lower down"–She pauses for dramatic effect, her fingers trailing down my torso to the clasp of my jeans. I glance around, but we're far enough away from the action that no one can see the way she's touching me–"and taking you in my mouth." She pauses again, pressing a kiss to my collarbone. "I guess we'll go to the damn parade."

A strangled sound jumps from my throat because *fuck*.

Her eyes flash. She knows she has me.

Everything in me wants to abandon the stupid parade and call her bluff. Weave my fingers into her hair and feel the back of her throat with the head of my dick.

But I rest my hands on her hips, my fingers digging into her skin in the way that makes those sexy little gasps fall from her mouth, and press my lips to her ear. "We're going to the parade and you're going to enjoy it, damnit."

She huffs. "Man, I really thought I had you there."

I keep my lips pressed against her ear. "But I look

forward to watching you struggle to swallow my cock down that pretty little throat of yours afterward."

She rears back, her eyes wide, and gently fans herself. "Wow, is it hot out here or is that a math teacher with a filthy mouth?"

I reach out and tug the zipper on her coat a little higher, giving her my best goodie two-shoes smile.

"Come on, Criminal," I say, grabbing her hand and dragging her across the parking lot.

There are a number of people ahead and behind us who also parked at the high school, and we meld easily between groups of them. I tuck Noelle under my arm, pleased that the only person I'm walking *with* is her. She smiles up at me, wrapping her arm around my middle and squeezing.

We head to the far end of the town square to avoid the crowd in the middle.

And then we wait.

We can see the parade in the distance, but they're not actually moving yet.

"Do you want coffee?" Noelle asks, eyeing the hut behind us as she rubs her hands together in front of her.

I take them in mine, trying to warm them with a bit of friction. "What, the dirty mouth wasn't enough to keep you warm all this time? Want me to come up with something else salacious?"

She snorts. "No. I'm already wet enough as it is imagining choking on your dick."

I'm momentarily rendered speechless, my mouth flapping about in the wind like I'm going to say something but nothing coming to mind.

She grins, cocking her head to the side. "See? I can do that too."

I let out a long breath. "I really do have my hands full with you, don't I?"

She nods, throwing me an indulgent grin. "So, coffee?"

"I can get it."

She shakes her head, stopping me. "I wouldn't want you to chance missing your parade. Save our spot."

I roll my eyes, but I take a moment to press a twenty into her begrudging hand and let her flit off to the coffee booth alone. She reaches for the heaters just outside as she passes them, taking a second to warm her hands. A moment later, she falls into conversation with the elderly woman manning the booth, who smiles at her sweetly and pours two cups of coffee. They chat for a moment, and after Noelle pays, the woman steps around the register to hug her.

I cock my head to the side, immensely confused at how she managed to befriend the coffee hut lady in the space of two seconds.

And then I hear a voice from behind me that reminds me viscerally of nails on a chalkboard.

"Nicky!"

I grimace before turning toward her.

"Wow, look at you without your glasses," she says, except her eyes are anywhere but my face

"Delia," I say, taking a step back from her so she doesn't get any ideas.

"I'm so happy I ran into you." She takes a step toward me, squeezing my arm. "How have you been?"

"Same as last time we spoke," I tell her, trying to gently move her arm away and only succeeding in pulling her closer. I very intentionally move my arm down and to the side so she can't pull that move on me again.

But she doesn't let go.

"Oh, well, I'm happy to hear you're still well," she says.

And then she smiles at me. That one she uses when she's going to be quiet until she gets her way.

I nod. *I will not ask her how she is.*

And she waits there. Hanging onto me. And it makes me irrationally angry because I *know* that she's waiting for me to break, like I might have before.

"Oh for fuck's sake," I hear over my shoulder, and I can't help it—my heart warms at the sound of her f-bomb as a grin spreads over my face.

Noelle doesn't hesitate knocking Delia's hand off my arm. She hands me the second coffee cup in her hand and turns toward her. "We tried to very surreptitiously let you know that Nick is not interested in you. But if you can't take a hint, I'll tell you straight out that *he is not*. So take your damn hands off him. You're being rude, and if you were a man doing that to a woman, I'd be calling the police for an escort home."

Delia rears back, finally taking her hand off my arm. "That's a little dramatic, don't you think? I was just saying hello."

Noelle fixes her with a glare. "Don't."

And then Noelle smiles.

And it is the longest, most tense silence I have ever been a part of.

But if there is one thing I know, it is that I should *not* speak at this moment.

After what feels like an eternity, during which I start counting seconds and then the number of breaths Noelle takes, Delia finally scoffs, turning and heading in the other direction with her head held high.

"Man, that woman has quite a set of balls on her," Noelle says, shaking her head. "Are you okay? You looked like a trapped cat about to scratch her."

I laugh. "Yeah, I'm fine. I was kind of hoping she'd lose interest."

Noelle pats my cheek. "Ridiculous that she feels like she can force herself on you like that." She stands on her toes to kiss my cheek. "I'm sorry you're such a catch, Saint Nick."

"Well thank you, Noelle, for giving her hell."

"That woman deserves a good egging," she says.

I let out a quick puff of air. "Noelle."

"What? I'm just saying, you've made it abundantly clear that you're not interested. Isn't there a point in time where you have to do something *other* than words?"

"She'll lose interest eventually."

Noelle grumbles. "So what, you just wait around and do your best to avoid her at town events?"

"It's not that serious, Noelle. So she grabs my arm every once in a while. *I* get to grab *you*," I say, wrapping my arms around her neck, careful not to hold my coffee in any way that could spill on her. I kiss her, closing my eyes briefly so I can imagine we're alone, just like this, in the confines of my house.

Someone remind me why I was so insistent on this stupid parade.

She grumbles, but I can tell by the way she nuzzles her head into my neck that she's ready to move on from this conversation.

"So who was your friend?" I ask, nodding to the coffee hut.

She shrugs. "My friend's mom. Mrs. Singh," she says. "Well, I guess my former friend's mom."

"What happened?"

She lets out a long breath. "Bullying. Loss of self-esteem. Loss of friends. Move to Philly. You know the story."

I nod. "She seemed like she liked you."

She unwinds her limbs from mine to take a sip of her coffee. "We were really close for a long time. She had a trampoline that we weren't allowed to go on unless we had adult supervision, but we did anyway. Made out with a boy for the first time on that trampoline. Smoked weed for the first time on that trampoline."

"You should reach out to her," I say.

She shrugs. "Why?"

"Wouldn't it be nice? To have a friend here?"

She blinks, her eyes connecting with mine. "You're my friend."

"Would it be the worst thing in the world to have two?"

She laughs, shaking her head, and leans over to kiss my shoulder. "Yes. Yes, it would."

I know that the tight feeling in my chest has nothing to do with her unwillingness to reconnect with a friend. That it has everything to do with the realization dawning on me that I'd do or suggest just about anything to make Noelle stay.

And I'm not sure it'll ever be enough.

17

NOELLE

Thursday, December 19th

Nick and I spend the night entangled, taking turns falling asleep and waking the other for sleepy, middle-of-the-night sex that's both lazy and incredibly indulgent. I've learned that running my fingers along his abs is a surefire way to make him growly and handsy with me, and that it takes only about twenty seconds from when I wiggle my ass back into his erection to him reaching into the drawer of the nightstand and fumbling around for a condom.

He wakes up early for his last day of work this year, but before he leaves, he leans down over me and gives me the sort of kiss that leaves me breathless when he finally unhands me and disappears through the door of his bedroom.

And I wander downstairs to start a pot of coffee and sign into work. Christmas is so close that most people aren't working anymore, but I usually hang around in case a client has a question or a request comes through. I'm not really *working*, but somebody has to man the ship.

So I spend my day wandering Nick's house, staring at the pictures of him and his mom. I connect my phone to his soundbar and play Christmas music even though it's really *not* my thing, but all of the damn town events have the songs running on repeat in my head. When that doesn't satisfy me, I put *The Grinch* on and sink down into his couch, my computer propped on a cushion next to me.

And when he finally gets home, I can't help darting into the entryway to greet him. He drops his bag by the door and immediately lifts me, his arms wrapped around my back and his face buried in my neck.

He walks me into the living room and sits us down on the couch with me on top of him, his hands splaying out across my ribs. "Mm, I could get used to this," he says, as I lean down and kiss him.

I grin. "Me too. It's kind of nice having a whole house to get lost in."

He raises his eyebrows. "Never thought of this as the sort of house you could get lost in." He pauses, and then pushes me to the side with one hand. When he looks at me again, one eyebrow is raised. "Noelle, were you watching Christmas movies?"

My breath catches. "No. It turned on by itself. And I couldn't change the channel. Or turn it off."

He grins, tugging me close to him again. "Noelle, are you turning into a little Christmas criminal?" I press on his chest to remove myself from his lap, but he only holds onto me harder, his grin widening. "Next thing I know, you're going to be dressing up like a little Christmas elf."

I narrow my eyes. "Yeah, you would love that, wouldn't you?"

"As long as it comes with a short little skirt just for me."

I press my finger into his chest. "You. Wish."

He shakes his head. "Nah, I like you the way you are. Grinch and all."

I crinkle my nose. "Stop saying cute things."

His grin grows wider. "Are you ready to go to the tree lighting?"

I huff. "No. Go back to saying cute things."

He slaps my ass. "Go get changed. I promise I'll give you a good dicking after."

I gesture to his body vaguely as I stand. "The dichotomy is so well done."

He snorts, standing from the couch and following me upstairs, where he grabs at my ass and pulls me into his chest and kisses my cheek from behind.

All the little things that make my heart race and face flush.

And then he also gives me a good dicking *before* the tree lighting.

WE PARK at the high school again and head over to the fair hand in hand. We get coffees and wander around the huts that line the town square. I have to head back into the city tomorrow to hand out everyone's Christmas bonuses, so I'll miss the frenzy of Shop Til You Drop in the square, but it's not really a shop-til-you-drop event, anyway. It ends at noon to give vendors time to spend with *their* families. It's really meant to encourage people to do their last minute Christmas shopping from locals rather than mass panic-buying at the local Target.

Nick throws his arm around my shoulders while we

wander, something he's been doing a lot lately. He's gotten so comfortable touching me and kissing me.

It's intoxicating.

"Do you want a snack or anything?" he asks, pressing a kiss to my temple in the place that always sends a little shiver down my spine.

I shake my head. "No. You're taking me to a real dinner after this, right?"

He doesn't miss a beat. "Of course." I grin up at him as his smile spreads across his face. "I wouldn't *make* you go to a stupid town event without taking care of your basic needs."

"You're smooth," I tell him.

He catches my eye before he speaks. "I just know you."

That sentiment sends all sorts of butterflies fluttering through my body. He's not wrong–over the past few weeks, we *have* gotten to know each other well.

A tightness blooms in my chest when I ask myself what happens *after* Christmas.

I hug him tighter. I don't want to think about this ending.

But what am I going to do, drive three hours every time I want to see my... boyfriend? Is that what we are now? A high schooler jokingly called me his girlfriend, and Nick didn't correct him.

We live three hours away from each other. My entire life exists in Philadelphia. Not to mention, he lives *here,* in a place that chewed me up and spat me out before I knew enough to know *better*.

"You okay?" he asks, his arm tightening around my shoulder. I squeeze him, letting my head drop to his shoulder for a moment before turning my attention back to the huts we're wandering past.

And then someone steps into our path, a wide grin on his face and a pretty blonde on his arm.

"Mr. Monroe," he says, his voice jovial. "And Noelle. Hi."

"Robbie," Nick says, his voice betraying his surprise as he steps forward to clap Robbie on the back. "Nice hair cut, dude. You look good."

It takes me a second to come to terms with the new Robbie standing in front of me. He's confident, wearing his full height proudly, and he meets my gaze with that same big grin he always wears. He's learned how to style his hair, and while his wardrobe used to consist of baggy, worn clothes, he's wearing a plain fitted sweatshirt over a brand new pair of jeans.

"I, uh, got a job at the gym." He shrugs sheepishly. "I liked what you said," he admits. "That I was strong. And I decided I wanted to build on that," he says, tugging the blonde girl on his arm toward us. "And this is Laura. She trained me." He grins at her. "And hasn't been able to keep her hands off me since."

"Robbie!" she squeals, her words quickly devolving into a giggle.

"Alright, I don't need to know all the gory details," Nick says, holding one hand up. "But happy for you, Robbie. And nice to meet you, Laura."

"Nice to meet you too," she says sweetly, smiling up at Robbie as he wraps an arm around her shoulders.

"Well," Robbie says, his voice almost professional as he nods to us. "It was nice running into you both. Happy holidays. And I'm glad you're finally together because that sexual tension was *uncomfortable*. Almost as bad as me and Laura."

"Robbie!" she squeals again. Nick runs a hand over his face, and I can't help the laugh that jumps from my throat.

"Enjoy the tree lighting," he says, steering her around us and continuing on their way.

Once they're out of earshot, we can't hold in the snorting laughter anymore. Nick turns to me, taking my hands in his and kissing them while shaking his head. "I feel like we just got bulldozed by a teenager."

I snort in response. "Not bulldozed, but definitely shown up. He did the whole glow up thing in the matter of a few weeks, found himself a sexy little workplace romance and somehow found the confidence that only a teen boy can have when he gets the girl of his dreams and knows there's nowhere to go but up."

"Yeah, you know, I was worried about him for a bit there. Over the past few weeks he's been quiet, and I was really worried his home situation was further falling apart. I guess he just found a purpose. I'm glad he's doing well."

I grin, turning to look over my shoulder at where they disappeared to. In the distance, I see them, his arm still around her shoulder and their heads turned in toward each other, sharing one of those intimate moments just between you and your person.

Nick tugs our hands into his chest, pulling me along with them, and kisses me. "You make me feel like a teenager again," he says.

"What, never-ending boners?"

"Exactly." He hums. "Plus maybe a little bit of giddiness. A little bit of optimism about what might come from this."

I swallow, his words bringing me right back into all of my concerns about making *this*–whatever *this* is–work longer than a season.

"I feel that way, too, with you," I say. While I have my concerns, what I say is absolutely true. *There's no one quite like you.*

He kisses me again, as if cementing our confessions.

And when he pulls away, he glances over my shoulder and clears his throat. "Uh, I think we have company."

My brow furrows, and I glance behind me.

Only to see my mom and sister, shit-eating grins on both of their faces.

"Oh, didn't see you there," Christina says, scooting over to us. "So is this what they call community service nowadays? Making out with the math teacher?"

I roll my eyes. "Christina! My community service is over."

"And you decided to stay in town regardless?" She turns to Nick, her eyes flashing with delight. "Wow, you must have made quite the impact."

He shrugs as he nudges me with his elbow. "I think somebody likes Christmas a little more than she lets on."

I scowl at him, my finger rising to point at him. "Don't say things you can't back up in a court of law."

His head tips back with his laughter, Christina and my mom following suit.

"Nick, nice to see you," my mom says. "I'm glad to see you're getting along with my daughter." She reaches out to pet my hair, and I feel the urge to crawl up into a tiny ball and rock back and forth. She turns to me. "It's so nice to have you here around Christmas, even if it's not with *me* specifically." She turns to Nick again. "I swear, as a mom, you can feel when your kids are nearby." She pats his shoulder. "You guys will understand one day."

"Mom!" Christina's laughter is uncontrollable.

Nick, to his credit, nods. "I understand the sentiment."

Good fucking answer, Saint Nick.

"So, what are your plans for Christmas?" my mom asks Nick.

And I have a feeling I already know where this is going, but it's not a train that I think I can surreptitiously derail.

He pauses for a moment, as if considering his answer carefully. "I usually spend Christmas at a friend's house."

My mom nods. "Well, we would love to have you if you have any time over the holiday. My house is always open. And I'm sure Noelle would appreciate the company." She winks at me.

I close my eyes. "Mom, you've got to be kidding me."

"That would be lovely," he says. "Thank you for the invite." He opens his mouth like he's going to continue–maybe weave some sort of excuse that would get him out of Christmas at the nuthouse–when my sister screeches.

"Dad!"

"Oh, for fuck's sake," my mom mutters. A quick puff of laughter escapes Nick. I roll my eyes, begrudgingly turning to where my sister is tackling him in a hug, his two teenagers flanking him on either side.

When he sees us, he heads our way, Christina doing a little loop and scooting along beside him.

"Ladies," he greets us, somewhat apprehensively.

"Dad," I say, even though I'd really rather refer to him as 'Sperm Donor.'

"Merry Christmas," he says. "I hope I'll get to see you girls this year."

Nick throws an arm around my shoulders, tugging me closer, and my dad's eyes track the movement.

"We can make it work. Maybe you can stop by for dessert," Christina says.

My mom's smile is tense.

"That would be wonderful. Maybe I can stop by earlier in the day, too. We can do some presents."

Nick clears his throat, his head dipping, and I realize this conversation might actually be upsetting him. I cock my head to the side, a small smile coming to my face when I catch his eye. He rolls his eyes as if to say, *God, what a jackass.*

"That would be great!" Christina says, her smile wide. My mom and I eye her, knowing we're going to end up *working* over the holiday to guard against her inevitable disappointment.

"Well, I'm really looking forward to seeing you girls this year."

Nick smiles, his voice easygoing when he speaks, but I detect an undercurrent that has my stomach clenching in response. "You say that like you don't normally get to see them at Christmas."

Christina waves him off before he can defend himself. "Things come up. With four kids, it's hard to always make the holiday perfect."

My dad nods, gesturing to her. "It's hard, with four kids."

The little one scoffs at that moment. "Especially when you only ever see two on Christmas."

My eyes snap to hers, a smile blooming across my face despite myself. She shrugs, averting her eyes.

"Naomi," he scolds. She rolls her eyes. He shakes his head. "Well, we'd better get going. Don't want to miss the tree lighting with my girls," he says, resting his hands on each of their shoulders. Naomi shrugs him off, walking ahead of them toward the center of the square where the tree looms above us.

"Looking forward to seeing you at Christmas," Nick says pointedly as they pass.

My dad pauses and, a second later, nods and continues after his new family.

Christina turns her sights on Nick. "Somebody's a little defensive of his woman, huh?"

He blushes, and it's adorable.

"Back off, Christina," I snap. "Dad deserves a hell of a lot worse than a little bit of accountability."

My mom rolls her eyes. "Come on girls, leave the fighting for the holiday." She turns to Nick, taking his elbow and tugging him away from me. "So I take it we *will* see you on Christmas?"

"Mom!" I shout, shoving myself in between them to protect this gem of a man from my family.

"I'm just asking," she says, holding her hands up.

"You can't accost people with invites without giving them time to think about it."

"I'm sorry," she says, and then turns to Nick. "You are always welcome." I give her a look. "And that's the last I'll say."

18

NICK

Thursday, December 19th

By the time we get back to my house, our limbs are icicles. When I lock my front door behind me, I turn to Noelle, taking her jacket and hanging it in the closet with mine, and then I wrap her up tight in my arms, running my hands along her skin to warm them up even though I can barely feel my own.

"Wine?" I ask, as we continue into the kitchen.

"Yes, please."

I pour us each a glass and we continue into the living room, where I get a fire started and we sit in front of it, each of us attempting to warm the other's skin because it's not as fun to rub *yourself* warm. I tug her between my legs, my hands running along her outer thighs and her upper arms.

She has her hands on my knees, squeezing and rubbing her way along my shins in a way that she doesn't intend to be sexual, but it's very much inspiring those thoughts. She's touching my *shins* and it's turning me on.

I leave a little kiss on her neck, brushing her hair out of my way so it doesn't get stuck in my stubble.

"Mm," she says, leaning into the kiss. "If this is what I get for going to the tree lighting, maybe it's worth it."

I snort, wrapping my arms tighter around her. "Please. You *loved* that tree lighting. You were staring up at it literally like a kid on Christmas."

She elbows me. "I was not!"

I laugh as I sigh into her neck. "Noelle, you were watching the tree lighting, but I was watching you. And I know what I saw."

Her head shakes, and I can only imagine she's rolling her eyes. "You *think* you saw me enjoying it. But it was really a strategic attempt to remove myself from the Christmas that has been thrust upon me. Sometimes you have to embrace your challenges in order to overcome them."

I kiss her neck again. "You're my little Christmas elf. My small little spitfire."

She nestles in closer to me and speaks in a mocking tone. "Well, if you're going to see what you want to see..."

I tug her closer and leave a triad of kisses along her shoulder.

She's quiet for a moment, tucked into my shoulder. "Hey, what's that?" she asks.

I lift my head to follow her gaze and realize it's hooked on the gift underneath the tree. "It's a present. Sometimes people do that, on Christmas. Give each other cute little things."

She twists to look at me. "Who's it for?"

"You, Criminal."

"You got me a present?"

"Well, yeah. You keep letting me play with your vagina, so I figured it was only right."

She snorts, elbowing me. "What is it?"

"You'll have to wait until Christmas to see."

She turns to face me fully, her eyebrows raised. "Are you coming to Christmas with my family?"

I gauge her expression carefully. Her mom's invite was incredibly thoughtful, but I don't want to impose on another family's Christmas.

It would be one thing if we were an established couple. If I didn't think she was going to run right back to Philadelphia once the season is over.

She's here now, and I'm loving every moment, but I'm under no false pretense that she's going to want to give up her flashy life to live in a town she hates.

"If you want me to, I'll go."

Her eyes narrow. "You sound uncertain."

"*You* sound uncertain."

She swallows, licking her lips. "I want you to come."

Lord help me, my chest swells. "Yeah?"

"I think that would be really nice."

I can't help the grin that spreads across my face. "Okay, I'll come for Christmas."

She giggles. "Just know there will likely be at least three fights and Christina is *going* to cry."

I only shrug. "Sounds like a fun time. Let me know what I can bring."

She nods, her smile widening.

I reach out and pinch her cheek, causing her nose to crinkle. "Look who's excited for Christmas."

"I'm not excited," she insists, even with that grin plastered to her face.

"Okay," I say, bundling her up in my arms and kissing her.

"I'm not!"

"Mm-hmm." I cup her jaw with one hand and tug her ass closer to me with the other.

"Nick!"

"I love it when you scream my name."

I lick at the seam of her lips and she opens to me, a breathy moan escaping her as I pull her closer. Her hands wind up into my hair, holding my lips against hers as she presses her body against mine. She throws her legs over mine so they wrap around my waist and pulls herself close to me. My hands dip to her ass, pulling her right up against me.

A minute ago, we were both freezing, desperate for warmth, but now the heat is overtaking us.

Noelle's hips push against me, the slightest pressure against my dick as we kiss.

Now that my hands are warm, I dip them underneath her sweater, along the skin of her back. I peel it up over her head and drop it to the ground next to us, anxious to feel her skin on mine. When she does the same to me, pressing her stomach against mine, my nerves light on fire.

This girl is something special.

I tug on her hips as they rock into me, and reach up to unclasp her bra. It falls between us and I waste no time taking one perfect pink nipple into my mouth. She moans, her body bowing to me, and my dick throbs at the noise.

I grunt as I clamp one arm around her back and press us up from the ground with one hand on the coffee table. She lets out a surprised gasp as I take a few steps toward the couch and throw her on it, taking the opportunity to unclasp her jeans and shimmy them down her legs, pulling her underwear with them.

And her pointed nipples might as well be the lights on my very own personal Christmas tree.

I nudge her knees apart with mine, settling myself between her legs and kissing her deeply. She writhes against me, her hands dipping to my pants to undo my jeans and push them down over my hips. She tugs at the waistband of my underwear, freeing me and taking me in her hand.

I breathe in sharply as I feel every single one of her fingers tighten around me. I let my head dip into her neck, smelling that delicious chocolatey rose scent of hers as she pumps me. A strangled sound escapes my throat as my hands roam her body, thumbing her nipples and grabbing at her hips.

"I want you," she breathes into my ear.

I nod, fumbling for my jeans on the floor. "Condom," I mumble in explanation, as I search my pockets.

And come up empty. I blink as I sit up and search again. "Fuck."

"Do you have one upstairs?"

I shake my head. "I put my last three in my pocket. I swear," I say. I think back through the night. I *did* put them in my pockets, I'm sure of it.

But I also put my wallet in that pocket.

And if I had to take a wild guess, I'd bet those three condoms are somewhere on the ground in the town square.

I hang my head. "They must have fallen out of my pocket."

"Nick," she groans, throwing her arm over her face.

And god, her tits look downright edible right now. I take an indulgent moment to torture myself, my eyes scanning her body. The slickness between her thighs glints in the light of the Christmas tree.

"I'm sorry."

She sits up, and it's like my hand magnetically attaches to her breast, my thumb running over that pointed nipple.

She runs her hands over my chest, my abdomen. When she looks up at me, she bites her lip. "We could go without, if you want."

I raise my eyebrows. "Yeah?"

"I mean, I'm on birth control and I trust you. And I mean, once you're the subject of a fake STD rumor, it's not like you forego testing." She shakes her head. "But I get it if you don't want to. I mean really, it's fine. We haven't known each other that long, so I really won't be mad if you're not comfortable with that."

A sense of relief washes over me that my fuckup is not the end of our night.

I rest my hand on the back of her neck and draw her lips to mine.

"I trust you, Noelle," I say against her lips as her hands land on my upper arms and slowly travel up around my neck.

"You do?"

I nod as I lay her back down on the couch, my hand trailing along her stomach as my lips press against her neck. I kiss her, my tongue winding into her mouth as I position myself at her entrance and slowly sink into her.

A strangled sound escapes me once I'm seated deeply inside her that matches her breathy moan.

"Fuck, Noelle."

Her pussy flutters around me, and the small movements send a shiver through my body.

If I'm not careful, I'm going to blow way too early.

"God, you feel so good," she mutters, her hips rocking up into me.

I groan, resting my head in her neck and brushing my lips against her skin.

I move slowly, intentionally. Pump into her rhythmically while making sure I hit that little bundle of nerves.

But god, the way she clenches around me has my orgasm building rapidly.

And as I feel that tension coiling in my lower abdomen, I realize I have to re-examine my strategy.

I pull out of her before I can lose it, and leave a quick trail of kisses along her chest, sucking each nipple into my mouth as I run my thumb over her clit.

"Nick," she gasps in surprise.

"You feel too good," I murmur against her skin as I struggle to catch my breath.

She groans, but it quickly morphs into needy little pants as I press my fingers inside of her and take her clit into my mouth. I've learned what she likes. A little twirl of my tongue, the most delicate suction.

Her hips are jumping, begging for more in only a matter of seconds.

When I've regained control of myself, I leave a wet trail of kisses back up her body and an indulgent kiss on her lips all while keeping up the movement of my fingers inside of her. As her back arches up, her stomach meeting mine, I press my dick inside of her again, and she gasps in response.

"Yes, yes, yes," she mutters, as I keep my thumb on her clit, giving her the gentlest of swirls as her pussy clenches around me.

I fuck her harder, sensing her orgasm building, and her nails dig into my back in response.

"I can't wait to feel you come on me bare," I whisper into her ear, running for the finish line as fast as I can because at this point, I'm just praying I can hold out for her.

She feels too fucking good.

When she tenses underneath me, I feel a sense of victory. She moans, the sound so light and delicate for a girl who's getting railed this hard.

I continue until she melts, her body going soft underneath me.

And with a few more jerky thrusts, I come.

We lay there for a minute afterward, her fingers running through my hair as I catch my breath.

"That felt really good," she whispers.

"Too good," I agree, coming up to my elbows and leaving a kiss on her nose. "I really thought I wasn't going to be able to hold on for a second there."

She raises her eyebrows. "Yeah?"

I nod. "It was scary."

She laughs. "You were very innovative."

I shake my head. "Just desperate to not be the kind of guy who leaves his girl high and dry."

"I'm sure you would have made up for it," she says.

"I do repent for my sins on my knees."

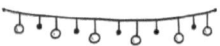

WHEN WE FINALLY STUMBLE UPSTAIRS, I pull one of my *I heart math* T-shirts over her head and we tumble into bed together, her head on my chest. I pull her as close as I can, my nose tucked in between strands of her hair, and listen to her breathing as it slowly deepens. She clings to me even in her sleep, and something about the way she nestles deeper into my shoulder in her dreams has my chest swelling.

I never meant to, but somewhere over the past few weeks, I've fallen head over heels for my criminal.

And I can't help but dread the end of this holiday, when

she's going to return to her apartment in the city and run her business like the smart, talented woman she is.

When she's not committing crimes, at least.

And I'm going to pine for the girl I only got to keep for a moment. The one who, in the quiet hours of the night, has me thinking, *This is it. This is what I've been looking for.*

19

NOELLE

Monday, December 23rd

I t is a sweet sort of torture to spend your night fucking someone's brains out and then having to get up the next day and go take care of *work*.

I know that I do this to myself. I've made it a priority every year to personally hand out Christmas bonuses to my employees because I think it's only right that their hard work is rewarded at the end of the year. Of course, there are some people who are traveling and some who don't want their boss showing up at their door the day before Christmas Eve.

And that's okay–I'll mail those.

But it makes me feel good to put in a little bit of work when other people are off. To be able to say thank you in person to the people who show up every day and make my little business what it is.

I unravel myself from Nick early in the morning and tip-toe into the shower so I don't get home smelling like sex, a fact that Christina is sure to point out immediately before spending every free moment pressing me for all the gory details.

Of course, he follows me in a minute later, and I'm not sure I'm actually any cleaner by the time we get out.

I kiss him goodbye at the front door, and he groans before he lets me go, his hair still wet from the shower and his gray sweatpants highlighting him in a way that really should be illegal.

"Text me when you're home, okay?" he asks, his lips against my ear. He gives me one last kiss on the cheek before letting me go, and I step out of the door into the harsh December air.

I nod, ignoring the intense pull in my chest that's telling me to stay here. To crawl back in bed with Nick and forget about Christmas bonuses and picking up my sister.

I may hate this town, but Nick makes me want to stay.

If I could pack him up in a suitcase and drag him to the city, I would.

But he wouldn't be happy.

He wants to teach at a nice school in a nice community, and despite that not being my experience *at all*, it's his.

And he deserves that, after everything he's gone through.

As I drive home, my mind runs off without me. I got myself involved with someone sweet–an actual *good* guy– from a place that I absolutely *hate*. *What was I thinking?*

Because now that I'm driving away from him, I feel a little tug on my heart with every mile.

Like the distance is too much.

I never intended to fall for someone like him. In fact, I don't think I've really *considered* dating anyone since college. I've had an array of sexual experiences that might border on enjoyable, but I've never felt like *this*. He makes me see stars when he touches me but also validates all of my harsh feelings about this town. He tries to cross out the terrible things that happened to me in high school by rewriting them with better experiences.

As much as I hate the town he lives in, I'm not sure I can leave him behind with it.

When I finally get to my apartment, Christina is sitting on the floor in front of the couch, wrapping presents while Christmas music plays through our bluetooth speaker. She grins when she sees me come in, but quickly shoves the present underneath the coffee table.

"Let me guess. Another of your famous scarves," I say, as I shrug off my jacket and leave it on the rack by the door.

She narrows her eyes at me. "You can *act* like you're surprised."

"Oh, I will. Christmas morning, I'll act like it's the most exciting gift I've ever received in my life. And I'll also act like I wasn't sitting on the other half of the couch while you knit most of it."

She huffs. "Well, consider yourself lucky to be getting one."

I collapse into the couch, throwing my feet up on the opposite side, and give her a sincere smile. "I do consider myself very lucky to have a brand new Christina Christmas scarf every year. It's my favorite thing about Christmas."

Her brow furrows. "What?"

I shrug. "I love your scarves. You always pick some fuzzy wool that's not scratchy or anything. And they're always fun colors. I think I have every single one you've given me, besides that one we learned we *can't* wash."

She crinkles her nose. "Yeah, that was not our best decision-making."

She scrambles up from the floor, her walking stunted by

the gigantic cast she still has on one leg. I move my legs so she can plop down on the couch where they are, and she rests it on the coffee table in front of us. I drop my legs into her lap.

"So what's got you suddenly so thankful for Christina Christmas scarves?" she asks.

I shrug, pursing my lips because I'm not sure how much to tell her.

She raises her eyebrows. "Maybe a certain math teacher who happens to love Christmas too?"

"I do not love Christmas."

She rolls her eyes. "Okay, Grinch. Is it him?"

I sit up, eyeing her as I cross my legs.

"I like him."

"Certainly seemed like it with the way your tongue was shoved down his throat."

"Christina!"

"What? I'm just saying, that was borderline pornographic. And in the town square, no less."

"You know what? I'm not talking to you about this," I say, turning to get up but quickly being blocked by a cast swinging toward me.

"You sit," she says. "You have an unfair speed advantage right now, but I won't hesitate to knock you in the head with this thing, and I swear it'll hurt."

I sigh. "Don't make fun of me for it."

She throws her hands out in front of her. "Okay. I promise I won't make fun of you for confessing to me that you're in love with the exceptionally hot Clark Kent-wannabe Snow Falls High School math teacher."

My nose twitches.

She raises her eyebrows. "That's what you were going to tell me, right?"

I make a face at her. "Maybe not in those exact words. And I mean, I don't know about *love*."

She rolls her eyes, waving me off. "Oh, stop. I've never seen you stare at someone all goony-eyed like that. And the last time *I* got you to participate in anything arguably Christmas-related, I had to buy our groceries for a month."

"In my defense, you made me dress up *like the Grinch I was*. I deserved free groceries for a month."

She grins. "That picture of you is one I will cherish until my dying day."

"And I can't wait for that day so I can finally delete it off your phone."

She leans back into the couch, searching for her coffee mug on the end table, and brings it to her lips for a quick sip now that she's sure I'm not going to do my best disappearing act. "So?"

I bite my lip.

"You're in love with him?"

I lean back into the couch. "I *can't* be in love with him. It's too soon." I rub my hand over the spot in my chest that hurts, thinking about the time we could be spending together but instead I'm here, without him. "But I'm literally *aching* for him."

Her face breaks. "Aw, Noelle. The tin woman found a heart."

I reach over and knock her arm. "This is why I don't talk to you about things!"

She takes the opportunity to wrap me in a big, one-armed hug, holding her coffee mug carefully out of spilling distance. "I'm so happy for you. You deserve a big love."

I shake my head. "Again, I don't know if I'd call it *love*. I just... I like who he is. Like, this kind of quiet guy who's nice to everybody but he doesn't hesitate to clap back at Dad–

even if Dad didn't realize it. I feel like I have somebody who's truly in my corner. Who... I don't know, maybe makes it worth going back to Snow Falls every once in a while."

She nods. "I mean, I won't take it as a slight that *I* won't be worth visiting in Snow Falls–"

"Christina! You know what I mean. Of course I'd visit for you."

She lets out a long breath as she takes another sip of coffee. Her voice is serious when she speaks again. "Honestly, Noelle, maybe it's time you give up the angry teenager act."

I blink, my heart dropping. "My... what?"

She shrugs. "It's like your *thing*. You hate Snow Falls because you had a bad experience in high school. You hate Dad because he had a second family. I'm not saying that either of those things aren't worth being upset over. They are. But Noelle, it's been almost ten years. Don't you think somebody like Nick is worth... I don't know... finding a way to get over it? By any means?"

I swallow. My sister and I mostly joke with each other– she's my best friend–but on the rare occasion she decides to deal me some truth, I know it's at least worth listening to. "How do I just... get over it?"

"That, I don't know. But Noelle, I've never seen you this happy. And sure, it boggles my mind that you've found happiness in Snow Falls. But don't you think maybe everything that you've been through put you in exactly the right place for something good?"

"You mean, if I didn't get bullied in high school and move here with you, and if Dad wasn't a dickhead deserving of a good egging, I never would have met Nick?"

She shrugs, a grin overtaking her face. "It's like a little Christmas miracle!"

I shake my head, pointing at her. "No. No Christmas miracles here."

"Come on, Noelle. Your name means Christmas. And he's Saint Nick! Don't you think it's a match made in heaven?" She starts laughing. "Wait, no! He's Father Christmas! Does he like it when you call him daddy?"

"Oh my god, Christina," I say, standing from the couch. "You are such a problem!"

She grins. "Sit down and tell me about the sex. This cast had seriously been a cock block so I need to hear it from you. All gory details included."

I roll my eyes. "Look, I have to hand out Christmas bonuses today. Why don't we get you all packed up and loaded in the car, and if you want to come with me, I'll tell you about Saint Nick with the big dick while we deliver them?"

She claps her hands. "I *love* bonus day! Yes! I want to be Santa!"

I snicker. "You sure know how to *ho ho ho*."

I slip out of reach before she can hit me with her cast.

20

NICK

Monday, December 23rd

Noelle is going to be gone for hours, so I head to the town square for the Shop Til You Drop event, and search for some little things that I can bring her family. I don't know them well, so I search for nonspecific, Christmas-themed things, because I *do* know they're big fans of the holiday.

I end up with a few stuffed animals and some generic ornaments. The town has themed ones every year, so I get one of those for Christina, since she'll be moving back, and a pretty silver snowflake for her mom.

And yes, when I see a Grinch-themed ornament, I get that for Noelle, too. It seems only right.

And when I can consider my shopping for the year done, I head back to my car, passing Hank's booth along the way. He's chatting jovially with someone, his laugh full and boisterous, and I get the distinct feeling that Hank would make a wonderful Santa. When he waves the person off, wishing them a merry Christmas, I stop by to say the same to him.

"Ah, done your shopping for the year?" he asks, rounding the table and clapping me on the back. He grins at me, hands on his hips.

"I am," I say, and it feels really nice to say that. To have people around me to get things for.

"Good, good." He gets a knowing glint in his eye as he eyes my bag. "Got a little something for Noelle in there?"

Heat rushes into my cheeks, and Hank only grins wider. "Yeah, I got her a little something."

He nods. "Good. I have a feeling in my bones that she needs somebody like you, just like you need somebody like her."

I can't help the laugh that escapes me. "Yeah? I feel like I can hardly handle her."

He waves me off. "She's not a difficult one. There's a lot of love underneath a hell of a lot of armor. The really difficult ones–they don't have love under there. Only needles. Noelle had it tough, but she came out on top. I have a lot of respect for that girl. For her mom and her sister, too. Great people, all three of them, who have been dealt a shitty hand."

"You really hate her dad too, huh?"

He lowers his voice, leaning toward me. "Look, don't tell anybody, but Noelle's mom called me when she saw her daughter taking off with a carton of eggs. She thought it might teach her a lesson to get caught, so she sent me over there to pick her up." He holds his hands out in front of him, as if to say, *well what was I supposed to do?* "When I got there, she was staring at his house, glaring. Seemed like she wanted to throw the eggs but she didn't have the nerve."

"What made her throw them?"

Hank shrugs. "Time, I guess."

I narrow my eyes. "You waited for her to throw the eggs?"

He shrugs. "Look, you didn't hear this story from me. But I sat there watching that girl fume for a good twenty minutes, working herself up to that point. And I swear, the whole time I was–pardon the pun–egging her on." He lets out a quick breath. "I honestly can't believe the amount of time I sat there, whispering to myself, 'Come on, Noelle. Throw the damn egg already.'"

I let out a disbelieving breath. "But why did you give her community service then?"

He shakes his head. "That was Helen's request. I would have picked her up and taken her right home, but Helen wanted to end the anger. She thought that might do it." He shrugs. "And hey, maybe I had a little trick up my sleeve that night that I wanted to see through."

"A trick?"

Hank winks at me, rounding the table between us. "Merry Christmas, Nick."

"What trick?"

He only gives me a look, and as if he planned the interruption, a man walks up to the booth to shake Hank's hand and wish him a happy holiday season. They must know each other well, because they quickly fall into an easy conversation, all happy laughter and questions about how the other is spending the holiday.

I wait for a moment, wondering if Hank is going to give me any clue whatsoever, until he turns to me and nods pointedly as if to confirm that he will not, in fact, be offering any further explanation.

Noelle normally comes to visit her mom on Christmas Eve and Christmas, but otherwise opts to hang out in the city for the holidays.

Except this year, she'll be visiting me.

She comes back late at night after dropping her sister off at her mom's, and nearly bowls me over as she rushes into the house, her arms loaded heavy with two duffel bags and a Santa sack.

She'll be staying through the new year, and *that* is the best Christmas present I could have asked for.

I take her bags and a quick kiss from cold lips, and follow her into the living room, where she promptly dumps out the Santa sack onto the ground and arranges the presents beneath the tree. I drop her duffel bags at the bottom of the stairs to worry about later.

"Noelle, what is all this?"

"Don't worry, it's not for you."

I laugh. "I wasn't worried. I thought it was cute. The Christmas elf strikes again."

She's on her hands and knees in front of the tree, stuffing presents underneath it, and she turns to shoot me a glare. "I am not a Christmas elf. But I hate the thought of Christmas presents being stuffed in a bag until the day of, you know? They should be able to breathe. Absorb the feeling of Christmas before doing their duty on the day of and being torn to shreds."

I grin, kneeling down next to her and helping her stuff them all underneath. They're mostly presents for her mom and sister, and a couple small ones for me, but I catch a few that surprise me. Mrs. Nguyen, the librarian who was nice to her in high school. Mrs. Singh, her friend's mom who ran the coffee hut. Naomi, her half-sister, and Cassidy who I can only assume is the *other* half-sister, considering the similar size and weight of the presents. I smile as I see that she even has one for Hank.

"Noelle," I say, that warming sensation spreading through my chest again. "You *are* a little Christmas elf."

"Can you please stop saying that?" she groans.

"You *love* Christmas."

"No, I don't!"

I gesture to all the presents underneath the tree. "You're *sweet*."

"I am not!"

I wrap my arms around her, pulling her into my chest and smothering her with every ounce of love I can give her because–like Hank said–she's got a whole lot of love under that prickly exterior of hers.

She's resistant at first, pushing against my chest and groaning. "I am not sweet!"

I kiss her forehead and her cheeks and her lips, and it doesn't take long for her to melt, to tug me closer and kiss me and start pulling at my clothes.

"Do you taste as sweet as you act?" I ask, as I trail my lips down her neck.

"I guess you'll have to find out," she says coyly, pressing away from me with a slick little grin on her face.

On my living room floor in front of the Christmas tree–a place we keep managing to end up naked–I eat my very favorite dessert to the tune of her pleasure ringing out around us. I tease her for being so sweet, and she threatens to throw my presents out and replace them with coal.

I don't have the heart to tell her the only real present I care about is *her*.

ALTHOUGH SHE REFUSES to admit she enjoys it, we spend the night listening to Christmas music, drinking wine, and making cookies that she decorates with curse words and penises, the perfect contrast to my lopsided trees and wreaths. I take her in the kitchen while she's chomping on chocolate-covered berries, and as I'm trying to clean up the mess of chocolate pieces on the counter beneath her, she sinks to her knees and cleans me right out.

We fall into bed tangled up with one another, and I wake in the morning to a smiling girl next to me. She claims it's not because of Christmas, but she grins when I ask her if she wants a special Christmas Eve breakfast.

As we cook in my kitchen, her prancing around in one of my *I heart math* T-shirts and her bare feet, I get lost watching her. I've wanted something like this for so long that I almost don't believe it. Someone who's a little goofy and a little prickly sometimes, but loves with unequaled ferocity.

She catches me grinning stupidly at her and eyes me, a piece of bacon halfway into her mouth. "What?"

I shake my head. "Just happy you're here."

Her eyes narrow. "And you call *me* sweet."

I shrug. "We can both be sweet. There's room for both of us to hold the title."

She laughs, shuffling over to me and leaving a kiss on my jaw that sends a shiver all the way down my spine and right back up. She isn't wearing anything under that damn T-shirt, and I can feel her breasts pressing against my chest through the thin fabric.

I thought I might calm down by now. That the frequency with which we've been fucking would let me go half an hour without popping a boner around her.

Apparently not.

So I bend her over my kitchen counter *again*.

Apparently I really am coming for Christmas.

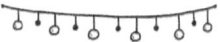

AFTER A LAZY DAY of food and fucking, we drag ourselves into the shower to get ready for Christmas Eve dinner at Noelle's mom's house. It's a low-key affair, according to Noelle, but she wears a pair of leggings and a sweater so soft that I have trouble keeping my hands off her.

We stuff the presents back into the Santa sack to bring them over for Christmas morning, but I let Noelle arrange them under her mom's tree. She glares at everyone, but I'm confident that inside, my little Christmas elf is enjoying herself.

Helen does a stripped-down version of seven fishes–she gets a pre-packed plate from the grocery store, so all she really has to do is throw it in the oven–and the girls *ooh* and *ahh* over the Christmas cookies I decorated, and roll their eyes at the ones Noelle very obviously did. She only grins at their reactions.

Christmas music plays in the background, and I'm just content to be a part of a Christmas Eve like this.

I feel like a kid again, when these traditions were just something I had to get through in order to get to the presents portion of Christmas morning. Except now I have a new appreciation for them. Noelle's family isn't flashy about the holiday, but they *are* together. And mostly happy about it.

In the years since my mom died, I've joined other families for Christmas. Friends or girlfriends whose families took pity on the kid without one of his own. I've had amazing Christmases and I've had so-so ones, but it feels like there's something more to this one.

It feels a little bit like home.

And that feeling hits me again. The one that tells me I shouldn't get used to this.

I rub the tightness out of my chest as Noelle refills my wine and returns to the couch, a grin on her face as she leaves a kiss on my cheek and takes the spot on the floor at my feet, resting her own glass on the coffee table in front of us. Her mom is next to me, still picking at her dinner because apparently that's how she eats, according to her girls—all the time and everything, but in bird-sized bites. Christina is on the couch adjacent to us, her cast propped on the arm and her phone in her hand.

"Dad says he's excited to see us tomorrow," Christina says, a smile on her face as she glances up at everyone.

Noelle's scoff carries enough weight for the both of us. "I bet he is."

Christina gives her a look. "He's only going to stop by for a little bit, so you can go hide in your bedroom if you're really that opposed to seeing him."

"Thank you. I'll definitely take you up on that offer."

Christina rolls her eyes. Helen sighs. "We're all going to have a very nice holiday. Whether or not your father shows."

Christina's eyes lock on Noelle's. "At least Father Christmas will be coming."

"Christina!" Noelle snaps, reaching over and slapping her on the cast.

"You realize I have a cast there, right? That felt like a light breeze lifting my hair."

"Well, I don't want to *actually* hurt you on a holiday. That's Dad's job."

Christina's nostrils flare.

"Girls!" Helen says. She turns to me, shaking her head.

"Every year, it's the same thing. I swear, their relationship hasn't changed since they were five and nine."

Both girls turn to her, grinning proudly.

"Consistency is key," Noelle says, mock seriously, and I get the feeling they've had *this* conversation before, too.

Christina nods in agreement. "You can't always rely on motivation, but as long as you've got consistency, you'll see success."

Helen rolls her eyes. "Motivational posters from a science teacher they both had."

I nod. "Mrs. Larson. She still has them up."

"Oh, really? That's too funny."

"To be fair, now that I've gotten to know her a bit, I think those posters are sarcastic."

Noelle raises her eyebrows. "You're kidding."

I shake my head. "She's a wild woman. Definitely the coolest teacher at school, but she has a *dry* sense of humor that I think goes right over most students' heads."

Noelle nods. "Well, I think I like her even more now. She was always one of my favorites."

"I'm surprised you didn't get her a Christmas present," I say, knocking her shoulder with my knee.

Noelle's face flushes, and Christina's eyes narrow in on her. "Did you buy a teacher a present?"

Noelle takes a quick sip of her wine. "Well, I had to get Nick something."

"And Mrs. Nguyen."

It takes Christina a second to recognize the name. "You *did*? You're such a nerd, buying the librarian a gift!"

Noelle points at her. "You should be thanking her because the love for reading she gave me is what eventually led you to those spicy cowboy novels you love so much."

Christina flushes. "Noelle!"

Helen sighs. "Oh, Christmas."

Noelle twists to face me. "You better be careful or I'm going to rescind next year's invitation."

"I was already given an invitation for next year?"

She shrugs sheepishly. "I mean, you know, it's implied, if..."

I rest my wine on the coffee table and reach down to tug her up into my lap, audience be damned, and give her an indulgent kiss on the cheek. "This is my favorite Christmas."

She raises her eyebrows, one elbow propped on the couch next to my head. "Yeah?"

I nod. "You're going to have to fight me off next year. But don't worry, I'll come armed with an array of things to roast you over."

"Yes!" Christina shouts. "I knew I liked him!"

Noelle rolls her eyes at her sister but gives me a small smile. "I think this is my favorite Christmas, too."

And then she kisses me, and there's a part of me that's aware her mom is grumbling and looking away, and her sister is saying, 'Eww,' repeatedly and telling us to get a room, but I can't get over how nice it feels to hold her in my arms and know that I'll see her grumpy, smiling face all throughout my holiday.

ON CHRISTMAS MORNING, I wake up to Noelle scooting her butt back into me. I give it a nice squeeze, groaning at the way it feels in my hand because it fits *just right*. When she notices I'm awake, she twists around and kisses me, hitching one leg around my waist and tugging me close.

"Merry Christmas," I say, as her lips brush against mine.

She hums. "Merry Christmas," she murmurs, her hand

dragging along my dick. My arms tighten around her, and she takes the opportunity to straddle me, to tug my underwear down and have her way with me.

And I realize very quickly that *this* was the Christmas morning I always wanted.

I know her body now, how she likes to be touched and what makes her cry out for me. I know the pinched look that overtakes her face as her movements become more languid means she's about to come.

I know she's going to whimper as I grab hold of her hips and tug her down underneath me. The feeling of her nails digging into my back and the way her legs will wrap around my waist and urge me deeper until I spill inside her.

And afterward, she's going to leave kisses all along my chest and my neck. She's going to make it to the coffeemaker first and somehow make it better than I ever do, despite using the same simple formula. She's going to smile as she opens her presents and laugh when she sees what I got her, and so help me god, I don't know if I can go back to Christmas without her after this.

Before we get out of bed, I hold her close, selfishly savoring this moment. I brush my lips over every part of her, hoping that one of these kisses might be the reason she stays.

When we get downstairs, we sit with our coffee in front of the Christmas tree. She unwraps her favorite *I heart math* T-shirt–the one that she keeps gravitating toward because it's a little old and worn out and very, very pink–as well as the Grinch ornament, a candle that smelled like something she'd like, and a crocheted egg that I found at the market a few days ago, because if it weren't for a damn egg, we wouldn't know each other.

She nearly falls over herself laughing as she realizes

what it is, and then crawls toward me, giving me one big long kiss in thanks.

And then I tear open my presents. A red and white striped blanket not unlike the one I saw in her mom's house last night. Christmas-themed cookie cutters. A mug that says *I heart math* and a Rubik's cube that spells out NERD-NERDNERD around the four sides when you solve it correctly.

Just like she did, I dissolve into a pile of laughter.

It's not an overindulgent Christmas—it's probably a lot for the short time we've known each other—but it's ours.

It's everything.

We whip up some scrambled eggs before heading over to her mom's house for Christmas breakfast and presents—Noelle said she usually makes a big spread, and I will not be the type of guest who shows up empty-handed. Eggs were the only truly breakfast-y thing Helen said she could use help with.

So, eggs it is. To our absolute delight. We can't stop laughing the entire time they're on the stove.

When we get there, large container of scrambled eggs in hand, Noelle transfers the dish to the counter where an array of breakfast food is already laid out. Bacon, sausage, various pastries, donuts, and plenty of fruit.

"Thank you for taking care of the eggs, that's so sweet of you. And now I have eggs for the week! No need to go grocery shopping tomorrow," Helen says to me, giving me a quick hug and a kiss on the cheek. "Thank you."

"Of course."

"I helped," Noelle insists.

"Sure, sweetie," Helen says, patting her hand. Noelle throws her hands out in front of her. Without another glance, Helen gestures to the counter. "We have so much food so please, eat up. It's not Christmas unless you've got a tummy ache."

So we fill our plates and move into the living room, where Christina is already propped up on the couch with one leg on a pillow. She waves hello as she spears a bite of sausage on her fork and pops it in her mouth. She's wearing Christmas jammies embroidered with her initials.

Helen follows us in a moment later, taking a spot on the floor with her plate to distribute the presents from underneath the tree.

"Can we wait until Dad is here?" Christina asks, her nose in her phone.

Even *I* balk at this question. Helen pauses and exchanges a look with Noelle.

"Honey, we don't usually wait for your dad to get here," Helen says, continuing to distribute the presents.

"I know. But he said specifically that he'd come in the morning. And I know he's flaky, but I feel like we can give him the benefit of the doubt. It's Christmas, after all. And we don't want to teach him that even when he *does* show up, we don't believe in him."

I press my lips together, suddenly insanely curious how this family handles Christina on Christmas.

Noelle raises her eyebrows and, with a pointed look at Christina, rips open her first present. "Oh, shoot. Looks like we already started without him. Too bad."

Helen rolls her eyes. "Okay, no need for that, Noelle," she says, and turns to Christina. "I have a little something special planned this year. So while we don't need to start *right* now, I would like to start sooner rather than later."

Noelle's brow furrows. "You have something special planned? What is it?"

"It's a surprise."

"Right, but what is it?" Noelle asks again.

Helen gives her a look. "Noelle, I'm not going to *tell* you if it's a surprise."

Noelle gestures to Christina. "Well, she's the Christmas one. I assume the surprise is for her, right?"

Helen shrugs. "It's for everyone. I just... don't want it waiting too long, you know?"

Noelle narrows her eyes. "Did you get a dog? Is it wrapped in one of these presents and you're worried about the air holes?"

Helen rolls her eyes. "No, honey. I wouldn't do that. It's dangerous."

"Okay," Noelle says, leaning over to take a bite of the scrambled eggs on her plate. "Then I guess we wait? Just a little?"

Helen nods, doling out the last of the presents right at my feet. "Just a little," she agrees.

I stare at the pile in front of me, feeling a little winded that it's nearly as big as the girls' piles. "I didn't get you enough," I blurt.

The girls laugh. Noelle pats my knee. "Half the fun of presents at Christmas is the unwrapping. My guess is there's a whole lot of fruit in there. Maybe a cookie or two if my mom was feeling a little whimsy last night. And I would bet good money there's at least one charging cable whose real home is a mystery."

Helen rolls her eyes. "That only happened one year."

"Old kitchen utensils," Christina contributes.

"DVD cases without the DVDs in them," Noelle says.

"Oh! Water bottles. Fresh from the fridge so the wrapping paper was wet."

The girls dissolve into laughter as Noelle finishes unwrapping the one that she started and holds it up for the group to see, hardly able to speak through her laughter. "A single roll of toilet paper," she says, wiping tears from underneath her eyes. "I think this one takes the cake."

"Just making sure you're Christmas isn't shitty," Helen says, and their laughter doubles. Noelle presses her face into my arm, the roll of toilet paper shaking in her hand.

"Thank you, Mom. I love you," she says, crawling forward to leave a quick kiss on her mom's cheek.

"Love you too, sweetie."

And then a booming voice cuts through the noise. "HO HO HO!"

Noelle jumps, Helen grimaces, and Christina twists on the couch with a look of delight on her face that drops when she realizes the voice is not, in fact, her dad's.

It's Hank's.

"MERRY CHRISTMAS!" he bellows, emerging from the hallway dressed in a full Santa suit with a sack thrown over his shoulder. He has a fake white beard attached to his face and waves at us like he's royalty.

"Hank," Helen groans, dropping her face into her hands.

"I COME BEARING PRESENTS FOR THE CHILDREN!"

Noelle's face is pure joy as she grins up at him.

"Hank, you were supposed to wait until I said the word!"

He pauses, shaking his head. "Helen, what was the word? I heard everybody laughing and I didn't feel like hiding out anymore. It's been *hours*."

Christina cocks her head to the side. "When did you get here?"

He clears his throat. Helen looks away.

"Were you here all night?" Christina asks, eyes wide as she looks from Hank to her mom. "Mom, was he here all night?"

She shrugs. "Yes."

"Oh!" Christina says. "And in the room right next to mine? Mom!"

Helen shakes her head. "Christina, I'm a grown woman with needs. Just like the two of you. And I'm happy, so you're welcome to go stay at your new apartment if it makes you uncomfortable."

She looks at Hank again, and he only shrugs in response.

"This is the best Christmas ever," Noelle mutters, and I can't help wrapping my arms around her and leaving a big kiss on her cheek. When she turns to me, she still has that big grin on her face, and she winds her arms around my neck to pull me close and kiss me. When she speaks again, her voice is lower. "*Now,* it's the best Christmas ever."

"Alright, so we've got a bunch of presents to hand out to the kids," Hank says, putting on his Santa voice again and kneeling in front of the tree. He reaches into the Santa bag and pulls out the first present, noting the name on it and passing it to Noelle.

"Thanks, Hanky Panky," she says.

He pauses, narrowing his eyes before giving her a quick wink. "Only your mother's allowed to call me that."

Noelle's nose crinkles. "Ew."

He grins. "Yeah, that's what I thought." He turns back to his Santa sack. "Christina!" He throws a present over his shoulder that she just barely catches.

"Hank, I'm broken!"

"You're as broken as your sister is a criminal."

Christina raises her eyebrows, her gaze catching mine for a second as she lets out a puff of laughter.

"Helen, dear," Hank says, handing a present back to her. I catch Noelle smiling to herself at the interaction.

We eat, and we accept presents from Santa, and we laugh hard enough that my cheeks hurt. Noelle leans against me and gives me surreptitious kisses every once in a while, a contented look on her face until she sees her sister frowning at her phone.

Noelle crumples up her discarded wrapping paper and chucks it at her, hitting her square on the nose. Christina flips her off in response.

"Pay attention to Christmas," Noelle says.

Christina huffs. "Dad isn't answering me back, and it isn't going to be morning for much longer."

"He's probably just busy, honey," Helen says, rubbing her knee.

"He said he'd *be* here."

Noelle sighs, reluctantly digging her phone out of her pocket to see if he texted her.

Her brow furrows as she taps and scrolls. "Naomi texted me."

Christina leans forward. "What did she say?"

Noelle starts typing back. "She said she hopes we're having a nice Christmas with Dad." She frowns. "She asked if we'd ever consider doing Christmas together so they could see him too."

Christina holds her hand over her heart. "Okay, that hit me where it hurts."

Noelle shakes her head. "I'm asking her to explain further."

With that, Christmas takes a more somber tone. Noelle sends her text, and then we wait, each of us picking at the ends of our food. Helen thumbs the edge of a piece of wrapping paper sticking out from one of her boxes. Christina purses her lips, staring at her phone. Hank sits on the ground in front of the tree, tugging his fake beard down around his neck.

And all I can do is suppress my anger that someone has all of *this*—has *two* of this—yet has the audacity to blow off people who love him. Who are so ready to look past all of his faults and accept him anyway.

I would give everything for a *fraction* of this.

And he can't even fucking show up.

When Noelle's phone lights up again, we collectively lean forward.

"She said Dad told her he'd be spending Christmas with us this year. That after all the time he's spent with them—" Noelle pauses. "That after all the time he's spent with them, now that her parents are separated, he needs to split his time better." She looks up at her mom. "They separated?"

Helen shrugs. "I don't talk to him. How would I know?"

Christina blinks. "So he told them he'd be spending Christmas with us. And he told us he'd stop by for a few *minutes*. Where the fuck is he, then?"

Noelle starts texting rapid fire again, leaving her phone unlocked on the coffee table since Naomi seems to be at hers.

I rub my chest where heartburn is threatening to take me down. *How dare he, how dare he, how dare he.*

A minute later, another text comes in, and Noelle summarizes it for the group, starting with a sigh and a, "This poor girl." She shakes her head. "She says Dad's been living at the Goldmans' old place. That he's been flaking out on them for a while now and she had a feeling he was lying about seeing his family this Christmas. That's why she looked me up and found my phone number. Because she wanted proof that he's the jackass she thinks he is."

Noelle taps her fingers along the side of her phone, glancing up at her mom. "Can I invite them here?"

Helen's eyes go wide. "You want to invite them *here*?"

Noelle shrugs. "They are technically *family*, right? And it sounds like they're having a rough day."

Helen swallows and nods. "Of course. The more, the merrier."

21

NOELLE

Wednesday, December 25th

I'm not entirely sure what I'm doing. Is it odd to invite your dad's second family for Christmas? Absolutely. Does it feel like the right thing to do right now? Kind of.

My mom is apprehensive, and I hate that I'm doing this to her on the holiday, but we've been running in circles for years, trying to stop Christina from getting upset. Trying to get him to show up when he says he will.

And Naomi... as much as I don't want to think we share some of the same genes, she reminds me of me. A little brash, with a healthy dose of skepticism. She looks like a little version of me, and I have a very strong feeling in my gut that I will regret not doing what I can to make things better.

How would my life be different if someone had been there for me when I was in high school? She might not have eczema or get bullied in the same way I did, but she's a human going through the same difficult realization that I did, at the same time I did: that unfortunately just because he's *Dad* doesn't mean he was ever qualified for the job.

They arrive half an hour later, with wide eyes and hesitant smiles. Naomi leads the charge, thanking my mom directly for having us and immediately clearing the air of any awkwardness by stating their intention–to have a nice Christmas with the family they *choose*.

I can't help but grin at her a little bit. My mom smiles at this too, shooting me a quick look like she notices the resemblance like I do. When she offers to host us next year, my mom thanks her for the invite and tells her the moms will have to discuss this and get back to her.

Cassidy beelines for Christina, and I can't help but notice the resemblance there, too. She asks how Christina's leg is healing and lets her know they've started thoroughly salting the driveway whenever the forecast calls for snow or ice.

Behind her, Harriet the Harlot walks in–who is definitely not a harlot, but that's the name Christina and I came up with when we were young and angry, and it rolled off the tongue so easily that it *stuck*. She nods to my mom, and like Naomi, clearing the way of any awkwardness, my mom wraps her in a big hug, thanking her for coming and gesturing to the array of food that's *still* overkill, even with eight people now in this tiny house.

Nick wraps an arm around my shoulders, pressing a kiss to my cheek and speaking softly against my skin. "I think somebody is feeling the Christmas spirit."

And instead of fighting him on this, I turn to him, brushing my lips across his jaw. "I'd rather feel your Christmas spirit."

He groans. "And I'd love nothing more than to give it to you." He leaves another kiss on my head, holding me close for a second longer than necessary. It feels needy, like maybe he's searching for a little bit of comfort this Christmas too.

I get the feeling that my dad flaking out upset him. He didn't say anything, but I could see his jaw clenching, the subtle shake of his head as the story unfolded through Naomi's texts. He says he's self-conscious about not showing enough emotion, but I can't help but wonder if whoever told him that was just trying to make him feel bad. It's written so clearly across his face and in his body language.

And I can't blame him for being upset by my dad. After what he went through growing up, it probably feels like a slight for someone to have everything he always wanted and not appreciate it in the same way he would.

I mean, he looked like a little kid this morning when the presents were being handed out. Not like he was excited to necessarily *get* things, but he watched the whole tradition unfold with rapt attention, one hand always on me but his focus on what my mom and my sister were doing. And he *grinned* when he saw Hank. Something tells me this is the first time Santa's made a cameo at his Christmas.

I smile at him and he looks right back at me, a softness in his eyes that melts me from the inside out.

"Hi, Noelle." I hear the voice behind me and turn to see Naomi waving at me, a small smile on her face that melds into an awkward shrug as she looks away.

"Hi," I say, realizing I invited these girls over and we're just kind of standing around, staring at each other.

So I take a deep breath and a step forward, and wrap my arms around a teenager I only barely know.

When she hugs me back, there's a part of me that warms to her. Like her hug is an indication I've been accepted. A moment later, I reach out and tug her sister into it too.

"Thanks for coming," I tell them, giving them one last tight squeeze before letting go.

"If it's okay with you, Cassidy wanted to call... Dad," Naomi says hesitantly, as if she's unsure whether that's what she should call him.

I raise my eyebrows. "Sure, whatever you need to do."

Cassidy purses her lips. "Naomi has been calling him all morning and he–"

"He doesn't like me, so he's not answering," Naomi says.

"Naomi," Cassidy scolds.

She shrugs. "What? It's true. But we think if Cassidy calls, he'll answer. Mom has refused to try," Naomi says, glancing over her shoulder and rolling her eyes. Harriet only shrugs, my mom reaching out to squeeze her elbow.

I'm sure my mom had many similar moments, dealing with me at that age.

Cassidy pulls her phone out of her pocket and calls him while we stand in a group around her, watching the phone ring.

And he actually picks up.

"Hey honey," he starts, his words a little drawn out. I can't help but catch Christina's gaze, her eyes narrowed as she listens. "What's up?"

Cassidy is quiet for a moment, and I get the feeling she didn't actually expect him to answer the phone. She looks to Naomi for guidance, and Naomi only widens her eyes, moving her hand in a circle as if to tell her to keep going.

"We were just wondering when you'd be here for Christmas," Cassidy says, shrugging at Naomi.

Naomi gives her a thumbs up.

"Ah, I got held up at Helen's. I'll be home soon, though," he says.

I blink at Christina when I hear the slur in his voice, and mouth, "Is he drunk?"

She shrugs, and I turn to Nick for an answer. He does the same.

Naomi and Cassidy are staring at each other, neither one of them speaking.

So I take a step toward them. "Hey, Dad."

The line is silent for a moment. "Noelle?"

"The girls stopped by to say hello and were surprised to see that you are not, in fact, held up at Helen's."

He grumbles incoherently. "I mean, I'm on my way over."

"From where?" I ask.

"From... my house."

"So after telling Christina you'd be here and then ignoring her texts, and telling Cassidy and Naomi that you'd be there and then flaking out on them, too, you're telling us you've been at home alone all morning. By yourself?"

"Look, I'm doing my best here, kid. Having so many people rely on me isn't exactly an easy thing and I'm doing my best to gather up all of your Christmas presents so I can treat everybody there, okay? So if you'd do me a favor and get off my back, that'd be great."

I rear back. "No one cares about your presents. No one even cares that historically you've proven to us time and time again that we can't rely on you. All any of us wanted was for you to show up. I would love it if you learned how to take accountability for what you've done. You're the reason you have two families to supposedly support–though I'm going to conveniently forget Mom working overtime when we were in high school to pay the bills and something tells me Harriet is in a similar position. But all anyone wanted was for you to show up and participate. In whatever way you're able to." I let out a quick breath, my eyes on Naomi's.

"But you chose to drink at home alone on the holiday instead of spending it with the people who care about you despite themselves." I scoff. "And you know what? I'm not even mad. I'm just disappointed."

I swallow, the silence around my words deafening.

And then the line goes dead.

I blink, staring at the phone in Cassidy's hand. Naomi nods as Cassidy slips it back into her pocket, and then takes a step toward me, squeezing my arm in a kind way that feels far beyond her years. "You did good," she tells me.

I kind of want to laugh and cry at the same time. I finally told my Dad what's what, and he had the audacity to just... hang up on me? And an arbitrary judgment from a teenager has my heart swelling with pride?

Who am I?

Nick throws an arm around my shoulders and tugs me into his side, pressing his lips against my head.

My mom steps behind the kitchen island, grabbing a bottle of wine and pulling the cork out. "Who needs wine?" she asks.

Naomi throws her hand in the air, and I grab it and tug it down to her side. "You're twelve," I say.

"I'm literally sixteen," she says.

"Really?"

She turns to me, her eyes scanning me in a way that has me feeling incredibly self-conscious. "What are you, forty-two?"

My mouth pops open as Nick snickers into my hair. Naomi gives us a devilish grin.

I roll my eyes. "Touche, small fry."

My mom and Harriet take two large glasses of wine, and Naomi and Christina go for the cranberry-flavored sparkling water from my mom's fridge. Conversation is stilted at first as we trudge through the awkwardness, but eventually there's mild laughter, though it's not the Christmas jolliness we might expect.

"You did do good, Criminal," Nick murmurs against my ear, pressing a light kiss there.

I let out a long breath. "Apparently it wasn't enough."

"You can't change someone else. All you can do is speak your truth. And you did that. Really well."

I turn to him, pressing my chest against his as he brushes the hair out of my face.

"Even though it fell on deaf ears?" I wrap my arms around his middle and squeeze him. "It's not very rewarding when the other person doesn't listen."

He nods. "And that, Criminal, is why you're a criminal."

I roll my eyes.

"But to be fair, I think your dad is the biggest fucking asshole this town has ever seen and I hope he gets a hell of a lot worse than an egging." He shakes his head. "This is *everything*," he says, his voice breaking just a tad over the last word. "This is everything and he's too much of an asshole to appreciate it."

I smile, standing on my toes to kiss his chin. "I'm really happy you're here."

He wraps his arms tight around my neck, squeezing me as tight as he can as his breath runs across my cheek. "I promise, I will never take a moment of this for granted."

I rest my hand on his jaw, my thumb running across the stubble there. "I know."

"And one day–mark my words–your dad will pay for this."

I can't help the laugh that jumps from my throat. "Wow, okay. What are you, mafia?"

He shakes his head, chuckling quietly. "No. I just... I'm so mad at him right now. His daughter told him to just show up and he can't even do that." He sighs. "I just don't get it."

"Because you're a nice person," I say, rubbing my hand along his chest.

He rolls his eyes. "You're giving him the most basic of tasks and he can't even do that."

I shrug. "I'm pretty used to it by now."

"That makes it even worse."

I press another kiss to his cheek. "For what it's worth, your support is really validating." I press my lips together. "And now that I know you, I just want to say fuck whoever told you you don't show emotions enough. Your simmer is everything."

He blinks. "My simmer?"

I nod. "Your mild rage on my behalf. Your subtle storm. I feel really supported."

He lets out a long breath as he tugs me close for another hug.

And then through the din of the chattering around us, someone starts crying.

My first thought is Christina, and my head whips toward the last place I saw her.

But I realize it's Harriet, my mom's arm around her shoulders as she sobs over one of the Christmas cookies I painted a dick onto.

I try not to think too hard about what *that* means.

Christina moves around the island as fast as she can with her cast weighing her down, and she and my mom flank Harriet, talking in soft voices as she wipes her tears.

I glance over at the couch, where Naomi and Cassidy watch with pained expressions on their faces.

I want to cry with Harriet. Cry *for* these girls.

But instead I gently extricate myself from Nick's arms,

grab the plate of cookies, and head to the couches. Harriet probably needs a good cry, and my mom and sister are more than qualified to help her through it. The girls, however, don't need to spend their Christmas watching it.

I sit in front of the tree and hold the plate of cookies out to them. They each grab one, cocking their heads at the designs.

"Are these supposed to be Christmas ornaments?"

No, it's a ball sack. "Yeah, those little dots are the sparkles."

"Is this a rose?"

I clear my throat. *Vagina.* "Yeah, it's a rose."

"Hm. I'm surprised you didn't put a poinsettia on it."

"Maybe I'll try that next year."

I grab a handful of presents from my pile and distribute them at the girls' feet as another sob breaks from Harriet's throat. The girls whip toward her, concerned.

"Hey, who wants to open a present first?" I ask.

Naomi eyes me. "They all have your name on them."

I shrug. "I'm pretty sure they're fruit so I don't really care." You can always tell which ones are fruit because my mom always does them last, usually the night before Christmas, and they're haphazardly wrapped, with the occasional drop of wine staining the paper.

Cassidy shrugs, reaching forward and ripping one open to reveal an apple inside.

I gesture to it as if to prove my point. I vaguely register Nick ducking his head into the fridge for a drink behind them.

"Your turn," I say to Naomi, and she grabs one from the pile, ripping it open. An orange.

She cocks her head to the side. "Why do you give each other fruit?"

I shrug. "Because we pretty much buy ourselves everything we want through the year, and half the fun of Christmas is destroying the paper. My sister and I always had a ball ripping it up over Christmas, so I guess that's kind of my mom's present to us. Lots of wrapped things that we can tear into wildly."

Naomi nods. "I feel that."

I raise my eyebrows. *Okay.*

I hand them each two more presents, and they unwrap them to find a mini tube of toothpaste and another roll of toilet paper.

"Ah, we've entered into the toiletries section of today's festivities."

They giggle, resting their presents on the coffee table in front of them.

"Hope your Christmas isn't shitty," I say, parroting my mom, but the words feel much more relevant now. Naomi dissolves into laughter, leaning back into the couch and crashing into Cassidy, who laughs but not quite as exuberantly.

I only vaguely register the sound of the front door shutting. A car coming to life in the driveway.

I glance around, searching for Nick, and realize he's gone.

My stomach churns as I reach for my phone and text him.

NOELLE

Did you leave? Are you okay?

He starts typing back almost immediately.

SAINT NICK

All is good. Just have to take care of
something real quick. I'll be back soon.

He starts typing again. And then stops. And starts again.

SAINT NICK

I can't even tell you how happy I am to be
spending Christmas with you and your
family. I'll be back as soon as I can.

I let out a long sigh, turning my attention back to the girls, who are thankfully now tearing into the piles at their feet without any prompting. Behind them, Harriet's tears are subsiding as Christina pours her an oversized glass of wine and holds it to her lips like she'd feeding a baby with a bottle.

Another Christmas, another drama-fest.

Christmases in the past haven't been quite *this* wild, but I'm relieved that for once, it's not Christina crying into her drink.

Naomi and Cassidy bounce off each other, their moods rising as they unwrap one downright hilarious present after another.

I can't help but think back to what Christina said the other day, that my shitty dad and a bad high school experience is what led me to run away, to be angry enough to throw eggs at his house, and ultimately led me to Nick.

I hate thinking about things that way–everything is meant for a reason, *blah blah blah*–but there's something begrudgingly nice about this. Having two teenagers around to unwrap presents and cackle over the crazy things my mom has decided to give us for the holiday.

I hate everything that led us here. I hate that Harriet is

crying and my half-sisters are as angry as I am. I hate that my sister's leg is broken and my mom is tending to a crying woman instead of her new beau.

But this, I don't hate. Sitting in front of the tree with family I didn't really choose, but I *did*, in some roundabout way.

When all is said and done, I might even admit to appreciating this holiday.

Chaos included.

WHEN HARRIET'S tears have subsided, the seven of us gather around the Christmas tree, distributing out presents haphazardly because half of them are now going to people whose names are not the ones scribbled into the wrapping paper.

As my mom lands on one with Nick's name, she glances around, realizing he's gone. She looks at me, brow furrowed. "Where's Nick?"

I swallow. "He said he had to take care of something."

Her eyes narrow. "On Christmas?"

I shrug.

Hank sighs. "Fuck."

My mom glances at him as he scrambles up from the floor, slapping his thighs and grabbing his keys from the hook by the door. "I'll be right back."

"Where are *you* going?" Helen asks.

He shakes his head. "Don't you worry about me. You girls do your best to enjoy the rest of Christmas. I'll be back soon."

Before he can leave, I run after him.

"Hank!" He stops, eyebrows raised as he twirls his keys around one finger. "Do you know where Nick is?"

He nods. "I've got a good idea. Turns out the two of you aren't all that different."

"Are you going to go get him?"

He shrugs. "Something like that."

"Okay, I'll come with you."

He shakes his head, resolute. "No. Noelle, you go spend Christmas with your family." He points behind me into the living room, where my mom and Harriet hesitantly laugh at something Naomi said. "I promise, we'll both be back soon."

"You think he's okay?"

Hank nods. "My guess is he's just fine."

He puts his hands on my shoulders and shoves me gently back toward the rest of the women. "Go, Noelle. We'll be back soon."

"Okay."

22

NICK

Wednesday, December 25th

I stare at the Goldmans' old house, fixated on the first floor window with the light on. Every once in a while, the shadow of a man passes in front of it, a beer in one hand.

It makes my blood boil. My hair stand on end. My fists clench.

It makes me feel all sorts of emotions that Noelle picks up on so clearly.

When she said that to me, it was a lightbulb moment in my head. This whole time, I've been worried that my emotions wouldn't be enough for her. That she'd leave just like Emily left, all the while telling me she wants more *passion* from me. That she wants me to *fight* for her.

Well, here's my fight.

Turns out it's easy when someone slights the one you love.

He's home alone, as far as I can tell, drinking by himself on Christmas instead of hanging out with the amazing group of women who are so willing to forgive him despite his shortcomings.

I'd be so lucky to have what he has.

And because I don't want to waste another moment away from them, I open the carton of eggs in my hand and take one out, throwing it gently into the air and catching it without breaking it.

This is the path Noelle took when she was angry.

Today, we're going to see if it truly is as cathartic as she said it was.

I chuck it at the house, feeling an immense rush of pleasure at the light cracking noise it makes against the front door.

The silhouette in the window pauses, and then takes a step closer. I can only imagine he's peering out, trying to determine what that noise was.

I chuck another egg, this time at that exact window, and see the figure rear back.

I throw another one at the front door before he storms through the house, flinging it open and screaming out at me.

"Hey man, I don't know what the fuck you're doing but you can knock it right off!"

I take another egg out, throwing it gently into the air again, and lob it at one of the second floor windows.

Good luck cleaning that, jackass.

"Hey, what the fuck?" he says, storming out further.

When he's only a few feet away from me, beer bottle dangling from between his fingers, he pauses. "Wait, are you the guy who's dating my daughter? I fucking *knew* you were bad news."

I scoff, taking another egg out and throwing it at the

front door. "Yeah, *I'm* bad news. I'm a fucking math teacher, dude."

He points at me, his beer bottle sloshing as he does. "Get the fuck off my property."

"Not until I've thrown all dozen eggs."

He shakes his head as he rushes toward me, but I hold them out of reach before he can grab them.

As I take another and attempt to throw it at the front door, he moves in just the right way that, instead, it hits him right on the forehead.

His eyes are wild when he fixes them on me.

And for the first time, I wonder if I made the wrong decision.

He charges at me, and in my state of surprise, I don't manage to move out of the way before his fist connects with my eye.

I see stars as I stumble backward, holding the eggs to my chest.

And then I realize it's not stars I'm seeing, but the red and blue lights of a police cruiser. It lets out a *whoop whoop* as it pulls gently out from behind an oversized van parked along the curb.

"Fuuuuuuck," Noelle's dad shouts, chugging the rest of his beer as the cruiser slowly moves toward us, turning at the last second so we have a clear view of Hank pushing the door open and stepping out, Santa suit and all.

"Back of the fucking car, Tom," Hank barks, opening it for him.

He throws the empty bottle onto the ground with a dramatic shatter and trudges over, tucking himself into the backseat while cursing both of us out.

Hank stalks toward me, hands on his hips. "Are you

gonna go ahead and finish off those eggs? Or are you going to take that punch for nothing?"

I don't hesitate. One by one, I hit each of his windows and the door a couple more times, too.

Hank sighs when I'm done and claps a hand on my shoulder. "Come on, let's get you back to the girls. Noelle is worried about you. And it's probably best to get you back there before that eye of yours gets any worse."

My hand flies up to my face, and as my fingers brush over the skin below my eye, I flinch.

"Yeah, you're gonna be looking real pretty for a couple weeks."

I swallow. "So I'm not in trouble?"

He sighs. "Look, I'll deal with you later. For now, let's get you back to Christmas."

Back to Christmas. Back to Noelle.

I can feel my eye swelling as I turn toward my car, and when I try to open it and pinch it closed again, my contact pops right out of my eye and falls to the ground.

Probably for the best, if it's only going to get worse.

But driving with one eye when it's starting to get dark out feels like a recipe for disaster.

"Uh, Hank? Could I possibly get a ride? I don't think I can see well enough to drive."

He lets out a long sigh. "Yeah. Hop in."

I get in the passenger side and spend an incredibly awkward ten minutes of silence with Hank and Noelle's dad until we finally reach the police station and Hank walks him inside. They're only gone for a few minutes before Hank comes out again, a certain lightness in his step.

He grins when he gets back in the car.

"What's got you so happy?"

He shrugs. "My girl Shelly is working the front desk, and

if there's one thing she hates more than crime, it's crime committed on a holiday. Tom is gonna be in for a long night, I can promise you that."

I can't help the laugh that escapes me.

"Alright, let's get you back to the girls," Hank says, turning the car on and directing us back to Helen's.

When I initially left with a carton of eggs in my hand, I felt it was my duty to tell Noelle's dad to fuck right off.

But now that I'm on my way back, I feel silly.

I left *Christmas* to enact my revenge on somebody who didn't even do *me* wrong.

But maybe that's the catharsis Noelle was talking about, big emotions evaporating with every egg thrown.

By the time Hank pulls in the driveway, I decide to ditch my second contact too, because I already have a headache. Whether it's from getting punched or being visually impaired, I'll never know.

I lean my head back against the headrest, trying to build up the courage to go in there and explain what the fuck happened that has me showing up with a black eye.

"Come on, Nick. Rip the Band-Aid off," Hank says, sensing my discomfort.

"This is going to be terrible."

"Only gets worse the longer you push it off." He pushes his door open and steps out. "Let's go!"

I begrudgingly follow him up the path to the front door. He pushes inside comfortably, like this is something he does all the time, and leaves his keys on the rack by the door. I follow him back into the living room, where six smiling faces drop at the sight of my eye.

"Nick!" Noelle's voice cuts through everyone else's. She's up in an instant, climbing over ripped open presents and her mom in between us. "What happened?" Her hands are on my chin, turning my face back and forth with strong fingers. Her brow is furrowed, her eyes wide with concern.

And I wrap my arms around her, squeezing her tight and breathing in that chocolate rose scent of hers that's become my *favorite* scent.

She squeezes me back, sensing my need for it.

"I'm sorry," I whisper into the skin of her neck, as everyone follows her over, face pinched in concern as they spread in a semicircle around us.

"For what?"

I swallow, lifting my head to look at her. She shakes her head, almost imperceptibly as she waits for me to answer.

Hank, apparently, is sick of waiting for the story to come out. "I picked up your boyfriend with a carton of eggs outside your dad's house."

I watch her expression carefully. She blinks, a grin slowly spreading across her face as she turns to Hank. "I'm sorry, what?"

"Apparently you're a bad influence," Hank tells her. "Here I was hoping it would work the other way around."

Noelle presses her lips together, trying her hardest to contain her laughter. She turns to me, her thumb brushing across my cheek lightly so she doesn't hurt me. "Why were you throwing eggs at my dad's house?"

I bite my lip before speaking. "Because he pissed me off. He's got a room full of good women who are willing to forgive him for any slight. To accept him for the sake of having family around at Christmas, and that asshole was in his shitty old house, drinking alone. When he could have *this*, just by showing up."

"Aw, Nick," Noelle says, wrapping an arm around my waist and pressing a light kiss to my cheek.

I shake my head. "I know that what I did was wrong

and stupid and ridiculous, but how dare he? *How dare he* see this and not recognize how lucky he is? I would have *killed* for this growing up. Especially after my mom died. And he can't even fucking show up. Fuck that guy. I hate him." And then I realize I'm in a room with people who love him, regardless. "I'm sorry. I know he's family and that things are complicated. I'm sure he's still a good dad sometimes. But today, he wasn't. And I will stand by that."

And then I tell myself that I need to *stop talking*.

Because everyone is staring at me. I have to squint to see their expressions and I probably look like a psychopath with my rapidly swelling eye. Christina has a slight smile on her face, and Naomi is grinning like the Cheshire cat. Noelle presses herself into me, her hands running soothingly across my back.

And apparently I *can't* shut up. "And I hate that he's part of the reason you hate this town. It's not fair that he's the one who fucked up but I'm the one who suffers for it."

"*You're* the one who suffers for it?"

I look at the ceiling through blurry eyes. "You don't want to be here. And that's *my* loss. Not his."

"Nick," she says. "I'll find a way to be here."

"What does that even mean? We'll take turns visiting each other on weekends? Every other Friday you'll work remotely and come an extra day? That's not good enough for me. I want more and I hate that it's on the tip of my fingers and I can't reach out and take it." My fingers dig into her skin like the harder I hold on, the more likely it is she'll stay.

She rests a hand on my chest. "I will be here," she says, her voice sure. "I promise you, right now, I'll be here. I'll figure out how to work remotely more often. I'll give up my apartment and move closer." She stands on her toes to kiss me, and it's all I can do to *hold on* to her.

She lowers her voice when she speaks again, her words only for me. "I want more, too. I want you. And I promise you that I will always let my love for you guide me rather than my hatred for him."

She's not saying she *loves* me, but she *is* saying that she's open to it. That I matter more than her experience here.

And I think there was a part of me that really needed to hear that, because my breath comes whooshing out of my chest like I've been holding onto it for the last few weeks.

"Noelle," I breathe, wrapping her tight in my arms and closing my eyes, my cheek pressed against her head.

"It's a Christmas miracle," Hank says, breaking the silence around us.

"Gross," Naomi mutters, as she turns on her heel and heads back to the couch.

Noelle leans away from me, running her thumb along my cheek again. "Who woulda thunk, a month ago when I started my community service, that we'd end up here?"

I see movement over her shoulder and squint in that direction.

And if I'm not mistaken, Hank winks at me.

Santa, indeed.

23

NOELLE

Wednesday, December 25th

We get Nick set up on the couch with a bag of frozen peas over his eye and continue Christmas where we left off. With the commotion of the day, my mom didn't have time to prepare her usual dinner, so she puts out the easy dishes–anything that she can microwave or throw in the stove for half an hour– and we put in an order at our favorite Chinese takeout place and fill the coffee table with food and drinks and the presents that we still haven't gotten through.

I sit on the floor in front of the couch, where Nick has his head tipped back so he doesn't have to hold the peas on his face.

While Naomi and Cassidy fight over who gets the surprisingly obscene apple my mom originally wrapped for Christina, I stand and lean over him so I can talk to him without drawing attention.

"We don't have to stay if you're in pain. I think we have

more than a good enough excuse to head out early if you want," I say, running my hand through his hair.

He shakes his head violently, holding onto the peas so they don't fly off his face. "No way. It's *Christmas*. I'm not leaving because of a black eye. You're going to have to try harder than that if you want to leave early."

I laugh, patting his knee and resuming my spot at his foot. "Well, at least we know that punch didn't break your Christmas spirit."

He pats along my arm until he can find my head, and runs his fingers through my hair. I rest my head on his leg, content to let him pet me until he's ready to go home.

Hank has offered to drive anyone and everyone home, if need be. Harriet has had more than her fair share of wine, and graciously accepted the offer so she could have another glass with my mom. Christina will be staying here for the night, though that plan didn't deter her from asking if Nick has a spare room because she'd rather hear *us* than *Mom*. I only raised an eyebrow at her and asked if she was sure about that, and she quickly swallowed her words, shaking her head.

We split our food family-style, filling up plates and passing containers and making the most of a holiday that turned out nothing like we expected but better than we could have imagined.

When our food is done and our presents have been distributed out somewhat evenly between all of us, Hank herds Harriet, Naomi, and Cassidy into his car to take them home, leaving the four of us sitting around a messy Christmas coffee table.

My mom brings over a trash bag that she hands to Christina to hold while we throw things in—wrapping paper, food containers, a few pieces of fruit that got squished in the Santa sack.

"How are you doing, Christina?" I ask her, knowing that while the rest of us roll with the punches, she's usually the one who ends up in tears over the holidays.

And she's been suspiciously level-headed.

She sighs, grabbing a piece of wrapping paper from the floor by her feet and shoving it in the trash bag. "I'm fine. I think I'm just a little disappointed, too."

"That's all?"

My mom gives me a look as if to tell me not to poke the bear.

She shrugs. "If I'm being honest, Thanksgiving kind of ruined any idea of what I thought this family could be. I mean, I'm willing to forgive and forget, but the other person has to *try*, you know? And I never felt like he was sorry about not being there for me."

I nod. "So why even try for Christmas?"

She lets out a long breath. "Well, to be honest, I was trying to train him like a dog."

Nick's head snaps up from where he had been resting it on the back of the couch, a laugh slipping from his throat. "Did I hear that right?"

"You were trying to train him like a dog?" my mom asks, her hand frozen in midair with a half-squished orange.

"Well, yeah. I mean, every year there's so much tension, you know? Even when we do see him, albeit accidentally, it doesn't exactly create this warm, welcoming environment. Thanksgiving taught me that he's not the person I wanted him to be. So, I guess I thought I could Pavlov him into thinking it's always a fun, happy time when he sees us. Like we're so thrilled to see him and he's doing such a good job. I thought maybe that might convince him to show up a little more, and showing up is the first building block to a good relationship." She sighs. "And he couldn't even do that."

My mom rests a hand on her shoulder. "I'm sorry, honey."

Christina shrugs. "Honestly, I told myself that I would give it one more try. I'm okay with being the person in this family that holds out. That gives a little more than she should. I *like* that that's who I am. But I told myself after carting this fucking cast around for the past few weeks that it's not worth it unless he can give a little extra, too." She presses her lips together. "Honestly, I think I'm disappointed about *not* being disappointed. We're a small family, but a happy one. And I think that's what matters."

My mom leans down to kiss her cheek. "Amen, honey."

"How was it, talking to Harriet?" Christina asks her.

She shoves another balled up piece of wrapping paper into the trash bag. "To be honest, it was kind of validating. I hate that she's going through the same thing I went through—I mean, it's a little different because he left me for *her*—but the feelings of self-doubt are the same. The overwhelm of having two teenagers to take care of. The fear of being a sole provider and a mom but also a friend as her girls get older." She throws one of the food containers into the bag. "I feel for her. But I'm also kind of proud of myself. It was like a mirror straight back into the past, and you know what? I did it."

"Aw, Mom," I say. "You did it *great*."

She rolls her eyes. "I wouldn't say I always did it great, but I now have two grown-up daughters who seem to be doing alright for themselves. I will take that as a win."

"And you have a Hank," Christina says.

My mom blushes. "And a Hank."

"Do you love him?" Christina asks, a grin spreading

across her face.

She shoots my sister a look. "It's new, okay?"

"New and fucking ancient," I interject. "Hanky Panky."

She lets out a long breath, her eyes flitting up to the ceiling. "We're seeing how things go. Hank is a very nice man."

I stop my cleanup to give her a quick hug. "Happy for you, Mom."

She throws an arm around my shoulders, giving me a quick kiss on the cheek. "Happy for you too, sweetie. Even though yours is broken."

We snicker as Nick lifts his head, his visible eyebrow raised. "Not broken. Just wanted a reason for Noelle to baby me for a few weeks."

I snort. "Um, have you met me?"

He gives me a big grin. "Yes. And I happen to know that underneath that prickly exterior, you've got quite a big heart."

And now it's my turn to blush.

"Aw, Noelle!" Christina shouts.

I crinkle my nose. "Stop. I hate Christmas. I hate joy. Take it all back."

My mom and sister cackle as Nick grabs my hand, tugging me down into the couch next to him and throwing his arm around my shoulders. He lowers the bag of peas from his eye for only a moment as he leans forward to kiss my cheek, and I get an unobstructed view of the puffy, bruised eye underneath.

I must visibly grimace because Nick's mouth tugs to one side in a frown. "It's that bad?"

I nod, grabbing his hand to place the peas back where they were. "Just keep that there, okay?"

He groans. "Fuck. What am I going to tell my kids?"

"Tell them you got in a fight with a goose. Good precautionary tale–I've heard they're psycho."

He shakes his head, letting out a long breath. "I'll have to think of something before school starts up again. Although I don't know, maybe it'll even be gone by then?"

I accidentally catch the gaze of my mom, whose eyebrows are raised as if to say, *Yeah, you wish*.

"Maybe it'll be gone by then," I repeat, even if it only gives him a few days of relief.

If it's not, I guess we'll be matching him with some drugstore cover up.

He nods, relaxing further into the couch as a car door shuts somewhere outside.

"Must be Hank," my mom says, dropping the wrapping paper in her hand and rushing off to greet him.

I catch Christina's eye, and she wiggles her eyebrows at me.

"You make that face now, but might I remind you you're sharing a wall with them tonight."

"Oh, Noelle!" She grabs the closest bit of wrapping paper and chucks it at me, but instead it brushes over Nick's chest and lands on the other side of us.

"Hey! I'm broken!"

I snort. "Two minutes ago, you insisted you *weren't*."

"Well, I'm broken now. Take pity on me. I think a kiss will make it better."

Christina rolls her eyes as she reaches for more of the containers on the coffee table. "Definitely not broken."

Hank and my mom enter the living room a minute later. He's abandoned the hat and the beard, but he still has his red velvet jacket and matching pants on. He smiles when he sees us. "Got the girls back home in one piece. I'll pick up Harriet tomorrow and bring her back for her car." He turns to Nick and me. "You kids ready to go? Want me to take you to pick up your car, or you want to go straight home?"

I look at Nick for an answer. "Home," he says, and turns to me. "If you don't mind driving me over tomorrow to pick it up?"

"Fine by me," I say, as we gather up the bags my mom separated for us. We leave with a round of hugs and kisses and well wishes for Nick, and when we fall into Hank's cruiser, I get two matching grins in the rearview mirror.

"In your rightful place, huh?" Nick asks, as I shoot him a glare.

"I've done my time," I tell him. "You, sir, have not."

He glances sideways at Hank. "Yeah, don't tell him that."

Hank only shakes his head as he pulls out of the driveway and heads toward Nick's. "It's Christmas, and I'm not about to come between two good people who happen to make bad decisions on occasion." He turns onto the main street. "But if I catch either of you throwing eggs again, it won't be the same story, you hear?"

I nod. "I hear."

"I hear," Nick repeats.

"Good."

WHEN WE GET INSIDE, we leave our bags of presents by the Christmas tree and head upstairs. He peels off his shirt and his pants and sits down in bed, still holding the somewhat soggy peas over his eye. I run downstairs and grab an ice pack from the freezer and a headband from my duffel bag so he doesn't have to hold it against his head the whole time, and when I get upstairs, I crawl into his lap and place it right over his eye.

"There. Is that better?" I ask.

He nods, his hands running along my thighs. When I go to get up, he groans. "Wait, now it hurts."

I sit again, adjusting it slightly on his face. "Good?"

He nods. "Better."

But when I go to get up again, the same thing happens.

"You just want me to straddle you, don't you?"

He shrugs. "Pain is pain, Noelle. It hurts when you're not sitting on me. I don't know what to tell you."

I run my thumbs along the underside of his jaw, and he hums in response.

"I would like to get changed for bed if you can deal with the pain for a few more minutes. And maybe we can watch a Christmas movie or something? It's still early."

He grins, his fingers digging into my hips. "You want to watch a Christmas movie with me?"

I roll my eyes. "Well, only if *you* want to. Since you're broken and all."

"My little Christmas elf strikes again," he says, his thumbs digging into my hips in a way that has a heat building in my core. I jump off his lap before my hips start moving on their own.

"I'll be right back," I tell him.

I bound down the stairs to grab the *I heart math* shirt he gave me, and I quickly strip down once I get back upstairs, throwing my dirty clothes into a pile by the door.

"Whoa, whoa, whoa," he says, as I tug my sweater over my head. "Slower! For Christ's sake, I'm working with one half-functioning eye here."

"I'm not stripping *for you*," I tell him.

"Damn straight you are," he counters, and the confidence in his words makes me immediately change my position. *Yeah alright, I'll strip for you.*

I take a step toward him and turn so he gets a full view of my ass as I push my leggings down over my hips. He reaches out and grabs me, palming me as I slowly stand again. "Mm, I like that," he says, his voice low as his thumb trails along my underwear.

I kick my pants off and throw one leg over his lap, seating myself right on top of his dick.

"I like the sexy stripper Christmas elf," he says, holding onto my hips as he says it because he knows I'm going to try to remove myself.

"I am none of those things!"

He grins. "Maybe for me? I'm so broken. Give me something to live for."

I roll my eyes. "Fine. Considering my dad punched you in the eye, it's probably the least I can do, huh?"

"Yeah, I'm sure that's not the outcome he was intending."

I laugh, and as his hands squeeze at my hips and run along my sides, I reach behind me and pinch the clasp of my bra, shrugging it off and tossing it to the ground. "Is this what you had in mind?" I ask, as I lean forward and press a light kiss to his jaw. My nipples brush against his chest with the movement, and we both shiver.

He takes a strangled breath. "Fuck, Noelle."

I swirl my hips, feeling him growing hard underneath me, and he grabs them, pressing down.

His hands run up my back, wrapping around me and tugging me against his chest. Careful to avoid the ice, I wrap my arms around his neck. I sigh, my breasts pressing against him as he rubs my back.

"Thank you, Noelle," he whispers.

"Tips are appreciated," I joke, and he lets out a breathy laugh into my shoulder before pulling away from me.

I sit up straight, and he runs his fingers through my hair,

brushing a strand behind my ear. "Thank you for today. It was the Christmas I never thought I could have."

I can't help but snort. "I really thought I could show you a fun Christmas, at least. And instead I showed you a shit show from beginning to end. So, sorry. But I'm glad to hear you enjoyed it."

He shakes his head. "It's not what you do or what happens that matters. It's the people. It's coming together and taking part in silly traditions even if it means the criminal of the family decides to decorate all of your cookies with genitalia."

I grin, proud of my artwork. "And I even passed off the balls as Christmas ornaments and the vagina as a rose when Naomi and Cassidy asked."

He rolls his eyes. "Very impressive."

I lean forward and kiss him. "I'm really happy you came."

He takes a deep breath, his free eye skirting over my body as his hands brush over my skin. He takes in a breath like he's going to speak, but decides against it.

I raise my eyebrows, my hands running across his chest. "What?"

He shakes his head. "It's dumb."

"Tell me."

He purses his lips. "Did you mean what you said? That thing about your love for me outweighing your hatred for your dad?"

My breath catches. I said it in a moment of emotion, but it wasn't untrue. As much as I want to say it's too soon, I know that what I feel for Nick is stronger than infatuation. I'm not about to move in and stop taking birth control, but with feelings like this, I need to give this thing between us space to grow into what I know it can be.

I nod, momentarily forgetting how to speak. My words

come out breathy and unsure as I say them. "I love you, Nick. And I'm going to make some moves so that I can be here in this stupid town, and love you as hard as I can."

"You're not saying that because it's Christmas and I took a punch from your dad?"

I laugh, shaking my head. "I don't know what the future looks like, but I know I want to do it with you."

He looks me in the eye when he speaks, no hint of a doubt in his words. "I love you, Noelle. I love your family. I love the prickly girl you show the world on the outside and the one that loves so fully on the inside. I love your brain and your snark, and there's nothing I want more than to have you in my house, in my bed, in my heart."

He lets out a long breath when he's done, and smiles at me as if to tell me that's the last of his monologue.

I can't help the grin that comes to my face, and he mirrors it right back to me.

"So why don't you stand up and put on a little show for the one you love."

I raise my eyebrows. "I literally only have my underwear to take off."

"Then I guess you better put some extra sexy into it."

I roll my eyes and slowly extricate myself from his lap. I stand, looping my thumbs in my thong, and shake my ass a little bit in his face. He slaps it, giving me a quick squeeze, and I slowly–*so slowly*–drag my underwear down my thighs, bending as I take them all the way to the ground.

"Fuck, Noelle," he says, palming one cheek. He runs his thumb along my center and I shiver at the touch. He groans as he presses his thumb into his mouth, tasting me. "Look how wet you are for me." He slaps my ass and runs his hand over the area, soothing the sting. "Now come sit in my lap and tell me what you want."

"Oh god," I say, rolling my eyes as I stand. "You did not just say that."

He shrugs. "Are you going to be naughty, or nice?"

I can't help but grin at him as I throw one leg over him. I reach below me–aware of the way his eyes are glued to my tits as they squeeze between my arms–and tug his underwear down, exposing him. I take him in my hand and pump him a few times as he groans, tipping his head back against the headboard.

"Oh, she's been a good girl this year," he murmurs, his hand drifting up my side and squeezing my breast.

"So you're going to give me what I want, then?"

He nods quickly, his breathing going ragged the longer I pump him. "*Anything* you want."

I lean forward, leaving a delicate kiss and a quick nip to the underside of his jaw. "I want you, Saint Nick."

I lift up, running his dick along my entrance and coating it with me before sinking down onto him, taking him fully. I moan as he thumbs my nipple, as he grabs the back of my neck and tugs me in for a rough kiss, his tongue winding into my mouth and tangling with mine.

I move my hips slowly, adjusting to the width of him inside me. He urges me faster, and I build us up to an indulgent rhythm that has his muscles fluttering underneath my touch, his hips bucking up into mine.

"Fuck, Noelle," he murmurs, his face tipping up to the ceiling as the tension pools in my abdomen.

My nails dig into the skin of his shoulders as my orgasm builds.

And as my movements become jerky, my orgasm reaching its tipping point and sending me over the edge, he pinches my nipple lightly, his groan reverberating throughout his entire body.

"Yes," he says, his voice a low grumble. I cry out as the pressure releases, and he holds me tight, pressing my cheek against his chest and brushing his lips across my ear. "I love the way your pussy flutters around my cock when you come."

"Oh god," I mumble, the last wave flowing through me and leaving me breathless.

"Mm," he says, slapping my ass. "You good, Noelle?"

I nod into his shoulder.

His hips move against me, anxious for his release. "Are you ready to hang onto the headboard for your damn life?" I nod exuberantly as he slaps my ass again. "Get up. Turn around."

With shaky legs, I do as he says, gripping the headboard with white knuckles and sticking my ass out for him.

He groans, running a thumb through my center and sending a quick shiver down my spine. It trails along the crease of my ass and pulls at my skin, spreading me for him. "Most beautiful pussy I've seen in my life," he says with another sharp slap to my ass that has me crying out.

He removes his ice pack, dropping it onto the bed next to us.

"Is that a good idea?" I ask, taking a quick look behind me. His hands move to my head, spinning my gaze forward again.

"That's not for you to worry about right now," he says. "You think about a second orgasm, okay?"

He presses into me again, as deep as he can, and lets out a string of expletives as his hips rock easily into mine. His fingers run along my spine, coming down to cup my ass and running up to tug on my hair.

"How's that feel, good girl?" he asks.

"Real. Ly. Fuck. Ing. Good," I say, as he tugs my head back

and pounds into me hard enough that I can barely get words out.

"Mm. You tell me if you want something different, okay?"

I nod. "Keep. Fuck. Ing. Me. Please."

He groans. "Your wish is my command."

He pounds into me harder, and my second orgasm builds like lightning in my abdomen, sharp and powerful and overwhelming.

I cry out as I lose control, my body clenching in his arms as he thrusts into me repeatedly, his rhythm pushing me right over the edge.

"Nick," I pant.

"I know. I'm coming right after you," he says, as the dam breaks and I turn to complete mush underneath him. His breathing heavy, he jerks into me hard, his grunts filling my ears as he layers himself on top of me, one arm clenched around my stomach and holding me in place.

"Fuck," he murmurs, his lips leaving rough little kisses along my shoulder blade as his thrusts become choppy and strained. And as I feel the warmth inside me, I reach behind me, resting one hand on his neck and keeping him close.

He holds me tight as our movements slow, his breath loud in my ear. He leaves a kiss there and slowly straightens, his hands running up and down my back so gently. He pulls out of me slowly, shaking his head as he struggles to catch his breath.

"Goddamn, Noelle." He sits back on his heels, one hand trailing up and down my thigh.

I can't move. I'm somewhere between numb and nerve damage.

And then I feel a trickle of warmth run down my thigh.

"Fuck me, that's hot," he says, running his thumb through it and following the trail back up. He presses his thumb briefly inside me as if to put it back where it came from, and it sends a little shiver down my spine. He slaps my ass again. "Naughty Noelle looks so fucking good with my come dripping out of her."

I groan as I straighten and another drop descends. "I have to go clean myself up."

"Let me do it," he says, and I only look at the surely sensitive skin of his face and raise my eyebrows.

"You're going to clean me up?"

He nods. "Come shower with me. I can soap you up, soap you down. Maybe give you a little massage."

I raise my eyebrows. "Yeah?"

"I love you, Noelle. Of course."

I don't know why his words hit my chest in the violent way that they do, but I feel them viscerally. *He wants to take care of me.* And it gives me this warm feeling like whatever I have to do to make *us* work will be worth it.

He follows me into the bathroom and starts the water, leaving little kisses along every bare inch of skin he can find. And once we're inside, he lathers me up with shampoo and gives me a scalp massage. Rubs body wash all over me and makes good on his promise to massage me. He gives me wet kisses whenever his hands aren't on my body, and afterward he rubs a towel all over me and pulls the pink *I heart math* T-shirt over my head.

And I take that ice pack and affix it to his head again because his eye looks absolutely terrible.

We settle in bed, and he picks the Christmas movie, me warm and cozy in the nook of his arm. I grow sleepy almost immediately, and with every minute that passes, curl tighter into him.

He leaves a kiss on my forehead, and before I finally drift off to sleep, he whispers softly, "I love you, Noelle."

24

NICK

Five Weeks Later

I wake to Noelle's hair strangling me. She's snoring softly on her side, her nose twitching in her sleep, and I weave an arm around her waist, tugging her back into me as I struggle to arrange her hair in some way that allows me to breathe. Early morning sun shines through the windows of my bedroom, giving her skin a warm glow.

I press my face into the back of her neck, savoring the moment. I've started doing that a lot lately.

Noelle is transitioning into an apartment about half an hour from Snow Falls. She still gets frazzled on occasion when she can't grab her things and run into the office, but she's getting used to the distance. Dare I say, enjoying that she's not always so available to other people. She officially broke her lease last week, and although she still has a lot of unboxing to do, she is officially closer.

Not close enough for me, but that will come in time.

Over the past few weeks, she's slept here more than she hasn't. The first few weeks she had the excuse of a long drive between here and her old apartment, but once she got the new one, nothing really changed.

I'm not going to goad her about it yet and risk her leaving just to prove a point. As frequently as she tells me she loves me, I know better than to give that girl a challenge.

So instead, I relish in these moments. Having her here with me and hearing her gentle snoring.

She twists toward me, as if she can hear my thoughts, her eyes blinking open as her hands drift across my chest.

"Why are you awake?" she asks.

"Because your hair was attacking me."

Her brow furrows. "No, it wasn't. *You* were attacking *it*. Stand down, Nick."

I roll my eyes, pressing a kiss to her forehead as she grumbles about being awake before dawn.

It's *after* dawn, but I don't tell her that. Noelle is crabby in the morning before her coffee and best left unprovoked.

"You're right," I say, running my fingers through her hair. "That was all me."

She turns onto her back to grab her phone from the nightstand, her *I heart math* T-shirt stretching across her chest in a way that makes my mouth water. "Ugh. It's not even worth closing my eyes again," she says, throwing the covers back and swinging her legs over the side of her bed. When she throws her arms above her head to stretch, it pulls her T-shirt up enough to expose her perfect ass underneath.

Fuck me, it somehow keeps getting nicer.

I swallow, willing the boner away. We fucked three times last night to celebrate her new apartment, and she has a big day ahead of her. I need to keep my hands to myself.

At least until tonight. Then all bets are off.

When Noelle started planning for her move closer to

Snow Falls, Hank quickly devised a plan to get Noelle to teach a web design class at the library. She was hesitant at first, but he wore her down over time by ordering food from her favorite places whenever she stopped by her mom's.

Eventually, she came back to my house one night and threw her hands in the air. "Hank fucking won, okay? He fucking won," she told me, before explaining to me that she didn't even know how he did it because one moment, she was eating pad thai, and the next she was exuberantly agreeing to teach a bunch of people who don't want to learn how to make websites, how to make websites.

I didn't have the heart to tell her that it's common knowledge in her family that if you're trying to get Noelle to do something she doesn't want to do, you give her something she really wants to eat.

Noelle pads into the bathroom, and a moment later the shower starts. She's heading over to the library early today to make sure everything is set up in the way she needs it.

And half an hour later, she emerges like the spritely goddess she is. She's wearing the *I heart web design* T-shirt I got her after she agreed to the class with a pair of jeans that hug her curves in all the right ways.

She leans over to kiss me, her wet hair dragging across my chest. "I'll see you there?"

I nod. "Let me know if you need anything once you're there."

"Thank you, Saint Nick."

"Anything for you," I say, my fingers brushing the underside of her chin as she presses her lips to mine.

She lets out a long breath as she heads to the door and rests one hand on the frame. "Well, wish me good luck. Or a quick death. I'll take either right now."

"Good luck, Criminal."

She rolls her eyes at me. "*You're* the criminal, here."

I shrug. "Yeah, but the nickname suits you better."

She shakes her head. "Bye!"

"Love you," I shout, as she turns and heads down the hallway.

"Love you, too!" she calls back. And a few moments later, the front door shuts behind her.

I'm meeting her there closer to the start of her class, so I take my time getting ready. She's about an hour early, so I shower and throw on a matching *I heart math* T-shirt, and make her a quick breakfast of eggs–because that's a running joke at this point–and the microwave mini sausages she loves so much.

By the time I get in my car to leave, there's a text from Noelle on my phone complaining that the library promised her an assistant but told the assistant to be there at start time–and what good does that do if all the setup needs to be done *before* the class starts?

Whoopsie.

I punch the gas to get there as quickly as possible, but when I arrive a few minutes later, Noelle seems calm and collected. Christina, Naomi and Cassidy are in the front row, standing behind three computers, and they chat easily like the close sisters they've become. Christina's in a different cast now–one that she takes on and off as the muscle in her leg builds up–and all four of them wave to me as I dart to Noelle's side with her breakfast. Behind me, a few attendees I don't recognize filter into the room, picking out computers and settling in their seats.

Her eyebrows jump up. "Oh, Nick. Thank you." I grin as she opens the lid and starts picking. "Oh man, I needed this. I was feeling grumbly this morning."

"You always are, in the morning."

She gives me a look that has Naomi and Cassidy snickering.

"What can I help with?" I ask. "You sounded panicked in your text."

She shakes her head, waving me off. "No, that was me being dumb. I happened to sit down at the one broken computer and I thought all of them were going to be like that. I took the chair away from it and left a note that it shouldn't be used. And honestly, the fact that they're even providing help for this is a godsend. Just somebody to close the door and make sure everybody is following along as needed? That's more than helpful."

I nod as Hank and Helen walk through the door and wave, Helen's face lighting up when she sees Noelle in the front of the classroom.

"Oh boy," she mutters, as she goes to greet them.

I follow her over, completely unsurprised to see their hands joined between them. Hank and Helen have been an official item since Christmas–to Christina's horror, having shared a wall with them–and they do new love better than the teenagers do. Always holding hands and shooting each other wistful gazes. He holds open every door for her, and she gazes at him like he hung the moon.

"Noelle!" Helen croons, immediately wrapping her up in a hug. Noelle's eyes follow another attendee as they take a seat near the front with a polite smile, before returning to Helen. "Look at you, teaching a class! Oh, I'm so proud of you, honey."

"Thanks, Mom," she says, catching my eye over her shoulder and pressing her lips together.

"You let us know if you need anything, okay? I don't know all the technical stuff you do, but if there is *anything* we can help with, you let us know."

"Mom, the library is providing an assistant. I'm sure I'll be okay," Noelle says.

Hank raises an eyebrow, catching my eye. "The *library* is providing an assistant?"

"Yeah," Noelle says, checking the time on her phone. "Although I'm starting to get a little nervous. It's almost start time."

"Well, you go do what you need to. If you need me, I'm here," Helen says, with another quick hug.

Noelle nods, wandering back to the front of her room where her laptop is set up and projected onto the screen up front. The room has filled in, most of the computers accounted for.

And I guess now is as good a time as any.

I follow Noelle to the front desk, reaching into my pocket for the piece of cardstock I stuffed in there before I left this morning.

After Hank caught me throwing eggs at Noelle's dad's house, he mulled over the best way to punish me without *punishing me*, like he did with Noelle. And as much as he wanted to find new, creative ways to torture people enough that they snap out of their bad behaviors, there was only one idea that truly made sense to him.

She raises an eyebrow as she watches me shuffle through my pockets, and a look of understanding spreads across her face as she eyes the lined paper and bursts into laughter.

With a grin, I press my timecard onto the desk between us.

"I'm here for community service."

NOELLE

EPILOGUE

Two Years Later

I tried my hardest. I really did.

But in the two years since I rented this apartment half an hour from Snow Falls, I've spent probably two full months there, collectively.

It makes more sense to crash at Nick's. He's close to my mom and sister, and after Christmas the year we got together, he turned one of his spare bedrooms into an office for me in the space of an afternoon. It's cozy and quiet, and when I'm there, I get lost in my work. After school, he comes home and knocks, asking if I have any thoughts about dinner, and we sit downstairs at the island together and give each other a quick download of our respective days.

Considering we're going on two years now, we think it only makes sense to make it official.

So a few weeks before Christmas, I give notice to my landlord that I'm moving out, and over the space of a few weeks, we move all of my stuff to Nick's. He grins with every box he carries in, like each one brings us closer to officially *living together*.

My lease is done at the end of the year, but my apartment is cleared out by Christmas, and we spend Christmas Eve at my mom's, like usual, but we come back early to spend our first official Christmas Eve together.

He lights a fire and we sit on the floor in front of the tree, two glasses of wine on the coffee table next to us. He throws an arm around my shoulders and tugs me close. "So how does it feel, living with a boy?"

I can't help the laugh that tumbles from my throat. "It feels okay, so far."

He nods. "Good."

"How does it feel living with a girl?"

He presses a kiss to my head. "Awesome. Really awesome. Looking forward to accidental nip slips. And every morning is a toss-up: Will your hair finally take me out, or will it take pity on me?"

I cackle as I press a kiss to his cheek. "You're nuts."

"You're nuts for me," he parries back.

I nod and rest my head on his shoulder. "Absolutely."

"I love you more than anything, Noelle."

I lift my head so I can kiss his cheek again, resting my chin on his shoulder. "I love you more than anything, too."

He's quiet for a moment. "I never thought I'd get this lucky," he murmurs, his lips against my head. "Never thought I'd be sitting in front of my Christmas tree with someone like you at the holiday. Since I met you, you've made every holiday special for me. Every *day* special for me." His breath runs hot across my cheek, and I close my eyes, squeezing him tight.

"Noelle, will you marry me?"

My eyes pop open and I turn to face him, my gaze connecting with his.

He clears his throat as he takes his arm from my shoulders. "I, uh, sorry." He reaches into his pocket and withdraws a little velvet box. He twists, so he's on one knee in front of me, as he pops the box open. "Will you marry me?"

I blink, the utter shock draining into a feeling of elation as I take him in, his wide, hopeful eyes and the perfect ring between us.

"Yes," I breathe.

"Yes?"

"Yes!" I say, and now I'm moving, wrapping my arms around his neck and tackling him to the ground. He laughs as he struggles to hold onto the box, to pluck the ring out and slide it on my finger as the light from the Christmas tree reflects off of it and bounces around the living room.

He laughs, his hands settling on my hips as I sit up straight to admire my ring. "You're going to marry me?"

"Nick, why do you seem so surprised by this?" I let my hands drop to his chest, my eyes still glued to the shiny diamond on my finger.

He shakes his head, his hands settling on my hips as a grin spreads across his face. "I don't know if I'm that surprised, but I'm... I don't know. Thrilled. Happy. Excited. It all just feels too good to be true."

"Well, it is, but it's true anyway." I lean down and kiss him, brushing my hair to one side so he doesn't have to fight for his life. He holds my chin with one hand, the other reaching down to grab my ass and give it a firm squeeze.

When I pull away, he drags his thumb along the line of my jaw. "I love you, Criminal."

"I love you more, Saint Nick."

Thank you so much for reading Christmas Criminal—I hope you
enjoyed reading it as much as I enjoyed writing it!

If you're looking to take a break from the cold, Advanced Reader
Copies of my next book—a charming small town romance set in
the idyllic fictional town of Sunflower Hill—are now available
when you sign up for my newsletter!

Get your free pre-release copy here:
authorallywilliams.com

THANK YOU FOR READING!

Thank you so much for reading Nick and Noelle's story! I hope you enjoyed their journey as much as I did. If you want to see more of these two, subscribe to my mailing list via the URL below for an exclusive spicy bonus scene.

authorallywilliams.com/bonus-content

ACKNOWLEDGMENTS

Thank you first and foremost to my readers. You guys are some of the most lovely people I've had the pleasure of knowing and it's because of you that I get to continually do this.

Thank you to my beta readers, who not only read for me but provide incredible feedback that helps me not only write better books, but become a better writer in general. Christina. Laura. Shanna. Lauren. Ashley. Dawn. Jessica. Stephanie. Nicole. Alexmary. Thank you so much for your feedback.

Thank you to my wonderful proofreader, Chelsea, who goes above and beyond in making sure my final product is everything I want it to be, while also managing to make me laugh harder than I'd ever expect a proofreader to. It is truly a delight to work with you.

And last but not least, thank you to my partner and our Pumpkin, who are endlessly supportive of this crazy hobby of mine.

ABOUT THE AUTHOR

Ally Williams lives in South Jersey with her loving partner and their crazy dog. She likes writing about real, flawed characters, who must work through their issues so they can be the people they want to be for those they love.

When she's not writing, you can find her devouring anything pumpkin spice, doing data-related things for her day job, or playing with 3d printers in her basement.

Connect with her at:

Email: allywilliams@authorallywilliams.com
Instagram: instagram.com/authorallywilliams
Website: authorallywilliams.com

ALSO BY ALLY WILLIAMS

The Love and City Lights Series

Things We've Lost and Found

Namaste and Code All Day

What Happens in Paris

Say Everything (coming early 2025)